RED MOON

RED MOON SERIES BOOK ONE

ELIZABETH KELLY

EK PUBLISHING INC.

For Jess.
Because she believed.

RED MOON

(BOOK ONE, RED MOON SERIES)

A dangerous desire in a strange new world.

Survival is paramount.

For humans and paranomals.

Avery is the eldest daughter of the man who brought light back to the world in the aftermath of the Great War's destruction. Now her comfortable life has taken a turn for the worse.

Branded as a witch and sold into slavery, Avery's only concern is keeping her sister safe. When Tristan, a powerful Lycan, is searching for a nanny, he hires her sister and is persuaded to purchase Avery as well.

Despite her attraction to the Lycan, she fears his reprisal should he learn who she truly is. After all, if her own people reject her for her powers, how could he accept her?

Even if Tristan's obsession with her is more than pure lust, he needs a Lycan for a mate, not a human.

But when she is stolen from Tristan, will he realize what he's lost and fight for the life they could have?

CHAPTER 1

Tristan rubbed his forehead and sighed irritably. He had grown weary of the man's fawning from the moment he had stepped into the building, and with an impatient grunt he held up one hand.

"Enough. Show me the slaves."

"Of course." The old man bowed low and pattered down the long narrow hallway. "Forgive me, my lord. It is not often we have someone of your stature visiting."

They walked out into the courtyard and the man stopped short, staring suspiciously at the large horses hooked to an empty wagon. There was a young man and a small girl sitting on the seat of the wagon and they stared back at him.

He glanced up at Tristan. "My lord, how many do you need?"

"I require six."

The man led him across the yard toward a second building. As they walked by the wagon, Tristan stopped and held his arms out to the young girl. She was no older than seven, and she hesitated briefly before allowing him to pull her from the wagon seat and set her on the ground.

"What are we doing here?" she asked.

"We're hiring some staff for our new home, as well as a nanny for you and your baby brother." Tristan smiled down at the girl.

She didn't return his smile, staring solemnly at him for a moment. "I can take care of Nicholas."

"I know you can, my love. But I think it would be best if you had some help." He squeezed her hand encouragingly as they approached the building. "I could use your help in picking out the right nanny. What do you say, Sophia?"

She nodded, watching curiously as the small, dirty man in front of them pulled out a giant ring of keys from a pocket hidden deep within his coat. He thumbed through them until he found the correct one and unlocked the door. Its rusty hinges squealed, and the little girl cringed but followed her father into the building.

They walked down the hallway. The man flipped a light switch on the wall and the overhead lights buzzed on weakly.

"You have electricity here," Tristan said.

"Aye - some days. We're close enough to the city to latch on to their grid. But it goes in and out." The man led them down the hallway to another door. This too was locked, and they waited patiently as he picked out the right key and unlocked the door. He ushered them into the room and shut the door behind him as Sophia peered from behind the safety of Tristan's legs.

The room quieted as the women in the room stopped their chatter and stared at the two strangers. Tristan grimaced. All of the women were dirty and unkempt, their hair uncombed and their clothing ripped and stained.

He swore softly and gave the man an undisguised look of disgust. "What kind of facility are you running here?"

The man bristled. "I can assure you, my lord, that our

slaves are of the utmost quality. Just because our facility is not as proper as you are undoubtedly used to, does not mean we don't offer excellent services."

Tristan rolled his eyes. "I'm sure." He eyed the women in the room with suspicion. "How many of them are suffering from the sickness?"

"None of them!" The old man puffed himself up, trying to match Tristan's formidable height. "If they suffer from the sickness, we banish them to the outskirts immediately." He paused. "Perhaps my lord would prefer to go somewhere else?"

"You know very well your facility is the only one within fifty miles," Tristan said. "Enough idle talking. I require a nanny and a house staff. Who do you recommend?"

The man didn't reply. Instead he hobbled toward the group of women and began pulling a few of them to the front. Out of the nearly fifty women in the large room, he separated fifteen of them into two groups before returning to Tristan and Sophia.

"They have experience in both cooking and cleaning." He pointed to the ten women on the left. "They have experience with child rearing." He waved his hand at the other five on the right.

Tristan moved forward, Sophia trailing behind him, and looked over the ten women. He stood in front of the oldest. "What's your name?"

"Marian." She kept her gaze on her bare feet.

"What experience do you have?"

"I was the head of the household for the Farthing family for more than fifteen years. Perhaps you have heard of them?"

"I am not from here. Why did you leave their employment? Were you fired?" Tristan asked.

She shook her head. "No, m'lord. Mr. Farthing grew ill and died. Mrs. Farthing could no longer afford my services and sold me to pay some of her bills."

"How long have you been here?"

She squinted in thought. "Not long, m'lord. Six months perhaps?"

He looked behind him. "I'll take this one. Who among this group of women would you recommend, Marian?"

She hesitated. "How many do you need, m'lord?"

"Five, including yourself."

She pointed to four of the other women. After questioning them, Tristan agreed to the ones she had chosen.

He turned to Sophia, crouching beside her and patting her back awkwardly. "Sophia, would you like to help me pick out your new nanny?"

"Yes, Tristan," she replied.

Tristan stared at the women critically as he and Sophia paced in front of them. "How many of you were nannies before?"

Three of them raised their hands and Tristan glanced at the other two. "You're dismissed."

They melted back into the crowd of women as Tristan questioned the remaining three women.

SOPHIA CLASPED HER HANDS BEHIND HER BACK AND STARED at the group of women behind Tristan. There was a flash of colour to her left, and she glanced over at the woman standing next to the window. Her long red hair glowed in the late afternoon sun and Sophia edged closer, fascinated by the red strands.

4

The woman smiled at her in a friendly manner as Sophia stopped in front of her. "Hello, little one."

"Hello," Sophia whispered.

"Your name is Sophia?" At Sophia's nod, she smiled again. "That is a very pretty name. My name is Avery."

"Avery," Sophia repeated, and the woman nodded.

"That's right. This is my little sister Maya."

There was a petite blonde woman standing behind Avery and she peeked around and smiled just like Avery. "Hi, Sophia. I like your dress."

"Thank you." Sophia ran her hands over the stiff fabric, wincing when it rubbed painfully against the cut on her finger.

"Are you hurt?" Avery crouched in front of her.

"I cut my finger." Sophia showed her the long cut on the pad of her index finger.

"Ouch." Avery frowned. "That looks very sore."

"It's not healing very well," Sophia said. "Marshall says if I don't make a better effort to keep it clean, he'll have to cut it off."

"Well that won't do." Avery smiled at her. "Shall I kiss it better for you? When Maya and I were little, our mother would always kiss our owies."

Sophia stared at her. "I like your hair."

A strange look crossed Avery's face, one that Sophia didn't understand, before she smiled at her. "Thank you, honey."

"Can I touch it?"

"Of course." She tipped her head forward so that her long hair fell over her shoulders, and Sophia rubbed it between her fingers.

"It's so soft, so pretty," she whispered. She ran her fingers down the strands and Avery smiled again at her.

"I'm glad you like it, Sophia." She captured Sophia's hand in her own. "Shall I give your owie a kiss?"

Sophia hesitated and then nodded. Avery bent her head and placed a gentle kiss on her finger, directly on the cut. Warmth surged down Sophia's finger and through her hand. She gasped and pulled her hand free, staring down at her finger.

TRISTAN LOOKED DOWN. "SOPHIA, DO YOU..."

He frowned when he realized she was no longer at his side. He glanced around the room, his scowl deepening when he saw her standing in front of the Red. The Red was holding her hand and when she kissed Sophia's finger, he stomped over to them.

"Get away from her." He pushed the redheaded woman to the ground with a hard shove. A blonde woman put her arms around the Red as Tristan pulled Sophia away. He took the little girl by the shoulders and shook her gently.

"Sophia, you know better than to leave my side. Did she hurt you?"

Sophia shook her head, staring with wonderment at her index finger. Where once there had been a long, swollen cut, there was now only smooth unbroken skin.

Tristan's expression softened and he smoothed her hair back from her face. She was still looking at her finger and he took her hand and examined it.

"Look at that - your cut has finally healed. That's good news. Marshall was getting ready to cut it off," he teased.

Sophia didn't smile, just looked at Avery with wide eyes.

Tristan took her hand and led her back to the three

women. "Which of these women would you like as your nanny?"

Sophia stared up at them for a moment before looking back at Avery and Maya. "I want her." She pointed at Avery and Tristan sighed.

"No, Sophia. You must pick from these three women here."

"I want her."

Tristan glanced at the man who was idly swinging his ring of keys from one finger. He shook his head. "No, m'lord, you don't want that one. She is contentious and disagreeable. You know how the Reds are."

Tristan looked back at Sophia. She was still staring at the redheaded woman and he frowned. "Stay here, Sophia."

He returned to the Red. She stared unblinkingly at him as he looked her up and down. She was wearing a dirty, grey dress that was too large. She practically floated in it. Her feet were bare, and her legs and arms were covered in grime and grass stains. Her hair hung halfway down her back, a cascade of fire-coloured locks with twigs and leaves stuck in it. Her light green eyes regarded him with a cool sort of haughtiness that belied her dirty and disheveled appearance. Her face was as dirty as her arms and legs, and he wrinkled his nose at her smell.

"Do you have any experience with children."

She shook her head. "No, m'lord. But she does." She dragged the small blonde woman out from behind her and pushed her toward Tristan.

"Avery no," the girl whispered.

"Hush, Maya," Avery said fiercely, and the girl quieted immediately.

"Have you nannied before, girl?" Tristan asked her. The blonde girl blushed and stared down at her bare feet, and

7

Tristan rolled his eyes with barely-concealed impatience. "Well, have you?"

"No, m'lord," she whispered.

Before he could turn away, Avery said, "She's had plenty of experience with our younger siblings, my lord. She practically raised both our younger brother and sister. She has a comforting touch with babies, and she can read and write. She taught our brother to read when he was only three."

Tristan stared at the trembling girl and then at her older sister. "Are you that eager to rid yourself of her?"

Avery flushed. "I want nothing more than a better life for her, my lord."

"And what makes you so certain I will give her a better life?" He arched his eyebrow at her.

She looked around the room and, in a voice filled with desperation, said, "Anything is better than this. She is too bright and too beautiful to live her life in a cage. Please, take her with you. She will serve you well. I swear this to you."

Tristan frowned. The woman's impassioned plea had moved him more than he cared to admit. "Very well then – we'll take the girl."

Avery nodded with relief, but Maya let out a loud wail. "No, Avery! I will not leave you!" She threw herself into the redhead's arms, sobbing brokenly. Rather than soothe her like Tristan expected, Avery grabbed her upper arms and pushed her upright.

She shook the young girl harshly. "Maya, enough! Stop your crying right now."

The woman struggled to obey, sniffing and hiccupping as a stray sob escaped. "Avery, please don't send me away."

He watched as Avery cupped her face, wiping away her tears with dirty thumbs. "Maya, listen to me. I love you. I will always love you. I do this for you. Do you understand?"

Sobbing quietly, Maya nodded, and Avery hugged her hard before kissing her on the mouth. Dry-eyed, she pushed Maya toward Tristan who took her upper arm and led her toward Sophia. He stopped when Avery dropped her hand onto his arm. He could feel the heat of her hand through his shirt. A shiver went down his back and he stared at her as she stepped closer.

"Keep her safe," Avery demanded, her green eyes staring into his. His eyes dropped to her mouth and then to her breasts. They were well-hidden beneath the sack of a dress she wore, and he looked back up at her, flushing a little at the wry look on her face.

"Promise me you'll keep her safe." She frowned at him, and with a small jerk he yanked his arm free. He pulled Maya toward Sophia. Already the girl's relentless sobbing was beginning to grate on him, and he was regretting his impulsive decision.

"Come, Sophia. Let's go," he said brusquely.

The little girl shook her head. "No. I want that one." She pointed again at Avery.

"No, Sophia. I do not have time for your games."

The small, dirty man gave an ugly laugh. "Listen to yer father, girl. The Reds are all witches or whores. No one with half a mind brings a Red into their household. They bring nothing but death and destruction they do." He picked his nose, staring at the green smear on his finger with interest before wiping it on his pant leg.

Tristan stared at him with disgust, and then at Sophia as she took his hand in her small one. She was staring up at him, her dark eyes large and wet with unshed tears. "Please, Papa. I want her," she whispered.

Sophia never called him papa. She kept her distance and referred to him as "my lord" or "Tristan" when prompted to interact with him. Hearing her call him papa made it difficult to resist her.

As though sensing his weakness, Maya said, "Avery is also very good with children, my lord. And she is excellent with plants. Your garden will thrive and provide plenty of food for your children's bellies."

Tristan scrubbed his hand across his face. "Fine. I'll take her as well."

Maya gasped with happiness, and Sophia grinned triumphantly as Avery joined them. Maya hugged her and Avery kissed her cheek before taking her hand. The four of them joined the others and as they filed out the door, the man grabbed Tristan's arm.

"Perhaps you would care for one more, m'lord." He looked down at Tristan's bare left hand. "Perhaps a fine wench to warm your bed?" He pointed to a dark-haired woman who was wearing a dress that left little to the imagination. She smiled slowly and invitingly at him.

Tristan pulled his arm free. "I have no need for a bed warmer. Let us agree over the price so I can leave this wretched place."

CHAPTER 2

"What on the gods' earth were you thinking, Tristan?" Marshall frowned at him as he clucked loudly to the horses. The wagon started with a jolt and Marshall slapped the reins gently on the horses' backs, encouraging them to move faster. They pulled onto the dusty road, the wagon creaking and groaning as they drove toward their camp.

"What do you mean?" Tristan asked.

"The Red? Are you deliberately trying to curse us?"

"That's nothing more than an old wives' tale, Marshall," Tristan scoffed derisively. "I didn't know you spooked so easily."

"I don't," he protested hotly. "But it's bad enough you're bringing more humans into the household. Did you have to bring a Red as well?"

Tristan rolled his eyes. "Afraid she'll cast a spell on you?"

"You laugh, but my mother used to tell me tales of the witches when I was still a small pup. Terrible tales they were. Women with flaming red hair, chanting and casting spells as they danced naked around their fires. Humans and paranormals alike have been destroyed by them, Tristan."

Tristan snorted with disdain. "You sound like a dithering old woman, Marshall. Tales of the witches are a human thing."

"You forget my mother was human."

"I haven't forgotten. Human blood runs within your veins, and yet you seem to loathe them."

Marshall refused to answer, staring forward moodily as Tristan glanced behind him at the back of the wagon. Sophia had insisted on joining Avery and Maya in the back of the wagon and she was sitting on Avery's lap, her small hand stroking the Red's hair repeatedly.

"Besides, Sophia has taken a liking to her."

"You don't need two nannies, Tristan. It's just another mouth to feed," Marshall argued in a low voice. "Tonight, after Sophia falls asleep, I'll take her to the outskirts and abandon her. You can tell Sophia in the morning that the Red ran away."

"That's a death sentence and you know it," Tristan said. "If the faeries don't capture her, the leeches definitely will."

Marshall shook his head. "I've never seen you bend so easily to a woman's will before."

"Sophia is my child. She has just lost her mother, and a father she barely knows is taking her to a home she does not remember. I will do whatever it takes to make her feel comfortable."

He paused and gave Marshall a hard look. "I value your opinion, brother, but the woman stays. Do you understand me?"

"Of course, I do. But when she's murdering our chickens and using their blood to write spells on our bedroom walls, you'll owe me an apology."

Tristan laughed. "Fine. When that happens, I'll apologize."

MAYA SMILED AT SOPHIA. "HOW OLD ARE YOU, SOPHIA?"

Sophia looked up from Avery's hair. "I'm seven."

"Seven. Wow. And can you read and write?"

Sophia shook her head. "No. Can you?"

Maya nodded. "I can. Perhaps I could teach you? Would you like that?"

"Yes. I have a little brother you know. His name is Nicholas."

"And how old is Nicholas?" Maya asked.

"He's seven moons old. He's sick a lot."

Maya glanced at Avery. "What kind of sickness?"

Sophia shrugged and stroked Avery's hair again. "He sneezes and coughs a lot. He's always throwing up his milk. Mrs. Lanning says it's the air. She says my mother should never have lived in the city."

She frowned, her hands tangled in Avery's hair. "I don't like Mrs. Lanning. She has bad breath, and she says mean things about my mother when she thinks I can't hear."

"Where is your mama?" Avery asked.

"She's dead," Sophia said matter-of-factly. "She had a friend who was a bad man. He took her to the leeches."

"I'm sorry, baby." Avery rubbed her back, and Sophia leaned companionably against her. "You must miss her very much."

Sophia shrugged. "She wasn't around a lot." She snuggled in closer, resting her head in the curve of Avery's neck. "I take care of Nicholas – I'm very good at it."

"I'm sure you are, baby."

Sophia wrinkled her nose. "You smell bad, Avery."

Avery grinned as Maya giggled. "I know I do. Perhaps when we get to your home, I could have a bath."

"We're not going home yet. We're going back to our campsite. Marshall says it will be another two days before we arrive home."

She sighed. "And it's not my home. Tristan says I used to live there but I don't remember it. Tristan says I'll like it. He says there are lots of places to explore and the house is very large. I'll have my own room, and he said he would buy me a pony and teach me to ride."

She hesitated. "I'm not sure I'll like living in the country though."

Marian spoke up. "The country is a wonderful place to live, young miss. The fresh air, big open sky…"

She sighed happily. "The Farthing's had the most beautiful country home. I've missed it. I'm so happy to hear we'll be living in the country."

"I'm not." The girl sitting next to Marian said. She had a thin and mousy face, and she sighed dramatically. "I hate the country. Give me the city any day."

"I miss the city too," Maya said.

Marian frowned. "It was the city living that got the ancients into trouble in the first place. All of those people crowded into the city with no place to turn without running into another human. "The Great War destroyed so many of us because we were crowded into the old cities like cattle. Three quarters of the population wiped out in an instant."

"We have seen an old city," Maya said.

The mousey girl's mouth dropped open. "You're lying."

"I am not!" Maya replied indignantly. "Our father took us to see one when we were young. Did he not, Avery?"

"Aye." Avery nodded. "He did."

"You would have the sickness if you had gone to the old city." A dark-haired girl, Avery thought her name was Nadine, said critically. "Your hair and teeth would have fallen out, and the sores would have appeared."

"Would have been a blessing for that one if her hair had fallen out." The mousey girl nudged Marian and looked pointedly at Avery.

"Don't be rude, Renee." Marian frowned.

Maya shook her head. "My father arranged for us to wear special suits. They had these small canisters attached to them that gave us our own air. That's why we didn't contract the sickness."

"What was it like?" Nadine asked.

Maya glanced at Avery. "I was very young, around Sophia's age, but I can still remember how tall the buildings were. They blotted out the sun. A lot of them had crumbled to the ground. Father said there used to be a great many more, but the Great War destroyed most of the buildings."

She shivered delicately. "It was so quiet. No birds sang or animals moved about. Although the sun shone brightly, there were no plants growing. There were no signs of life at all – even after all the years."

"Why did your father take you there? What if you had gotten sick?" Nadine wondered.

Avery shifted Sophia on her lap. "My father was fascinated with history. He had a thirst for knowledge, particularly about the ancients' lives, and he wanted to share it with us. He wanted us to learn from the ancients' mistakes. He believed it was worth the risk."

"He sounds crazy." Renee sniffed.

Maya frowned but Avery smiled. "Aye. I guess he does."

"I still wish I had been bought by someone who lived in

the city." Renee sighed. "The lights are so pretty at night, and there is music and dancing and parties."

Marian rolled her eyes. "What do you know of the parties? You, who was born into slavery."

"My lord's son favoured me." Renee gave her a haughty look. "I pleased him well, and in return he showered me with gifts and took me with him to many gatherings."

"A fat lot that did you, didn't it?" Marian glowered at her. "You still ended up being sold when the household could no longer afford to feed you."

"It doesn't matter. Now that we're going to the country, I'll never hear music or go dancing again," Renee said.

"Tristan says there is a village not far from his home," Sophia said. "Perhaps they dance there?"

Renee smiled at her. "Perhaps, young miss. But I would still prefer the city."

Marian frowned. "With the leeches and the faeries and the Lycans just running rampant? No, thank you. Do you know how many people go missing every day from the city? Why, before Mrs. Farthing sold me, there were five people in the city not five miles from our home that went missing all in one night. Of course, no one knows for sure what happened to them. Some swear it was the faeries, but I heard from Mr. Windon next door that it was the Lycans. It was a full moon that night."

Sophia was visibly trembling in Avery's arms and she squeezed the little girl soothingly. "Are you okay, my pet?"

She nodded as Tristan turned around. His gaze landed briefly on Avery before he scanned the rest of the women. "Quiet your tongues. All of you."

"THE GODS BE DAMNED, LORD WILLIAMS! YOU SAID YOU would be bringing no more than six back with you."

Avery stared curiously at the woman holding the crying baby. She was tall and thin and looked to be close to fifty. She had deep wrinkles on her forehead and around her eyes, and her black hair was pulled back into a severe bun.

She jiggled the baby impatiently as he screamed louder. "This one has done nothing but cry since you left."

Tristan took the baby from her, patting his back and lightly bouncing him up and down, as the others climbed out of the wagon. They stretched their legs and stared curiously at the campsite.

Maya held Avery's hand and squeezed it nervously. Avery smiled reassuringly at her. "It will be fine, Maya."

They were in a large clearing in the forest just off the main road. A number of horses, their short leads staked to the ground, were grazing at the edge of the clearing. A small carriage was standing close to the road, and there were four tents situated around a large campfire. Two men approached the horses and helped Marshall untie them and lead them to where the other horses were grazing. Two women were in the campsite. One was tending to a pot of boiling liquid over the fire. The smell of cooking rabbit drifted to them on the soft breeze, and both Avery's and Maya's stomachs growled in response.

The other was sitting close to the fire, a basket of mending in her lap, and she stared at the small group. When her gaze fell on Avery, she actually gasped and crossed herself nervously before standing and backing toward one of the tents.

Avery, used to the reaction, winked at her and the woman covered her mouth and stumbled into the tent, closing the open flaps firmly behind her.

"What is that?" The older woman stared in horror at Avery. "You bought a Red? What – what were you thinking?" She glanced down at Sophia who was holding Avery's hand firmly. "Tell me she is not the nanny for your children!"

Tristan was still trying to soothe the wailing baby. "Mrs. Lanning, these women here," he nodded towards Marian and the others, "will be your new house staff."

He stared at the women. "Mrs. Lanning is the head of the household. You will obey her without question. Do you understand?"

They nodded as Tristan approached Maya and Avery. The baby was really screaming now, his small fists flailing and his thin face bright red. His tiny body twisted and squirmed in Tristan's arms, and his nose was running steadily. His screaming turned into a bout of coughing, and Avery winced as his small body was racked with sudden shivers.

Tristan held the baby out to Maya. "Your sister says you have a way with babies. Now is the time to prove it."

Maya took the shrieking, wailing baby and glanced timidly at Tristan. "Do you have a blanket for him?"

Tristan nodded and turned to the girl who was standing by the pot. "Laura, grab his blanket please."

She disappeared into one of the smaller tents before returning with a small, thin blanket. Maya took it from her with a nod of thanks and knelt on the ground, holding the wriggling baby carefully against her. She spread the blanket out and laid the baby in the middle of it. With quick, prac-ticed movements, she wrapped and folded the blanket around his body until he was swaddled completely. Only his thin, red face peeked above the blanket, and Maya picked him up before standing. She placed a soft kiss on one red cheek and swayed back and forth, crooning softly to him under her breath. The baby quieted and stared at Maya's face as she used one edge of the blanket to wipe the snot and tears from his face.

"Husha, baby," she sang softly. "Go to sleep, little baby."

Avery gave Tristan an 'I told you so' grin, and he snorted and turned back to Mrs. Lanning.

"This is Nicholas and Sophia's new nanny. Her name is Maya." He cupped the back of Sophia's head. "Sophia, show Maya to yours and Nicholas' tent. I need you to show her where all of Nicholas' clothing and supplies are. You and Nicholas will sleep with her in the tent tonight."

Sophia nodded and Maya held her hand out to the little girl. She took it willingly enough and led her to the tent that Laura had pulled the blanket from. Avery could hear her chattering to Maya about Nicholas as they disappeared into the tent together."

"What about this one?" Mrs. Lanning looked at Avery with revulsion. "What am I to do with it?"

Tristan smiled at her. "I bought her for you, Mrs. Lanning. She has experience with plants, and I know how much the gardening hurts your back. She'll relieve you of your garden tending duties and allow you to focus more on the house."

"Do you really trust her with our food, my lord?" Mrs. Lanning argued.

"I do." Tristan spoke in a tone that brooked no refusal, and Mrs. Lanning sighed before looking over the group of women.

"They smell horrible and they'll all need new clothes. They probably carry bugs, and the gods only know what other diseases."

Tristan glanced at the darkening sky. "They can go to the lake tomorrow and bathe and wash their clothing before we leave. Tonight, we'll get food into their bellies," he glanced at Avery's thin face, "and give them a good night's rest."

"And where do you propose I put all of them? We have only one tent for the household staff – we'll never fit all of us in there." Mrs. Lanning looked at Avery as she spoke.

Tristan smiled at her before leaving to join Marshall and the other men. "I'm sure you'll think of something, Mrs. Lanning. You always do."

AVERY PICKED HER WAY CAREFULLY ACROSS THE CAMPSITE toward the tent. She had stopped by Maya's tent to say goodnight, and dark had fallen like a thick blanket. The campfire was down to coals and she could barely see the man standing guard in the trees just beyond the clearing. She nodded in a friendly way to him and he nodded back impassively.

She stepped on a rock, hissing as it dug into her bare foot, and lifted the flap of the tent. Mrs. Lanning appeared immediately at the entrance. "There is no room for you in here."

"Where would you suggest I sleep then?"

"You can sleep beside the wagon." She held out a thin blanket to her.

"I'll join Maya and the babies in their tent," Avery said.

Mrs. Lanning grabbed her arm and dragged her toward the wagon. "You're not going anywhere near those babies. You heard the lord Williams. I am the head of the household and you'll obey me without question."

"I am not sleeping outdoors!" Avery tried to dig her heels in, but her body was weak from months of poor nutrition, and the larger Mrs. Lanning easily overpowered her.

She pushed her to the ground next to the large wooden wagon. Before Avery could rise to her feet, Mrs. Lanning had pulled a metal cuff from deep within a pocket in her skirt and latched one end to the wheel of the wagon and the other to Avery's left wrist.

Avery pulled on the cuff. "Have you gone mad, old woman? Release me now before I start screaming."

Mrs. Lanning crouched next to her. She had a short but sharp knife in her hand, and she traced it across Avery's cheek. "I wouldn't do that if I were you. You may have the Lord Tristan fooled, but I know exactly who and what you are. I won't hesitate to slit your pretty throat. Do you understand me?"

Avery nodded, her body tense, as Mrs. Lanning smiled. "Good. Obey me, witch, and we'll have no quarrels between us. Disobey me, and I'll do everything in my power to convince Lord Tristan that you should be burned at the stake. I've been in his employment a long time, and he trusts me. If I tell him that you and your pretty little sister have been practicing witchcraft, he'll light the fire himself."

Avery stiffened when she mentioned Maya, and Mrs. Lanning stood and smiled down at her before tossing the thin blanket at her. "Make not a peep, little witch, and I'll release you in the morning."

She turned and disappeared into the tent. Avery sighed and curled up into a small ball before wrapping the blanket around her shivering body. It would be a long night.

CHAPTER 3

"How did your first night go with the baby?" Avery gave Maya a tired smile.

They were sitting on the soft grass close to the water's edge, and she lifted her face to the sun. The days were growing cooler, but it still felt good to be in the outdoors. They had bathed in the lake and washed their clothing, and Avery couldn't get over how much better she felt after having her long hair and body scrubbed clean for the first time in months.

"He has a fever. And he threw up nearly everything I fed him in the night," Maya said worriedly.

"He always has a fever," Sophia said. "He rarely eats without throwing it up."

She kissed Nicholas, who was lying wanly on his back on Maya's lap, before looking at Maya. "Can I play in the water?"

"Yes, love, but you must stay where I can see you at all times and you must not go any deeper than your knees. Do you understand?"

Sophia nodded and skipped down to the water's edge.

They watched as she waded in before glancing behind her to see if she could still see Maya. She waved cheerfully at them. They waved back as she bent over and began to bring up handfuls of stones from the bottom of the lake.

Avery glanced to her right. The other women were checking their clothes that were laid out in the soft grass to dry. They had all but avoided Avery and Maya the entire time they were bathing and washing their clothes, and Avery was glad. She had no patience for women and their gossiping and clucking about, and much preferred Maya's quiet company.

She checked to make sure that both Mrs. Lanning and Marshall, who was keeping a close eye on the women, were not watching them and then held her arms out.

"Give him to me."

Maya handed Nicholas to her. She laid him on her lap and quickly undressed him down to his cloth diaper. She stared sadly at the tiny baby on her lap. She could count every one of his ribs, his breath wheezed in and out, and already his skin was starting to turn blue from the cool air.

"Poor baby," she whispered. Her dress was drying in the sun next to Maya's, and she was wearing a plain white shift that stopped just above her knees. She quickly unlaced the top of her shift and slid Nicholas inside until his naked body was resting against her naked skin.

She kissed his head repeatedly and whispered to him as he stiffened. He uttered a small hoarse cry before falling silent and collapsing weakly against her. Avery rested her lips against his forehead and cupped his tiny head as she closed her eyes and concentrated.

Maya watched as the baby's pale skin began to take on a rosy, healthy glow. Avery continued to hold him, rocking back and forth a little, and didn't release him until he began to squirm against her. She pulled Nicholas free from her shift and handed him to Maya.

Her sister gave her a worried look. "Avery? Are you all right? You're very pale and I can see you trembling."

She nodded. "Aye. He was just more ill than I anticipated." She coughed and then looked at the baby fondly. "He's a tough little one. I have no idea how he survived this long."

"What was wrong with him?" Maya asked.

Avery smiled at her. "You know that isn't how it works, Maya. I have no idea what his illness was."

She coughed again, wincing and holding one hand to her head, as Maya stared at her with alarm. "Are you sure you're all right?"

Avery nodded again. "Yes. I didn't sleep well last night, and it's been a long time since I've had to heal such a deep sickness. I'm just not used to it. I'll be fine once I get more sleep."

Maya held out her hand. "Here, take my hand. I'm healthy."

Avery shook her head. "I'm fine. Do not worry yourself _."

"Take my hand," Maya insisted. Avery sighed and linked fingers with Maya. They sat silently for a few minutes as Maya crooned softly to the baby, and Avery closed her eyes and breathed deeply.

She looked up when Marshall whistled and waved his arm at them. The other women had gathered their clothes, and Maya squeezed her hand before standing. She called for Sophia who wandered out of the water and toward them.

"Come, Avery. We'll get you some breakfast."

Avery shook her head. "I'm feeling better. I think I'll take another swim. It's been many moons since I've gotten to swim, and the gods only know how long it will be before I get another chance."

TRISTAN GLANCED AROUND THE CAMPSITE. MARSHALL HAD returned with the women nearly half an hour ago and Avery, easily noticeable with her bright red hair, was missing.

He stood next to Maya who was feeding Nicholas his bottle. The baby was eating enthusiastically for once, grabbing Maya's hands with his tiny fingers and gulping hungrily at the milk. "Where is your sister?"

Maya gave him a nervous look. "She is still at the lake, my lord. She wanted to swim for a bit longer."

He shook his head, cursing under his breath before storming over to Marshall. "You left the Red at the lake alone?"

Marshall shrugged. "She said she wanted to swim for a while longer. I wasn't going to argue with her – she'd probably turn me into a lizard."

"You know it's not safe in the woods, Marshall." Tristan frowned at him, but the younger man just shrugged again.

With a harsh sigh, Tristan turned and headed for the lake. As he jogged through the trees, he cursed his decision to buy the Red. It didn't take long before he was at the lake and he scanned the shore for her. Her dress was lying on the grass, but she was nowhere to be seen.

He searched the water and caught movement in the corner of his eye. He turned to see Avery surface about twenty feet from the shore. She pushed her hair from her face before floating lazily on her back.

"Girl!" he shouted irritably. She jerked and disappeared

under the water for a moment before popping back up, coughing and sputtering.

"What?" She shouted back.

"Get out of the water. We're leaving."

She nodded and swam toward shore with long, powerful strokes. He envied her obvious confidence in the water. He could swim, but it was little more than a doggy paddle and deep water made him nervous. He would get her to teach Sophia to swim, he decided.

As she drew closer, a strange scent drifted to him and he closed his eyes and inhaled deeply. He turned his back to the lake and stared suspiciously into the trees before inhaling again.

"Hurry up, girl!" he barked over his shoulder. Dimly he was aware of her splashing her way onto shore as he stared into the trees. The scent was fading rapidly, if it had even been there in the first place, but he continued to stare intently into the trees.

"What?" She asked, peering curiously over his shoulder. "What do you see?"

"Nothing." He turned around and faced her. "But we should get back to the others. It's getting late and we need to get back on the road before..."

His voice died as he stared at the Red.

She was wearing a short white shift that the water had turned translucent. The wet fabric clung to every curve of her pale body, and he grew hard as he stared at her. The grey dress had done an excellent job of hiding her curves and although it was obvious she was much too thin, the fullness of her breasts and the swell of her hips had him aching to touch her.

He looked up at her face. She had bathed and scrubbed her face and body clean, and he could see a tiny smattering of freckles across her nose. Her skin was the colour of milk and other than the freckles, completely unblemished. He was suddenly itching to touch her skin and see if it felt as soft as it looked.

"What's wrong?" She frowned at him.

His eyes dropped back down to her breasts. The wet fabric and cool air had hardened her rose-coloured nipples and he had a sudden image of sucking gently on them.

She looked down at herself. "Gods!"

She blushed and pulled the wet fabric away from her body before searching frantically for her dress. She spied it on the grass but before she could reach for it, he took her by the arm and pulled her close.

"My lord..."

She gave him a warning look and he grinned wolfishly at her. "You smell much better."

"Thank you." She tugged against his hand, but he refused to let her go. He reached out and pushed the wet strands of hair from her cheek. She inhaled sharply when he ran his fingers along her cheekbone.

"You're too thin," he informed her. She didn't reply, just continued to stare at him with her clear green eyes, and he frowned. "You need to eat more."

"Whatever you say, m'lord."

He scowled at her insolent tone before cupping the back of her head and pulling her forward. "You belong to me now," he whispered. "You will do what I tell you."

THE TOUCH OF TRISTAN'S HAND SENT WEIRD TINGLES OF pleasure down Avery's spine. Trying to ignore them, she scoffed in his face. "I belong to no one."

He bent his head until his mouth was hovering over hers.

"You belong to me," he repeated himself, his warm breath washing over her face, and Avery felt a surge of warmth in her belly despite her annoyance with him. "And I want you to kiss me."

She shook her head. "No."

She hoped she sounded more confident then she felt. She had no idea what was happening to her. His deep voice and warm hand were playing havoc with her system. She felt weak and disoriented and when he had told her to kiss him, she had damn near obeyed him immediately.

"Yes," he demanded.

"No." She swallowed hard, her lips trembling.

He ran his thumb over her mouth and at his touch, her lips parted. He groaned a little when her tongue flicked out and licked at her dry lips, brushing against his thumb in the process.

His eyes were dark like Sophia's and to her horror, her body was responding shamelessly to the look of need in them. He suddenly pulled her wet body against his and ran his hand down her back through the wet fabric of her shift.

"Kiss me, girl." He hesitated. "Please."

She pressed her lips quickly and lightly against his. "There, I kissed you."

"Again," he muttered.

Feeling like she was drowning, she pressed her mouth against his again. This time she let her lips linger on his. When the tip of his tongue probed gently at her closed lips, a shudder of desire went through her. His hand was against the small of her back and he pressed her so close she could feel his erection against her abdomen.

"Open your mouth," he breathed and then flicked his tongue against her upper lip. She moaned and obeyed his whispered command. He stroked her tongue with his and explored her mouth with demanding urgency. Warmth was rushing through her, and her hips bucked against him compulsively when she slid her tongue timidly into his mouth and he immediately sucked hard on it.

An ache was starting in her belly and pelvis and when he cupped her ass, squeezing it familiarly, she didn't protest. He lifted her until she was on her tip-toes, his hands still holding her ass firmly, so that he could press his erection directly against her warm center. She groaned at the contact and tore her mouth free from his. She pushed on his chest, trying to put some distance between them.

He growled low in his throat and moved one hand to the back of her neck, holding it with his large, warm hand. "Can you feel how much I want you, girl?"

When she didn't answer, he pushed her more firmly against him. "Can you?"

"Aye," she moaned.

He kissed her again, sucking on her lower lip, and she stopped trying to escape his embrace and pressed herself against him. He smiled his approval and pulled her head back so he could kiss her throat.

He let go of her ass and took one smooth thigh in his hand. Gripping it tightly, he lifted it up around his hip. The cool air slipped between her thighs, caressing her heated skin and bringing her back to her senses.

"My lord, stop. I – I'm getting you wet," she whispered. She could feel streams of water from her clothing trickling down her legs and arms, and the front of his dark shirt was wet and sticking to his chest.

He grinned at her. "Aye, so you are."

He kissed his way to her ear and then breathed quietly, "Shall we see if I'm getting you wet?"

A vision of his warm hand between her legs, his rough fingers touching and stroking her, rushed through her and she couldn't stop the long, shuddering moan from escaping her lips.

He nipped her earlobe. "That sounds like a yes to me."

Still gripping the back of her neck, he let go of her thigh and pushed his other hand between their bodies. He traced the tips of his fingers across the front of her thigh. Avery knew she should have been moving her leg from where it was still wrapped around his hip, but instead she squeezed her leg more firmly around him and held her breath. Her entire body tensed as she waited for his warm touch.

There was a sudden, loud noise in the woods behind them. He pushed her away immediately, spinning around and scanning the trees.

Her mouth red and her body trembling, Avery quickly stripped off her wet shift and struggled into the shapeless dress. She tapped Tristan on the back with one finger. "What is it?"

She watched curiously as he lifted his head and inhaled deeply. Without looking at her, he held out his hand. "Let's go."

She took his hand and allowed him to lead her back toward the campsite.

CHAPTER 4

"Why are you walking?" Tristan rode up beside Avery who was trailing behind the wagon. She was nearly jogging to keep up with it, and her cheeks were red and flushed looking.

"It's too crowded in the wagon," she panted without looking at him.

He glanced at the wagon. The wagon was full, although he supposed she could have squeezed in if she was determined enough. He couldn't blame her for not wanting to. Even from here he could feel the tension and distrust radiating from Mrs. Lanning.

"You cannot keep up this pace all day," he said. "It's only been an hour, and we'll be travelling until dusk."

"I have excellent stamina." She winced as she stepped on a rock and he studied her bare feet.

"You'll rip your feet to shreds."

"I'm fine," she said.

He grunted irritably and then moved his horse in front of her, forcing her to stop. He reached down, wrapped one powerful arm around her waist, and hauled her upward as she squeaked in alarm. He positioned her thin body in the saddle in front of him, grimly ignoring the feel of her ass pressing against his groin.

"I can walk, m'lord," she said through gritted teeth and tried to slide out of the saddle.

"Be still for the gods' sake," he grumbled. He put his arm around her waist and pulled her back against his chest.

She squirmed against him, and he grimaced as her soft ass rubbed against his crotch. He squeezed her waist. "I said be still." .

He pulled away from the wagon, ignoring Mrs. Lanning's look of disapproval, and dropped back until they were trailing behind the group.

"Could you loosen your grip, my lord?" she asked. "You're hurting me."

He realized he was still squeezing her waist and released her with a muttered, "Sorry."

She rubbed briefly at her side before beginning to cautiously sit forward. He immediately pulled her back against him.

"I'm not going anywhere," she protested.

"No, you're not," he agreed amicably and shifted her until she was pressed more tightly against him.

A lovely feeling of warmth was rushing through him, and an odd sort of contentment filled his big body. He glanced down at Avery. She was visibly trembling. The wind had picked up, bringing dark stormy clouds, and he frowned at the way the wind was rippling through her red hair. Her dress was thin, and he reached between them, unbuttoning the cloak he wore over his shirt and pants and wrapping it firmly around them both.

"You're freezing," he said gruffly, slipping his arm back around her waist and resting his large hand against her hip.

"Thank you."

She tried again to put a little space between them, and he tightened his hand on her hip. "How did you end up at the slave house? Neither you nor your sister were born into slavery, that's obvious enough."

She shrugged. "Nothing more than a bad luck story and it's a boring one at that."

"I would hear it anyway," he prompted.

"I would prefer not to share it."

"I don't care what you prefer. Tell me the story, now."

She cleared her throat angrily. "Fine. My father was a very wealthy man. Many years ago, when he was a young man, he figured out how the ancients had created their electricity.

Tristan stiffened behind her. "Your father was James Hendrin?"

She nodded. "Aye."

"He's one of the most famous humans in the history of the new world." He grabbed her chin and turned her face toward his. "Are you telling me that I purchased the children of James Hendrin to be my nanny and gardener? Your father was the wealthiest man in the country."

She wrenched her head free. "I am well aware of that, my lord." The bitterness in her voice was undeniable.

"How did he die?"

She sighed and although she began to tremble again, her voice was steady enough. "We were at our country home. My mother took Maya and me back into the city. There was a play that Maya wanted to see. My father stayed home with our two younger siblings. While we were gone, there was a fire in the house and both my father and our siblings died in the blaze."

"Was it an accident?"

"It appeared so, but my father had many enemies."

"I still do not understand how you and your sister ended up in a slave house."

"My mother is not a strong woman. After my father and siblings died, she – she became completely unglued. My father had always encouraged a frugal lifestyle, much to my mother's dismay, and once he was gone there was no one to stop her. She threw elaborate parties, took expensive trips and bought several houses. She met the wrong people, fell in with a bad crowd, and before long they had her hooked on the cocakin."

Tristan frowned. He had tried the human's cocakin once, many years ago. The fine white powder had burned his nose and given him an instant headache, along with strange and disturbing hallucinations. He had not touched it again.

"It took my mother less than nine months to burn through my father's considerable wealth," she said. "Maya and I begged her to stop, begged her to get help, but she had gone mad with grief."

She sighed again. "When she ran out of money, she sold both Maya and me to the slave house in order to buy more drugs. She told us we were going on a holiday. Instead, she brought us to the slave house. We were taken and chained before we even really knew what was happening. We didn't even try to fight the man at the slave house… we were in too much shock."

She lapsed into silence for a moment. "She promised she would return in less than a week to buy us back and that was the last time we saw her. We have no idea where she is now or if she's even still alive."

She winced when Tristan squeezed her waist involuntarily. He was horrified by what she had just told him. Sophia's mother had been a terrible mother, but even she would not have sold her children for drugs.

"My lord," she said, pushing at his arm.

He relaxed his grip. "How long were you at the slave house?"

She mulled it over for a few minutes. "I'm not entirely sure. I would think at least ten or eleven months. I was sold once but returned back to the slave house the next day."

"Why?"

She appeared to be choosing her words carefully. "Most of the men that go there are looking for a companion or a housekeeper. The ones who are looking for a housekeeper would sooner scrub their own toilets then bring a Red into their household. Those who are looking for a – a companion, are leery of the stories of men who have tried to take Reds into their beds."

"What stories are those?"

She gave him a strange look. "Surely you know them, my lord?"

He shook his head, and she suddenly grinned ferociously. "Take a Red into your bed and you risk having your cock turn black and rot. If you manage to fuck one without catching their whore's disease, you don't dare fall asleep while they're in your bed."

"Why not?"

She wrinkled her nose at him. "While you sleep, we wrap our long red locks around your throats, mutter the spells of the ancient ones and turn our hair into fire. Humans burn to a crisp while we remain unharmed."

"Bullshit," he said.

"You're one of the few humans I've met who doesn't believe the stories."

He rolled his eyes. "Tell me why you were returned to the slave house."

"A truly disgusting man bought me to be his companion. Apparently, he was willing to risk losing his cock or having his bed set on fire." She paused. "The first night he took me to his bed, I broke his nose and bit off his right earlobe before muttering nonsense under my breath and threatening to set him on fire."

"Gods be damned," he grunted.

"He returned me the next day for a full refund." She smiled prettily, her even white teeth flashing at him.

He shook his head, smiling despite himself, and after a moment she sobered. "It's why I was so desperate to have Maya go with you. She is young and – and untouched, and I did not want her to be sold as a companion. I deliberately stopped her from bathing and tried to keep her as undesirable looking as possible. She's so beautiful, so pure and sweet. Your children will love her – I promise you."

"Aye," he answered.

She was silent for a few moments and then glanced up at him. "How did Sophia's mother die?"

"She, how did you put it? Fell in with the wrong crowd? Only they handed her over to the leeches as payment for their debt."

"I'm sorry," she said. "You must miss your wife."

"When Sophia was two her mother left our home and took her to the city. I did not see my child again until a week ago."

She remained silent and he found himself opening up to her. "I knew she hated the country, but I thought once Sophia was born, she would change her mind. Our – our people normally live in the country, we avoid the cities, but her family were one of the few who found comfort in the city. I lived there briefly, met Sophia's mother, and convinced her to marry me and move back to the country. She agreed but was almost instantly unhappy. A few months into the marriage she became pregnant with Sophia. She did her best to adapt to country living but it was clear she was miserable. I was away tending to matters dealing with my father's death, and she used that opportunity to take Sophia and leave."

He cleared his throat. "When I returned from my parents' home I immediately left for the city. I searched many moons for them, but she had hidden herself and Sophia well. I did not speak to them again until just over a moon ago when I received word that she had died. She had obviously spoken about me to Sophia. She knew who I was and that I was her father. But she wants little to do with me."

"So that's why she calls you Tristan," Avery said.

"Aye."

"And Nicholas – he isn't yours."

"No. I do not know who his father is."

"That was kind of you to take him in."

He shrugged. "Sophia loves him very much. I did it for her. Besides, he is a thin and sickly baby. I doubt he will see his first birthday."

"You might be surprised. I have a feeling that the fresh air will suit him well."

"Perhaps," he agreed.

They rode for the next half hour in silence. He was surprised when Avery, who'd been yawning repeatedly, slumped against him, pushing her face into his neck and muttering softly in her sleep.

He gritted his teeth at the feel of Avery's mouth moving against his throat. He shifted her into a more comfortable position and slid his hand upward until it rested against her ribcage. He knew she was naked under the dress, and his groin tightened uncomfortably at the memory of her body in her wet underclothes.

He was aching to touch her breast, to feel the firm weight of it in his hand, and he slid his hand upward. He slipped his hand inside the loose neckline of her dress and cupped her bare breast gently. It fit perfectly in his large hand and he ran his thumb over her nipple, smiling when it hardened under his touch. He pulled lightly on her tight nipple and she arched her back a little, muttering something low in her throat. He snatched his hand away, his pulse beating thickly in his veins and shame flowing through his body.

He was no better than the man who had bought her to be his companion. Despite his shame he wanted to touch her again, and he wrapped his hand around her hip to stop himself from cupping her breast. He clucked to his horse, encouraging him to move faster until they had caught up to the others.

CHAPTER 5

"You're very good with him."

Maya blushed. "Thank you, m'lord."

He sat down beside her with an easy grace. "Call me Marshall. And you are?"

"Maya." She looked back down at the baby in her lap, smiling and kissing his forehead as he giggled up at her.

Marshall watched as Nicholas kicked his feet and giggled again. The boy's normally pale skin was flush with colour, and at supper he had drunk two bottles of milk without throwing up.

"He's like a different baby."

Maya shrugged. "The fresh air must agree with him."

"Indeed." Marshall smiled at her. "How old are you, Maya?"

"Twenty, m'lord - I mean Marshall."

"You're very pretty. Did you know that?" He brushed a stray piece of hair away from her face and Maya blushed bright red.

"Thank you, Marshall," she whispered.

"Would you care to go for a walk with me?"

She shook her head, glancing down at the baby. "I cannot leave Sophia and Nicholas."

"I'm sure one of the other women would be happy to watch them for a while." He smiled encouragingly at her.

"I'd better not. I'm sorry." She gave him a look of regret.

"Do not be sorry, little Maya. I can visit with you just as easily here."

"Maya!" Avery was sitting on a fallen log and Sophia was standing behind her, running a comb through her long, red hair. Avery patted the spot next to her. "Come sit with me for a bit."

She stared distrustfully at Marshall as Maya obediently circled around the campfire and sat next to her. Maya handed her the baby as Sophia crawled over the log and into Maya's lap.

"Sing to me," she demanded, curling up against Maya's thin body. Maya sang softly as Avery placed Nicholas on his back on her lap and lifted his shirt. She leaned over and blew raspberries on his belly, grinning when he screamed delightedly and kicked his feet against her sternum.

"Does Nicky like that? Hmm?" She crooned before leaning down and blowing another raspberry on his bare skin. He giggled and shrieked before snatching a hank of her long red hair and yanking on it.

"Ouch, baby!" Avery winced and tried to unclench his tiny fist. "No hair pulling."

"Here." A familiar voice came from above her and she groaned silently when Tristan sat next to her and began to untangle her hair from Nicholas' fingers.

He pulled the last of her hair free and then brushed it back and over her shoulder, out of the reach of Nicholas' waving hands.

"Thank you," she murmured. Her stomach was in knots

and she prayed to the gods that he couldn't see the way his presence was affecting her.

He frowned and stared down at the baby, and she took the opportunity to study him. His dark hair was long, and he kept it tied back from his face in a low ponytail. His face was tanned from the sun and he had high, wide cheekbones. His eyes were so dark they looked nearly black, and he had a generous mouth and straight, white teeth. She had always admired tall men with broad shoulders, and his shoulders were so wide both she and Maya could have easily hidden behind them.

He was attractive. Avery could admit that to herself. She could also admit that she was attracted to him. But it didn't mean that she could allow herself the luxury of taking him into her bed. Her first priority had to be Maya and ensuring her safety. Mrs. Lanning's almost immediate hatred of both her and Maya meant she needed to be careful about what she said and did. She had a feeling that sleeping with the lord of the house would not help her worm her way into Mrs. Lanning's good graces.

"You were right," Tristan murmured.

"Hmm?"

"About your sister having a way with babies. I think this is the first time I've seen Nicholas happy." He tickled the boy under his chin and smiled when he giggled.

He plucked the thin baby from her lap and held him up in the air, looking him over critically. "He seems healthier as well."

Avery smiled. "The fresh air is good for him."

"I guess." He tossed the baby into the air, catching him gently, and Nicholas laughed and squealed.

Maya leaned over Avery. "My lord, Sophia has fallen asleep. Would you help me carry her to our tent?"

"Of course." He handed the baby to Avery and stood, reaching for Sophia. He picked her limp body up and cradled her against his shoulder, burying his nose in her cloud of fine hair and inhaling deeply. She snuggled into him and he rubbed her back as he carried her toward the tent. Maya smiled at Avery and took the baby from her.

"Good night, Avery. I love you."

"Good night, baby sister. I love you too."

TRISTAN WAS JUST CRAWLING BETWEEN THE BLANKETS WHEN he heard Marshall's voice outside the tent.

"Enter," he called, and Marshall ducked inside. The storm had started just shortly after they had retired to their tents and after only a few hours on watch, Marshall was soaked through.

"What's wrong?" Tristan frowned at him. "Where's Leo?"

"Nothing's wrong. Leo just took over for me and I'm headed to the tent to dry off and get some sleep, even with Jeffrey's awful snoring. I'll thank the gods when we're finally home and I can sleep in my own bed."

"Is that what you came in here to tell me?" Tristan said irritably.

"I thought you should know the Red is huddled next to the wagon."

"What?" Tristan stared at him. "What do you mean she's huddled next to the wagon?"

Marshall waved his hand impatiently. "I mean she's huddled next to the wagon. I was heading to my own tent and that damn red hair caught my attention."

"Why is she not in the tent?" Tristan asked.

"I don't know." Marshall gave him another look of impatience. "Perhaps she's doing some sort of spell, or perhaps she finds the rain refreshing. I just thought you should know."

He stretched, his back cracking loudly. "Good night, Tristan." He slipped out of the tent and into the darkness.

Tristan cursed and dressed quickly before throwing on his cloak and heading out into the dark. It was black out and the rain was pouring down but he could see nearly as well in the dark as a cat. He had no trouble finding Avery curled up in a small ball next to the front left wheel of the wagon.

He strode toward her, crouching and touching her shoulder. She had a thin blanket wrapped around her body and her head was bowed against the steady downpour. The blanket was soaked through and her hair was clinging limply to her skull.

"Girl, wake up!" He shouted to be heard over the sudden crash of thunder.

She looked up, her face pale and dark circles under her eyes.

"What, my lord?" She asked wearily.

"Why are you out here?" He shook her. "Have you gone mad?"

"There is no room in the tent." She curled up into herself again, her body shaking violently.

He cursed and grabbed her arm. He pulled away the blanket and tried to yank her to her feet, but she cried out and fell back against the wheel. He stared in disbelief at the metal cuff around her wrist.

"What in the gods name is going on here?" He grabbed her chin and made her look at him. "Who chained you to the wheel?"

Her mouth set in a thin line. "Please, my lord. I'm very cold. May I have my blanket back?" She reached with trembling fingers and he threw the sopping wet fabric angrily onto the ground.

"Hold still." He held the chain next to the cuff on her wrist with his right hand and grabbed the other end of the chain with his left. He pulled, the cords standing out in his neck and the muscles in his arms bulging, and Avery's mouth dropped open when the chain snapped in half.

He picked her up and carried her to his tent. He dropped her to her feet, and she stood dripping water on to the floor of the tent as her entire body shook violently. He cursed again and turned around, digging through his bag to find a dry shirt and a towel.

"Here, girl. Put this on." He handed them to her, and she nodded gratefully. He turned around to give her some privacy When she tapped him on the back, he turned back to face her. His shirt fell past her knees and despite drying off with the towel, it was already starting to stick to her damp skin.

She handed him his towel. "Thank you, my lord."

He stared at her. Her lips were blue, and her face was so pale the freckles on her nose stood out in stark relief.

"Turn around," he demanded. She turned and flinched a little when he rubbed her hair dry with the damp towel. He squeezed the water out quickly and efficiently as her teeth chattered, and she wrapped her arms around her body in an attempt to warm herself. The cuff around her wrist jingled softly as she shook.

He threw the towel into the corner and picked up the top blanket from his bed. He wrapped it around her, and then pushed the rest of the blankets back before picking her up and placing her on his bed. He took off his cloak and shrugged out of his clothing before climbing into the bed behind her. and pulling up the blankets.

He pulled her blanket-wrapped body back against his and

wrapped one arm around her waist. He rubbed her body roughly through the blanket as she shook and shivered. After almost half an hour, her trembling finally began to subside.

He leaned over her, inspecting her face closely. Her lips had returned to their normal pink colour, but her skin was still pale, and she looked exhausted.

"Warmer?" he asked.

"Aye," she whispered.

"Who chained you to the wheel?"

She sighed. "Please, my lord. I am very tired, and it will be morning soon. Could I sleep for a few hours?"

He nodded. "Go to sleep. We will speak in the morning."

AVERY SIGHED AND STRETCHED LANGUIDLY. SHE COULD HEAR Maya snoring softly behind her and she frowned a little, not understanding why her normally soft bed was so hard. She was much too warm. Maya was wrapped around her like a vine and she was positively radiating with heat.

She tried to wriggle away but Maya snorted softly and buried her face against the back of her neck. Her stubble scraped – *stubble*?

Avery opened her eyes in a hurry. She stared upward, expecting to see the familiar ceiling of her bedroom, and frowned in confusion at the ceiling of the tent. After a few seconds, reality flooded through her. She had been dreaming of home.

It was early morning. The rain had stopped, and the tent was washed in cool sunlight. She looked under the blankets. When she had fallen asleep last night, she had been wrapped in a blanket cocoon. At some point in the night she had wiggled her way free and now her body was pressed intimately against Tristan's. She blushed when she realized he was naked, and she tugged nervously at the shirt which had risen up in her sleep and was just barely covering her ass.

She moved his arm off her waist and eased her body away from his. He snorted in his sleep, threw his arm back around her, and yanked her against him. She could feel his erection pushing against her ass, and she was helpless to stop the small moan from escaping her lips when he slipped his hand inside the neckline of her shirt and cupped her bare breast.

He sighed and buried his face into her hair, inhaling deeply as her nipple hardened against the palm of his hand. Still asleep, he plucked gently at her nipple and she moaned again, covering her mouth to dampen the sound as he shifted against her. He moved his hand to her other breast, cupping and kneading it before pinching her nipple. Against her will, her back arched, pushing more of her breast into his hand and making her ass press against him. He groaned and thrust his erection against her in response.

He was awake now. She could feel it in the way his breathing had quickened against her skin, and she wasn't surprised when he pushed her hair away from her neck and trailed a path of hot kisses down her soft skin.

"Please, m'lord," she moaned. "We should not be doing this."

"I think we should," he whispered against her skin before kissing the spot behind her ear. He squeezed her breast, rolling her nipple between his finger and thumb, and she cried out with pleasure as he sucked her earlobe into his mouth.

He reached down and quickly tugged her shirt up around her waist. She inhaled sharply and tried to wrench her lower body away from his, but he was too quick and too strong. He pressed his hand against her flat abdomen and pushed her back against his body.

He groaned loudly into her ear at the first feel of her naked ass against his hard cock.

Get out of his bed, right now, her mind screamed at her. Instead, to her horror, her body rubbed against him shamelessly.

He kissed the curve of her shoulder, running his tongue along the soft skin before nipping lightly with his teeth. His hand stroked and rubbed one pale thigh until her tightly-closed legs loosened and relaxed. He moved his hand back under her shirt and cupped her breast again, his fingers rubbing and pulling on her nipple until she was gasping.

Her head spinning and her body aching and throbbing with need, she didn't notice he was moving his hand between her legs until it was too late. He was cupping her warmth, his finger sliding through the soft red curls and into her with shocking intimacy, before she could stop him.

She clamped her legs shut around his hand and grabbed his wrist with trembling fingers. "My lord – stop!"

He stopped, holding his hand perfectly still against her, but continued to place soft kisses on the sensitive skin of her neck.

"Are you sure you want me to stop? Your wetness would suggest differently." There was more than a hint of arrogance in his voice.

She hesitated and then nodded. When he made no effort to move his hand, she blew out her breath in a shuddering sigh.

"My lord," she prompted.

When he spoke, his voice was tinged with amusement. "You'll need to loosen your legs then, girl."

She realized her thighs were still clamped tightly around his hand and heat flooded her face. She relaxed her thighs but kept her fingers wrapped around his wrist and, with an agonizing slowness that had her moaning softly, he slid his finger out of her. He let his thumb brush against her clit, and she gave a loud cry and squeezed her thighs around his hand, trapping it against her again.

He chuckled, a warm sound that she felt more than heard, and sucked on her earlobe again. "I'm starting to think you don't want me to stop, girl."

He circled her clit with the pad of this thumb before rubbing it firmly. "Should I stop?"

"No! I mean aye. I mean - I - I don't know," she whimpered helplessly.

"Take your time to decide," he breathed into her ear and stroked and rubbed her clit once more.

With a soft moan of need she opened her legs wide and released his wrist. He chuckled again. She knew she should have been embarrassed but his fingers were rubbing and exploring her with a rough and exciting urgency. Every touch of his fingers against her clit was sending bolts of pure pleasure through her pelvis and legs.

She was panting and moving restlessly against him when he stopped and grabbed the shirt that was bunched around her waist. He pulled it up and over her head and then pushed her onto her back. He pressed his upper body against hers and kissed her slowly, pushing his tongue at her closed lips until she opened her mouth and allowed him access. He stroked her tongue with his own and they kissed hungrily for a few moments, before he pulled his head back and stared at her naked body.

He made a low murmur of appreciation at the sight of her naked breasts before dipping his head and sucking her nipple into his mouth. She arched her back, her fingers threading through his long hair as he sucked gently. He rolled her nipple between his teeth before laving it with his tongue. He kissed his way to her other breast and tugged lightly on her nipple with his teeth. She could feel his cock hard against her hip, and she reached down and took him into her hand. He groaned before suddenly pushing her thighs apart and lowering his body between them.

"M'lord," she moaned.

He stared down at her. "Tristan. Say it."

"Tristan," she whispered, and he shuddered against her. He took her hands, linking their fingers and pinning her arms above her head, admiring the way it lifted her full breasts. He nudged her thighs farther apart and she moaned when his cock rubbed against her clit.

"Tristan, I -"

She cried out, her body arching against his when he entered her fully with one smooth thrust.

He groaned with pleasure, releasing her hands so he could prop himself up above her. He stared down at her and she blinked in surprise. His dark brown eyes were now green and glowing with a fierce light.

TRISTAN STUDIED AVERY'S FACE IN THE COOL SUNLIGHT. "Kiss me, girl."

She obeyed him immediately, kissing him hard on the mouth. He withdrew, staring down at her as he pushed slowly back into her. From the moment he entered her, his entire body had been filled with a strange and powerful warmth. Avery's walls clung wetly to him, and he gritted his teeth and ignored his almost immediate need to both climax and to shift. He took several deep breaths as she wiggled and arched beneath him.

"Please, Tristan," she panted softly.

He slid in and out of her in a slow, deep rhythm as she moaned his name repeatedly. He was just reaching between them to rub her clit when a scream pierced the silence. She stiffened underneath him.

"What was that?"

"Stay here," he ordered.

He pulled out of her and stood, throwing his pants on before leaving the tent. He squinted in the sunlight. Mrs. Lanning was standing next to the wagon, her face white and her body trembling. She held the broken end of the chain in one shaking hand and she stared wildly at the group who had gathered around her.

"The Red is gone!" She stared down at the broken chain and then held it out to the others. "She is a witch! We need to find her and burn her before she kills us all."

"Mrs. Lanning, calm down!" Tristan scowled and pushed his way through the crowd of women who had gathered around her. From the corner of his eye he could see Maya emerging from her tent, Sophia clinging to her leg and Nicholas still asleep in her arms.

"She's a witch, my lord!" Mrs. Lanning grabbed his arm and squeezed it anxiously. "She has disappeared into thin air and we must hunt her down and burn her."

"Avery?" Maya appeared next to him. She shifted the sleeping Nicholas against her. "Where is Avery? What's going on?" He could hear the panic in her voice, and he rubbed his forehead.

"She's fine, Maya. She's -"

"Your sister is a witch!" Mrs. Lanning shouted, spittle flying from between her lips. "We should use this one to lure her back into the open."

She reached for Maya and Marshall stepped in front of her. "Don't touch her, you old bag."

"Marshall – enough," Tristan barked at him. "Mrs. Lanning, calm down. Avery is not a witch. She hasn't disappeared. She's -"

"Maya?" Avery's soft voice called out worriedly, and Maya breathed a sigh of relief as everyone turned to see Avery standing in the opening of his tent.

She tugged nervously at his shirt as Maya hurried over to her. "Avery, are you hurt?"

"No, I'm fine." She smiled reassuringly at her younger sister as Sophia joined them.

"Hi, Avery. Why are you wearing Tristan's shirt? Were you sleeping in his tent?" she asked.

"Um…"

He could see Avery's blush from across the clearing as Mrs. Lanning moved toward her.

"Whore!" She hissed, pointing a trembling finger at her. "You seduce our lord with your whoring ways."

"Hold your tongue, Mrs. Lanning." He pulled the older woman around to face him. "Was it you who chained her to the wagon last night?"

The woman hesitated. "She was being insolent, my lord. She threatened me and the others, and I chained her out there for our own safety."

He looked at Avery. She stared calmly back at him, and he had a quick memory of her voice moaning his name as he fucked her.

He cleared his throat roughly and looked at the other women. "Is that true?"

They hesitated, and Mrs. Lanning gave them a threatening look before her gaze narrowed in on Laura. "Laura – tell him."

Laura swallowed. "It's true, m'lord. She was – was threatening us."

"How?" Tristan arched his eyebrow at her.

"She was chanting spells and…." Laura trailed off.

"What does it matter how?" Mrs. Lanning spat. "She was threatening us. You need to either burn her now or dump her at the outskirts."

"I trust you're not trying to tell me how to run my household." His voice was soft but Mrs. Lanning shrank back.

"Of course not, m'lord," she whispered.

He stared at the group. "We need to get back on the road. I have every intention of being in my own bed tonight."

"But what about her?" Mrs. Lanning pointed at Avery.

"We'll deal with her at home. Bring me the key so I can unlock the cuff around her wrist." He turned to the others. "Get moving, people. I want to be on the road in an hour."

CHAPTER 6

"Avery, are you all right?" Maya asked in a low voice.

Avery looked up from packing Nicholas' bedding.

"I'm fine."

"What happened last night?"

"The hag chained me to the wheel, like she did the night before. Tristan discovered me, broke the chain and took me back to his tent." Avery shoved the blanket into the canvas bag and reached for his bag of clothing.

"Did you have sex with him?" Maya asked.

Avery stared at her. "Why would you ask me that?"

"Because he seems very robust this morning."

Avery cleared her throat nervously. It was true. Tristan seemed even larger and stronger than usual this morning and despite the drama from earlier, he was in a surprisingly good mood. She glanced over at him. He was throwing Sophia up in the air, catching her before tossing her into the sky again and the little girl was giggling with delight.

"I was soaking wet and freezing. He put me in his bed to warm me up and we fell asleep. He slept against my body all night. Of course, he's going to feel good this morning," she replied.

Maya frowned. "How do you feel? Does he have a sickness?"

"No. I feel perfectly fine."

It was another lie. She felt more than fine. In fact, she couldn't remember the last time she felt this good. He had unwittingly fed off her power all night, but she had taken her own dose of his good health when she had allowed him to fuck her.

Her face flushed at the memory of how quickly she had stopped protesting and parted her legs for him. She had been like a cat in heat and even now, her body was aching and throbbing with a need for release. She had spent the last hour alternating between cursing Mrs. Lanning for interrupting them and breathing a sigh of relief that it had gone no further than it did.

Not that it mattered. Mrs. Lanning had already labeled her as a witch and a whore, and she would undoubtedly make both hers and Maya's life hell when they finally arrived at Tristan's home. She stared down at Nicholas' clothing and wondered if it wouldn't be better if she just slipped away when they reached his home. She could wait until their guard was down and disappear in the night. Maya had already proven her competency with his children, and Tristan would not send her away. If she disappeared, Mrs. Lanning would calm down and Maya would be safe.

"Avery?" Maya said.

"Aye?"

"Are you sure you're all right?" She placed a worried hand on Avery's arm, and Avery forced herself to smile at her.

"I'm positive." She glanced down at herself and smoothed

Tristan's shirt down. "Although I wish I had more clothing."

Maya smiled at her. "Your dress is still soaking wet. I'm afraid it's his shirt for now."

They carried the children's things to the carriage, handing them to Jeffrey who secured them carefully to the roof of the carriage. They returned to the tent and Avery hooked the baby sling around Maya, tying it tightly at the back. Avery disassembled the tent as Maya slipped the sleeping Nicholas into the sling before helping her.

"Here, let me." Marshall appeared beside her and began to tear down the tent as Maya smiled gratefully at him.

"Thank you, m'lord."

"Marshall." He reminded her.

"Marshall," she repeated shyly.

"You're looking very lovely this morning." He smiled at her as he carefully folded the tent and slipped it into the carrying case.

"Thank you," she murmured.

Marshall slung the tent bag over one arm before offering his other to Maya. She took it with another shy grin, and he led her toward the carriage. Avery followed them, stopping a few feet away from the carriage and suppressing a grin when Marshall whispered something in Maya's ear and she giggled and blushed, smacking his arm lightly.

He helped her into the carriage as Tristan approached with Sophia tucked into the crook of his arm. He kissed the girl's cheek and deposited her in the carriage as Maya stuck her head out the door. "My lord, may Avery ride with us? The wagon is crowded."

Tristan took her by the arm. "She'll ride with me for a bit."

"I would prefer to ride with my sister." Avery tried to pull her arm free.

"And I would prefer if you rode with me for a while." He refused to let go of her.

"I'd be more comfortable in the carriage," she said.

A look of irritation flashed across his face. "Stop your arguing and do as I tell you, girl."

Her cheeks reddened with anger as he marched her to his horse and lifted her easily into the saddle. She pushed his shirt down, but her nakedness rubbed uncomfortably against the cold leather, as he wedged his body behind hers.

"I'm not wearing any underclothes," she said in a low voice.

"I am well aware of that." He grinned wolfishly.

She did her best to ignore the shudder of need that went through her at his grin. "The leather is cold and uncomfortable."

"We definitely don't want that." He reached into one of the saddle bags and pulled out another of his shirts. "Here, place this underneath you."

She looked at the shirt in his hand. "Are you kidding me? Just let me sit in the carriage with my sister."

She had braided her long hair and secured it with piece of leather, and he tugged gently on the end of it. "Your choices are the cold leather or my shirt. Take your pick."

She continued to hesitate, and he leaned forward, his breath tickling her ear. "Or perhaps you would prefer to have my hand there?"

She shivered violently as the memory of his hand between her legs went through her head and he grinned again. "It seems as though you would prefer option three."

Quickly, before he could do what he threatened, she plucked his shirt from his hands and tucked it beneath her. She arranged it so that it was covering the saddle and protecting her from the leather.

"Better?"

"Aye," she muttered.

"Good." He clicked his tongue to the horse and wrapped his arm around her waist, rubbing her abdomen through his shirt as they followed the others. Like yesterday he dropped back until there was some distance between them and the other riders. She squirmed nervously as he placed a soft kiss on her neck and cupped her breast familiarly.

"Please stop that." She pushed his hand away from her breast and leaned forward.

He frowned and tugged her back against him. "Why do you deny me the pleasure of touching you?"

She swallowed. "My lord -"

"Tristan."

"My lord," she said pointedly, "what happened this morning was a mistake. I should not have allowed you to touch me so intimately."

"You seemed to enjoy my touch this morning." He stroked her bare thigh and she shivered again.

"Please, my lord," she said. A frown crossed his face at the obvious distress in her voice. He stopped touching her, holding the reins with both hands and allowing her to lean away from him.

"I'm sorry. I did not mean to lead you on this morning," she said. "The other women are already agitated by my presence. If they find out that I am warming your bed, I'm afraid they will make my life difficult."

She cursed inwardly at how weak she sounded, but she needed him to believe that she was worried only for herself. She feared that if he realized it was Maya she was concerned about he would send Maya away despite her abilities with his children, in order to indulge in his obvious desire for her. She was not completely naïve to the ways of men, and she knew there were many who could be like a dog with a bone when it came to sex.

He didn't reply but he made no move to continue touching her either. They rode in silence for a few minutes. Avery watched the rest of the group disappear around a curve in the road ahead.

"May I ask you a question, my lord?"

"If I can ask you one."

She thought about it for a moment. "Fair enough. What's your question?"

"Were you casting spells on the other women in the tent last night?"

She shook her head. "No."

He waited for her to elaborate and when she didn't, sighed in irritation. "Ask your question."

"Why do your eyes change colour?"

He stiffened behind her. "They don't."

"They do," she insisted. He remained silent and she twisted her upper body to look at him.

"Earlier this morning when we were -"

She paused awkwardly and he grinned at her. "When we were fucking?"

She blushed and he suddenly slid his hand behind her head and gripped her neck. He kissed her deeply, pushing his tongue into her mouth as she moaned.

With a low gasp, she tore her mouth from his. "Stop distracting me. Your eyes turned green – why?"

He shook his head dismissively. "You imagined it."

She glared at him. "No, I didn't. Tell me why they -"

There was a sudden scream ahead of them and, with a loud curse, Tristan dug his heels into his horse's side and the horse galloped forward.

They rounded the corner and Avery made a cry of dismay. "Faeries!"

Their small group had been surrounded by a dozen of the creatures. Avery shuddered in disgust at the sight of them. They were short but powerful, with large, grotesque leathery wings sprouting from their backs and bodies covered in strange markings. Their hair was wild and knotted with twigs and leaves, and they carried short and razor-sharp spears. It was nearly impossible to distinguish the males from the females, and Avery watched in horror as one flew down and lifted Renee from the wagon.

She screamed in terror, struggling and kicking as the faerie flew to the soft grass next to the road. He dropped her onto the grass and fell on her before she could rise to her feet. He pinned her down on her back and held his face above hers.

He squealed in delight and opened his mouth. It was filled with pointed teeth, and his long, lizard-like tongue flicked out and licked Renee's cheek lightly and delicately before he inhaled. Renee went still and her eyes shut as her mouth opened and a fine grey mist rose from her open mouth.

"No!" Avery cried.

Faeries were fierce and wild and had a taste for humans. Before they killed and cooked the humans they captured, they sucked the essence of a person from them. Avery had met a person once long ago, who had been rescued from faeries before they could devour him. However, he had not been spared from having most of his essence sucked away. He had been like a dead man that still breathed, and Avery could still remember the horror she had felt at seeing his blank eyes and limp body.

As Tristan urged his horse toward the carriage, she looked behind her to see a large black wolf come bounding across the road and attack the faerie on Renee. The faerie screamed as it tumbled off of the girl and jabbed at the wolf with the spear it carried in his right hand. Before the spear could penetrate the wolf's thick pelt, the wolf tore the faerie's throat out.

Blood and black liquid poured from the faerie's throat as it made a weak gurgling sound and collapsed on the hard ground. The wolf raised its snout to the sky and howled triumphantly before racing toward another faerie.

Tristan slid off his horse and threw open the door of the carriage. He lifted Avery from the horse and tossed her inside the carriage. She landed with a hard thud on the floor of it and Maya, crying and trying to soothe a screaming, frightened Nicholas, helped her to the seat.

Tristan looked at Sophia. His entire body was shaking and rippling, and Avery could see the beard growing on his face.

"It's fine, my love." He spoke in a near growl. "Stay in the carriage."

He glanced at Avery, his eyes glowing bright green, before he slammed the door shut. She pushed away from Maya and slid across the seat to the window, looking out just in time to see Tristan's clothing explode from his body as he transformed into a giant grey wolf.

She let out a breathless little gasp as he howled deafeningly before he crouched to the ground and then leaped into the air, snatching a faerie out of the sky above him. The faerie screeched and beat at Tristan's head, but Tristan threw him to the ground, placing his front paws on the faerie's chest and his mouth around its head. With a muffled growl, he tore off the faerie's head with a wet squelching sound.

Avery winced in horror as a jet of blood and black liquid squirted out of the faerie's gaping neck. Tristan dropped the faerie's head on the ground and ran toward the other wolves.

"Avery!" Maya let out a wailing cry and she turned to see Sophia on the floor of the carriage. Her small body was shaking and rippling, and low growls and snarls were emitting from her throat.

"What's happening to her?" Maya moaned as Nicholas screamed and wailed in the sling.

"She's a Lycan." Avery knelt beside Sophia. "Honey, it's okay. Calm down, baby. Everything's fine."

With another low snarl, Sophia looked at her and Avery jerked back. Like Tristan, her eyes had gone from dark brown to green, but they were filled with fear and confusion.

Maya, jiggling Nicholas frantically, knelt in front of her. "Sophia, my love? Shhh…it's okay."

With a loud scream that was half-howl, Sophia's clothes burst apart and she shifted into a small grey wolf. She crouched on the floor of the carriage, growling and snapping her teeth at them.

"Sophia?" Maya whispered.

Sophia leaped for her throat.

"Sophia, no!" Avery screamed as Sophia landed with a thud on Maya and Nicholas. Maya fell onto her back, her head hitting the door of the carriage with a loud bang, and threw her arm up as Sophia lunged for the soft flesh of her neck.

She screamed in pain as Sophia's small, but needle-sharp teeth tore into the flesh of her forearm.

"Sophia – stop!" Avery grabbed the scruff of the wolf's neck and yanked as hard as she could. Maya screamed again as Sophia tore a chunk of flesh from her arm. Avery wrestled the small wolf to the ground, flinching back just in time to avoid having Sophia sink her fangs into her face. She used her weight to pin Sophia to the floor and as the wolf howled and struggled beneath her shaking arms, she looked at Maya.

"Maya, are you all right?"

Maya, bleeding profusely from the wound in her arm, sat up and nodded. "I'm all right."

"Here, give me your hand." Avery reached for her with one hand.

"No," Maya gasped. "I'm fine for now. We'll heal it later."

She looked at Sophia. "What do we do with her? Should we *"

The door of the carriage ripped open and a faerie peeked in. He grinned and clapped his hands together. "Hello, my pretties!"

He looked at Maya and the baby. "Ooh, two for the price of one!"

Before Avery could move, he grabbed Maya by the hair and yanked her from the carriage.

"Maya!" Avery screamed. She threw Sophia onto the seat and scrambled out of the carriage, slamming the door shut just as Sophia leaped from the seat and thumped against the door.

Avery looked around frantically. The faerie had dragged Maya to the edge of the road, and three other faeries were crowding around them.

"A baby! I want the baby! C'mon now, give me a taste!" The three of them jostled for position. Avery snatched a large rock from the ground and ran toward them.

There was a loud howling and a large white wolf slammed into the three faeries, sending them tumbling and scattering across the road. He turned and pulled the faerie that was pinning Maya down, away from her. With a fierce snarl, he bit into the faerie's face, pulling and tearing off the flesh as the faerie shrieked and beat weakly at the wolf's head. There was a loud crunching noise as the wolf bit through the faerie's skull, and the faerie went limp.

"We'll kill you, Lycan!"

The white wolf twisted around as the other three faeries hovered above him. He bared his teeth as they fell on him, snapping and snarling as they pinned him down and began to stab him with their spears.

Avery was nearly there, the rock raised above her head, when hard hands suddenly grabbed her arm and she was yanked off her feet. The rock tumbled to the ground as a faerie, its wings flapping and cutting through the air, grinned down at her.

She screamed and reached up with her other arm, sinking her nails into the scaly arm of the creature. It gave its own scream of surprise and dropped her. She hit the ground hard. The breath was knocked from her and she rolled onto her back, staring dazedly at the grey sky above her.

The faerie's face appeared above her as he landed on her soft body with a hard thud. "I've never tried a Red, I haven't." He giggled and winked at her. "I bet you taste delicious."

He leaned over her, and Avery gagged as his hot and fetid breath washed over her.

"I'm going to enjoy this dearie," it simpered.

As it opened its mouth wide and inhaled, there was a flash of grey and the faerie was knocked backward. Before it could rise to its feet, Tristan was crouching over it.

The faerie had time to whisper weakly, "No, please...." before Tristan ripped its throat out.

Avery gasped for breath. She laid on her back, staring wide-eyed into the sky as the large grey wolf approached her. It whined softly, and she reached out a trembling hand and stroked the side of its face. "Tristan?"

He licked her hand and she closed her eyes, forcing

herself to take long, deep breaths. There was a soft popping noise and then she felt Tristan's warm hand on her belly.

"Avery, are you hurt?"

She shook her head and opened her eyes, giving him a weak smile when he helped her into a sitting position. "Maya?"

"She's fine. We've destroyed the faeries but we need to get -"

"Marshall!" Maya's loud cry made them both look, and then Tristan was yanking her to her feet and nearly carrying her across the road.

Maya was kneeling next to Marshall's naked body as an equally naked Jeffrey and Leo crouched helplessly next to them.

"He's not healing. Why isn't he healing? They did not administer the kiss!" Jeffrey gave Tristan a look of panic as Tristan took Marshall's cold hand.

"There are too many wounds. The spears carry their own poison."

Avery looked at Marshall's body. He had been stabbed multiple times with the spears of the faeries, and each wound was oozing a foul-smelling yellow liquid.

"He saved Nicholas and me," Maya whispered.

"Marshall, can you hear me?" Tristan squeezed Marshall's hand and although they could see the slow rise of his chest, he neither moved nor responded.

"What do we do?" Leo had left and returned with pants for all three of them, and a blanket for Marshall. Mrs. Lanning and the other women approached, and she gave Tristan a hard look.

"You know what we need to do, lord Tristan. He will not survive this, even with his Lycan healing powers. It is cruel to leave him to suffer this way."

Tristan cursed vehemently, bowing his head as Maya looked at Avery.

"Avery, please," she begged.

Avery knelt next to Tristan, putting one hand on his arm. "My lord, I may be able to help him. Will you let me?"

He looked at her, confusion in his eyes. "What do you mean, girl?"

"You need to trust me. I might be able to save his life if you will trust me."

Mrs. Lanning froze. "You cannot possibly trust her, lord Tristan. She's a witch. She will mutter a spell that she says will heal him, but it will destroy us all. We do not have time to - "

"Shut up, Mrs. Lanning!" Tristan suddenly roared. He stared at Avery. "Save his life."

She nodded and slipped under the blanket next to Marshall. She wiggled out of Tristan's shirt, and tossed it aside before wrapping her naked body around Marshall's. She kissed him several times on the face and mouth before resting her forehead against his.

She winced and Maya said worriedly, "Avery? Are you all right?"

She nodded. "He's badly injured. I'm sorry, Maya, but it may be too late."

Maya, her eyes filling with tears, rubbed Nicholas' back through the sling before taking Tristan's arm. "Leave them alone for a bit. She won't hurt him, I promise."

He stood up, glancing at her bleeding arm. "Did a faerie bite you?"

She shook her head. "No, m'lord. Sophia, she – she turned and attacked me. She is still in the carriage. I wasn't sure what to do."

He swore violently and struggled into his pants before

crossing to the carriage. Maya hurried after him. He opened the door of the carriage and peered inside.

Sophia was sitting naked on the floor, her legs drawn up and her thin arms wrapped around them. She raised her head and stared at him with a tear-stained face.

"I'm sorry, Papa. I did the bad thing. I didn't mean to do the bad thing. I was so scared. I couldn't help it, Papa," she moaned.

"It's okay, Sophia," he soothed. "It's not your fault, baby."

"I hurt Maya." She sobbed brokenly and then Maya was pushing him aside and shoving Nicholas into his arms. She climbed into the carriage and Sophia scrambled away from her, cringing and covering her head with her arms.

"Don't spank me, Maya! I'm sorry," she cried.

She flinched when Maya scooped her up, but the young woman simply hugged her against her chest. She sat on the seat and picked up a blanket.

"Shh, my Sophia, shh." She wrapped the blanket around the young girl and rocked her back and forth. "Don't cry, my love. You've done nothing wrong. It's all right, everything's all right."

She sang softly to the young girl and, with a watery gasp, Sophia wrapped her thin arms around Maya's neck and clung tightly.

"I didn't mean to hurt you, Maya," she whimpered.

"Of course, you didn't, my love. I know that. It was very scary, and you can't help what happens when you're afraid."

She continued to rock the young girl and, still holding Nicholas, Tristan quietly closed the carriage door and returned to Marshall and Avery.

CHAPTER 7

Maya stood next to Tristan and stared down at Avery and Marshall's entwined bodies. Tristan glanced at her and she answered the question in his eyes. "Sophia fell asleep in the carriage."

She reached for the sleeping baby in his arms and he handed him to her. She quickly tucked him into the sling.

"How is he doing?" she murmured.

"He's starting to move and crying out a bit," Tristan replied.

She breathed a sigh of relief. "That's a good sign."

"What is she?"

"She is not a witch, m'lord. I swear to you."

"That's not what I asked," he said impatiently.

"She's a healer."

"A healer?" He frowned.

"Aye. She can touch people and heal their sicknesses."

"What do you mean?"

She shrugged. "I mean that if someone is hurt or sick, Avery can touch them, hold them and something inside of her heals them."

He stared at her. "Has she always been this way?"

"No. She did not develop her ability until her monthlies began."

"The gods be damned. I have never heard of such a power."

"My father's grandmother had the same ability."

"How does she do it?"

"We're not quite sure, my lord. My father believed that she absorbs the sickness and the pain into her own body and then somehow heals herself."

He frowned, remembering the way she had winced when she first touched Marshall. "Does it hurt her?"

She gave him a cautious glance. "She says it does not, but I do not believe her."

"Who else knows of this?" He glanced around them. The others were crowded in and around the wagon. Some of the women were sobbing quietly, and Leo and Jeffrey were keeping a grim watch of the skies above them.

"Until now, no one outside of our family. My father kept it well-hidden from others."

"He was wise to do so. This type of power…"

He glanced at her. "I admit I am not sure that I entirely believe it."

She rolled her eyes. "Really, my lord? Marshall was close to death not half an hour ago and now look at him. His colour has returned, he is moving and making sounds."

"Lycans have their own healing powers," he said.

"You yourself said it was not enough," she said.

When he continued to stare doubtfully at her, she sighed impatiently. "You slept beside her last night. Tell me, in the morning did you not feel good? Did you not feel happier, stronger, more rested than you should have?"

He stared at her and she smiled wryly at him. "You

soaked in her power as you slept next to her. Even those who are perfectly healthy benefit from touching her."

He paused, remembering the strange feeling of power and warmth when he had entered her. He frowned as another thought hit him. "Sophia's finger – Nicholas."

She nodded. "She kissed Sophia's finger at the slave house, and our first morning by the lake she held Nicholas until he was better."

She stared solemnly at him. "Nicholas would not have survived much longer if it hadn't been for Avery. She said it was a miracle that he had survived for as long as he did. He should have died many months ago."

Marshall made a low groaning noise and opened his eyes. He blinked and stirred in Avery's arms, wincing and groaning again.

Avery opened her eyes and smiled at him before placing a soft kiss on his mouth. Marshall stared blankly at her and she kissed him again, urging him to kiss her back. After a moment he returned her kisses. Tristan watched, tension growing in his belly when Marshall leaned over her and deepened the kiss. She didn't resist, opening her mouth and allowing him to slip his tongue between her lips. Tristan was unaware that he was growling until Maya pressed her hand on his arm.

"She's doing this to help him."

"Help him?" he grunted. Jealousy was flooding through him as Marshall continued to kiss Avery. Even as he watched, he could see Marshall's skin starting to glow and Avery's grow paler and paler.

"Aye," Maya said. "The more of Avery they can touch, the more intimate she is with them, the faster they heal. It's why she held Nicholas against her bare skin, why she kissed

Sophia's cut directly, and why she allows Marshall to kiss her now."

He glanced at the girl, saw his jealousy mirrored in her eyes, and forced himself to relax. When he thought he had it under control he looked back down at Avery and Marshall. It was the wrong decision. Although they were hidden under the blanket, it was clear that Marshall was cupping her breast as he kissed her and with a low, angry growl he started forward. If he was well enough to do that, he was well enough for his own healing powers to kick in.

Before he could rip them apart, Avery shoved at Marshall's shoulders. He released her mouth and fell onto his back, staring up at Tristan.

"Tristan? What happened?" He looked in confusion at the pale and panting Avery.

"Faeries," Tristan grunted.

He helped Marshall to his feet and Maya handed him his pants. Marshall put them on, buttoning them up quickly as Tristan stared at his torso. Earlier there were at least a dozen stab wounds, oozing blood and foul poison, and now his torso was perfectly smooth. There were no open wounds and no scars.

"Maya? What happened?" Marshall stared at her arm. The wound had clotted but there was a large chunk of flesh missing from the top of her arm.

She shook her head. "I'll explain later."

Tristan squeezed his bare shoulder. "How do you feel?"

Marshall stared at him. "I feel...good. I mean, really good. Like I could run for miles, you know? I'm hungry."

Behind him, Tristan could hear Avery stirring and Maya ducked around him to help her. "Go to the wagon, brother, and help Leo and Jeffrey watch for more faeries. We'll be leaving shortly."

"Aye." Rubbing his head, a confused look on his face, Marshall left them. Tristan turned to see Avery rising to her feet. She had slipped into his shirt and she weaved unsteadily.

"Avery? Do you need to sit down?" Maya asked, a worried look crossing her face.

Avery's face was completely void of colour and there were deep, dark circles under her eyes, but she said, "I'm fine. I need to rest though."

She suddenly coughed harshly, holding her side and wincing. "I just need sleep." She staggered forward and collapsed.

"Avery!" Maya crouched down next to her and hesitated, looking at her arm as Tristan knelt beside her.

"I cannot touch her," Maya said. "If I do, her body will try to heal my arm. She's too weak. I've never seen her like this before."

Tristan reached for Avery, and Maya grabbed his arm. "Were you hurt in the attack? Is there any part of you that needs healing?"

He shook his head. "No, I'm fine." He picked up Avery and carried her to the carriage. "We need to get her to my home. There will be a soft bed and food waiting for her there."

"We should hurry," Maya said as she followed him to the carriage.

"I know," he replied grimly.

"WHY DOES SHE NOT WAKE?" TRISTAN STARED AT THE STILL-unconscious Avery. They had travelled the rest of the journey to his home without incident and he had immediately carried Avery to his room, Maya following at his heels. He had tucked her into his bed and Maya had sat beside her. She was careful not to touch Avery, and they had been waiting for close to an hour for her to wake up.

"I do not know, m'lord," Maya said. "Usually she only needs to rest for a bit and then she is fine. But I have never seen her try to heal someone hurt so deeply. Perhaps she just needs more time to heal her own body?"

"There must be something we can do." Tristan paced the large room, staring out the window at the growing darkness.

Maya hesitated. "There may be something we can try."

"What?"

"Avery does not just absorb people's sicknesses. She can also absorb their health. She uses it to help herself heal faster. If you're sure you are not hurt in any way, it may help if you lie with her."

"Why did you not say something sooner?" he said angrily. He pulled his shirt over his head and started to unbutton his pants. "Naked helps, right?"

"Aye."

He stripped and climbed into the bed beside Avery. He pulled off her shirt and gathered her naked body into his arms. He lay on his side, pulling her flush against him. He stared up at Maya as Avery's head clunked down onto his chest. He could feel her soft breath stirring the hairs on his chest and it comforted him.

"Will I feel anything? How will I know it's working?"

She shook her head. "No. If you do feel something, warmth or tingling, it means she's trying to heal you. Let go of her immediately."

"I will."

Maya hesitated and then glanced at the door of the bedroom. "I should be with Sophia and Nicholas. Will you stay with her for the night?"

"Yes. She'll be fine by morning." He wasn't sure if he

was trying to convince himself or Maya. "Go and get some rest. I will send for you if anything happens."

"Thank you, m'lord." She kissed Avery's cheek and then slipped out of his bedroom.

Tristan stared up at the ceiling. He was tense, waiting anxiously for any sign that Avery was trying to heal him, but when nothing happened, he let himself relax. He closed his eyes, listening to Avery's soft and steady breathing, and drifted into sleep.

CHAPTER 8

Tristan woke in the darkness. Avery was stirring against him and he stared anxiously at her.

"Hi." She smiled faintly at him.

"Hi. Do you feel better?"

She moved cautiously. "Aye. How is Marshall?"

"He'll live, thanks to you."

She turned her head slowly, groaning a little, and he sat up. "Should I get Maya?"

"No. Please - lie back down with me. It helps."

He relaxed back against the pillow and she curled up against him, staring up at him.

He cupped her face, stroking her pale cheek with his thumb, and then dipped his head and placed a gentle kiss on her mouth.

She returned the kiss, smiling a little, and he kissed her again. When she didn't resist, he turned until he was facing her and tugged gently on her braid until she tilted her head back. He kissed her neck, sucking and licking at the soft skin until she was moving restlessly against him.

"Tristan." She sighed and he captured her mouth with his,

kissing her until her lips parted and he could push his tongue between them.

"Tristan, what are you doing?" she whispered when he trailed a path of hot kisses across her jawline.

"Maya said this would help," he murmured into her ear before tracing the curve of it with the tip of his tongue.

She moaned quietly and clutched at his shoulders.

"Is it?" He sucked lightly on her earlobe, making her shiver.

"Aye."

"Good." He kissed her again, and she opened her mouth immediately and slipped her tongue into his mouth. He sucked hard on it until she was thrusting her hips against him, and then released her.

He cupped her breast, rubbing his thumb over her nipple and pinching it lightly. She arched her back as he bent his head and placed a gentle kiss on her nipple before sucking it into his mouth. He traced her smooth hip, running his fingers along her leg before slipping them across the top of her legs and tracing circles in the soft hair between her thighs.

"Tristan, wait…"

He stopped. "I want to make you feel better, Avery. Let me help you."

"I know, but the others…"

He kissed her cheeks and then the tip of her nose. "Just for tonight, Avery. Let me touch you tonight. Let me make you feel good, and I promise I won't touch you again after this. No one needs to know about it."

She stared doubtfully at him and he picked up her hand and placed a gentle kiss in the palm of it. She shivered and cupped his face. "Do you promise?"

"I promise."

She hesitated and then nodded. "All right."

He smiled and immediately slipped his hand back between her legs, cupping her warm sex and parting her lips so he could rub her clit.

She gasped at the sudden intimacy, her hips jerking against his hand as he rubbed and pressed her small pink nub. It swelled and hardened against his fingers, and she moaned in pleasure before sliding her hand down his abdomen and wrapping her fingers around his cock.

He groaned, his own hips thrusting helplessly as she stroked him. She kissed his neck and then ran her tongue along his collarbone, tasting the saltiness of his skin as he inhaled sharply and slipped his longest finger inside of her. She stared sightlessly at the ceiling above her as he rubbed her clit with his thumb and slowly slid his finger in and out of her.

"Please, Tristan," she moaned, her hand squeezing around his cock.

He pushed her onto her back and she parted her thighs eagerly as he knelt between them. She wrapped her legs around his waist and urged his body down onto hers. He reached between them and positioned his cock at her warm, wet opening. He pushed into her, groaning at the feel of her smooth walls, and she cried out with pleasure. Immediately, warmth and power flooded through him and he stopped as he remembered what Maya had said to him.

"Don't stop." She pounded him on the back and arched her hips against his, taking him fully inside of her.

"Wait, girl," he gasped out.

"Why?" she muttered. "Tristan, I don't want to stop."

"Are you – are you trying to heal me?"

"What?" She groaned. "For the gods sake, Tristan! No!" She moaned in frustration and kissed him frantically, thrusting her tongue into his mouth.

"There's nothing to heal. I swear it," she whispered against his mouth. "We're so good together... can you not feel it?"

He stared down at her. Her face was flushed with colour, and her light green eyes were shining with excitement and need. The dark circles under her eyes were completely gone and she was practically glowing with pleasure.

She smiled up at him. "Make me feel good, Tristan, please."

He groaned and plunged in and out of her, leaning down to kiss her as he propped himself on his hands above her and began a steady rhythm. She made small sounds of excitement and pleasure, her hands clenching and unclenching on his chest as she met him stroke for stroke.

As her smooth walls squeezed and released his cock repeatedly, his groin tightened, and he lost his smooth easy movement within her.

"Avery," he groaned. "I'm so close."

"Me too," she panted. "Don't stop."

He thrust harder and her moans grew steadily louder until her body suddenly stiffened under him and she came with a loud, hard cry. Her muscles clenched tightly and as she climaxed around him, a powerful wave of such intense pleasure surged through him that he came immediately. He shuddered and moaned above her, desperately controlling the urge to shift, until he collapsed weakly against her.

He breathed harshly, resting his head on her breast as she stroked his long hair until he finally forced himself to roll off of her. She curled up against him like a small cat.

"What in the name of the gods was that?" He stared at her with a combination of shock and awe.

She coloured slightly. "What?"

He stared down at her, his chest heaving for air. "I've never felt anything like that before."

She stared solemnly at him for a few seconds before her face broke out in a huge grin. "You're welcome."

THEY HAD BEEN LYING TOGETHER QUIETLY FOR OVER AN hour, Avery believed that Tristan had fallen asleep, when his voice drifted out of the darkness.

"How many men have you been with?"

She hesitated and he squeezed her gently. "Tell me."

"Only one before you. He worked for my father. We were together a few times."

He stroked her bare back leisurely. "Only a few times?"

He was quiet and when he spoke again, it didn't seem to be directed at her. "How in the gods did he resist? How it feels to be inside of you... I've never felt anything like it."

She stiffened against him. "This was a one-time thing, my lord. Do not forget that."

"I remember." He spoke absently. "Where is he now?"

"He was at our country home that night. He perished in the fire as well."

"Were you in love with him?" he asked.

She hesitated again. "I was – I was very fond of him."

She closed her eyes. Being with Daniel had been very nice. He'd been a kind and soft-spoken man, and he'd been gentle with her in bed. She had enjoyed his touch but whether it was from her nervousness, his own inexperience or a combination of both, he'd not been able to make her orgasm.

Being with Tristan, the way he touched her with his hands and mouth, made her feel nearly crazy with desire. Already, with just the touch of his hands stroking her back, she could feel the heat returning in her belly and pelvis. She shivered a little, and he pulled her closer against him. She could not continue to sleep with him despite how good he made her feel. She knew that Tristan desired her, but she also knew that he did not entirely trust she was not a witch. She could see it in his eyes when he looked at her. Especially since he had seen how she had saved Marshall.

She had a feeling that Mrs. Lanning would not rest until she had convinced Tristan she was a witch and perhaps her sister as well. Maya was what mattered. She was the only family she had left now, and she would do whatever it took to keep her safe.

She shifted her head on his chest and ran her fingers through the coarse hair that covered it. "Were you bit?"

He shook his head. "No. My family have been Lycans for generations."

"Was Sophia's mother a Lycan?"

"Aye."

"What about Nicholas' father?"

He shrugged. "I do not know. Sophia could not tell me. When he shifts for the first time, I'll be able to tell if he is full Lycan or not."

"Earlier when the faeries attacked, Sophia could not control the turning."

"Our young have to be taught to control the shift. Sophia's mother did not spend the time needed to teach Sophia what to do. She shifts when she is too tired, when she is excited or frightened. She did not mean to hurt your sister."

"I know." Avery took a deep breath and forced herself to ask the question she was dreading. "She bit Maya. Will Maya become a Lycan?"

Tristan shook his head immediately. "No. A human will only turn from a Lycan's bite if it's during the full moon."

Avery released her breath in a harsh rush.

"I will teach Sophia how to control the shift. She's a bright girl and it will not take her long to learn. Your sister will be safe. In the meantime, on the night of the full moon I will keep Sophia away from humans," Tristan said.

"And yourself as well?" Avery said.

"I can control the shift, even during the full moon." Amusement was etched in his voice.

"Can you? Whenever we are – are together, your eyes turn green and your hair thickens. I'm not stupid. I know what that means."

HAVING THE RED NOTICE AND POINT OUT HIS TROUBLE controlling the shift was humiliating. A blush was rising on his face and he was thankful for the darkness of his bedroom. He hadn't had trouble controlling the shift during sex for years, and to be struggling now was shameful.

"I can control it," he said more harshly than he intended.

"Is it because you're with a human woman?" She wondered out loud. "Perhaps it's the novelty of it."

"I have been with human women," he said.

"Did you have trouble controlling the shift with them?"

"No! Avery, I can control the shift when I'm with you, I swear. Can we please drop this?" He was starting to sweat a little. He didn't want to admit to her that he didn't know why he was having trouble controlling the shift when he was fucking her. He hoped it had something to do with her powers. He thought back to the way it had felt when she had climaxed, how it had immediately made him come too, and just the memory of that was making his cock stir against the sheets.

She was saying something to him, and he forced himself to concentrate. "What?"

"I asked if it's unusual for a Lycan to sleep with a human."

"No. Most Lycans sleep with humans at some point. The ancients used to forbid it. Humans were widely regarded as weak, and Lycans were encouraged to stay away from them. Of course, there were some that disobeyed and mated with them anyway. Then the Great War happened, and there were so few of us left afterward that many Lycans started mating with humans as a way to continue the bloodlines."

"Really?" she asked.

"Aye. Half-breeds are better than no Lycans at all. In fact, many Lycans purchase human women from the slave houses in order to mate with them. They produce Lycan babies and _"

She sat up, the sheet falling to her waist and he took a quick look at her naked breasts. She slapped him hard on the chest. "Are you kidding me?"

"No."

"So, your kind buys human women and treat them like some kind of breeding machine? They're only good for one thing to you? Why not just find Lycan women and convince them to have your babies? Or are they repulsed by your piggish behaviour as well? Do they ask these human women if they want to be popping out babies? Do they give them a choice in the matter at all or are they just expected to lie on their backs and open their legs?" She was shouting now, her pale skin flushed with colour and her hands squeezed into tight fists.

He kept his voice low and calm. "Avery, these women are slaves. They belong to their lords and it is their right to do what they will with them. I do not agree with the practice and I would never do it myself but it's the way of the world."

She snorted loudly. "This idea that one man can own another and force him to bend to his will is ridiculous! Only someone ignorant believes that it's the way it must be. Did you know that the ancients had abolished the practice of slavery? Before the Great War, no human could own another. Everyone was free. My father believed we could have that again."

"That's rich, coming from a man who purchased and owned more slaves than most people could even imagine," he said.

She glared at him and he raised his eyebrows. "Even an ignorant country Lycan like me hears the rumors and reads the stories about the man who brought light back to the world."

Her face had gone pale and she was staring at him like she was trying to set him on fire.

"You're right, my father did purchase slaves," she said through gritted teeth. "He brought them home, fed them, clothed them, and gave them a soft bed for the night. And in the morning, after they had rested, he gave them a choice. They could work for him, earning a wage, or they could leave as free men."

His mouth dropped open and she gave him a look of disgust. "They never mention that in the stories, do they?"

"Avery, I -"

"My father was a good man. The best man I knew. He believed that all men deserved to be free, and I will not let you or anyone else speak ill of him."

She threw back the covers and slid to the edge of the bed. He reached out and caught her by the wrist. "Where are you going?"

She refused to look at him. "I did what you asked of me. I laid on my back and spread my legs for you. Now I want to check on my sister. She needs healing." She tugged at his hand and he tightened his grip.

"Avery, I'm sorry for what I said about your father. I made an assumption and I shouldn't have. Stay the night with me - please." He leaned forward and placed a gentle kiss between her shoulder blades.

She inhaled sharply, her back straightening. "You promised."

He sighed and released her wrist. She quickly put on his shirt and, without looking at him, walked to the door. "Where is she?"

He sighed again. "Down the hallway, last door on the left."

She walked out the door and closed it gently behind her.

CHAPTER 9

"Witch! Hurry up!" Renee hollered from the back door of the house.

Avery picked up a pile of wood from the woodpile, wincing as a large splinter dug into the palm of her hand. It had been nearly two weeks since they had arrived at Tristan's home and in that time, she had hauled wood, lugged buckets of water and scrubbed floors.

Mrs. Lanning was determined to make her miserable and had assigned all the hard labour duties she could to Avery. Tristan's home was a large sprawling rancher. The size of it rivalled her father's home and she spent many hours by herself, needlessly scrubbing the floors of rooms that were rarely used.

She had seen neither Maya nor Tristan. Two days after they arrived, he and Marshall had left for his mother's home taking Maya and the children with them. Last week, Mrs. Lanning had sent Avery to the barns to clean out the horse stalls. After only an hour, Laura, a fresh bruise on her face, had shown up. She had dropped a dish while dusting and as punishment was sent to help Avery. She was so scared at first that she could barely stop from shaking, but Avery spoke kindly to her and it hadn't taken long for Laura to warm up to her.

She was close to Avery's age and had been purchased by Tristan when she was only twelve.

"I was born into slavery," she said. "My original lord sold me to lord Tristan when he moved to the city. He took my mother with him and my older brother, but he had no use for me."

"I'm sorry," Avery said.

Laura shrugged. "Lord Tristan has been very kind to me. I was very frightened when I realized he was a Lycan. My mother used to tell me stories about how Lycans bought girls just so they could hunt them during the full moon, but lord Tristan is not like that."

"What was his wife like?" Avery asked.

Laura wrinkled her nose. "She was very odd. She was beautiful, I have never seen someone as beautiful as her, but there was a coldness to her. She hated the country. She would speak often of the city and how much she missed it. When Sophia was born, she did not even seem to warm up to her own child. Lord Tristan took over most of her care very quickly after she was born. When she left him and took Sophia with her, I thought lord Tristan would go mad. He was very different when he came back from the city without Sophia. These last few weeks of having his child back have turned him into the man he was before."

"Do you know when he will be back with Maya and the children?" Avery pitched clean hay into the stall closest to her.

"I do not know. He is trying to convince his mother to come and live with him. His father died nearly five years ago, and I believe his mother is not well. Leo says lord Tristan believes that the children may convince her to come back with him."

As Avery carried the load of wood towards Renee, who was standing impatiently at the door, a small smile crossed her face. She could still remember the look on Laura's face and the way her cheeks had coloured when she had asked in a hushed whisper if Avery had any potions that would work on a man.

"What do you mean?" Avery had asked, watching amused as Laura's blush deepened.

"I just thought perhaps you had some kind of potion that would show Leo that he should be with me."

Avery had bitten back the laughter bubbling in her throat. Laura was looking at her so earnestly she didn't want to hurt the girl's feelings.

"I'm sorry, Laura. I'm not a witch. I know of no spells or potions that will help you win Leo's love. Have you tried talking with him?"

Laura sighed. "Aye, we do nothing but talk. I have tried to make it perfectly clear that I am interested in him but so far...." She trailed off looking miserably at Avery. "Are you sure you're not a witch?"

"Positive," Avery said.

"Mrs. Lanning says only a witch could heal Marshall the way you did. She says you healed him to try and win favor with lord Tristan, to get him to lower his guard so that you could burn us all in our beds."

"Lycans have healing powers. I did nothing but help keep Marshall warm while his body healed itself." Avery said.

Laura had looked at her doubtfully but let it drop.

"For the gods sake, witch, could you be any slower?" Renee grumbled at her as Avery eased by her and dumped the load of wood into the box next to the door. She cuffed her on the back of the head.

Anger made an unexpected appearance in her belly, and Avery turned and shoved Renee against the door. "Call me witch one more time and you'll regret it."

Renee blanched, her mouth dropping open with fear before she pushed herself away from Avery.

"I'm telling Mrs. Lanning," she warned in a shaky voice.

"Go ahead," Avery turned and headed to her room in the slave quarters.

Her room was small, barely the size of a closet, at the very back of the quarters. It had no fireplace to keep it warm and no bed, only a thin blanket on the floor. She sat cross-legged on the blanket and carefully picked the large splinter from her hand. Despite her care, the wound began to bleed. She stared at her hand for a moment, frowning when it didn't heal.

She rubbed her face wearily. She should not be surprised that she wasn't healing. Her healing powers worked best when she was well-rested and had access to healthy people. She'd gotten very little sleep since that night in Tristan's bed, and shoving Renee today had been the first time she touched a person since the morning Maya had left.

She was tired and her body ached so badly she wanted to cry. She sniffed back the tears. In her entire life she had never felt as tired and sick as she did now. Her healing powers had never let her get so much as a cold and now, sleep deprived and miserably lonely, she was having a hard time adjusting to the weariness and pain her body was feeling.

She was just about to wrap the blanket around herself and lie on the floor when the door to her room burst open. Mrs. Lanning stood in the doorway glaring at her. Avery glanced at the short, thick stick she carried in her hand and stood.

"Did you threaten Renee?" Mrs. Lanning asked.

"No. I simply asked her not to refer to me as a witch any longer," Avery replied.

"Do not lie to me. You shoved her and threatened her." Mrs. Lanning took a step into the room and Avery straightened her back.

"She should learn not to call me names then."

"I am the head of this household, and I will not tolerate anyone threatening or hurting a member of this house. You will be punished. Turn around and take off your shirt," Mrs. Lanning said furiously.

"Come anywhere near me with that stick, and I'll use it to beat your face in," Avery said.

Mrs. Lanning paled and then sneered at her. "And what do you think will happen to you when the lord Tristan comes back to find me beaten? I have been with him for many years. You're nothing but a Red whore who cannot be trusted."

"I don't care what happens to me. You're not touching me with that stick," Avery said.

"It won't just be you." Mrs. Lanning took another step forward. "I'll make sure your darling baby sister burns at the stake beside you. I promise you that."

Avery paled at the mention of Maya and Mrs. Lanning smiled triumphantly. "Turn around, remove your shirt and lean against the wall."

Avery turned slowly and pulled off her shirt. She pressed her hands against the cold wall, steeling herself as Mrs. Lanning approached. The woman raised the stick and slammed it against Avery's bare back. Avery bit her lip, her back bowing and her nails digging into the wall, but she refused to cry out as Mrs. Lanning hit her repeatedly.

She stared blindly at the wall, tears flowing down her

cheeks. When darkness crept across her vision, she dove into it with a feeling of relief.

MAYA SCANNED THE COMMON ROOM ANXIOUSLY. THEY'D been back for over two hours and she still hadn't seen Avery. It was dinnertime and she should have been in the room, bringing food in with the others. She jiggled Nicholas on her knee as Sophia sat down on the bench beside her and began to eat.

"Wait, my love, for the others," she admonished gently, and the little girl obediently put her fork down and folded her hands in her lap.

"Where's Avery?" Sophia asked as Tristan, his mother walking slowly but steadily beside him, entered the room and guided her to the chair beside his.

"I do not know, my love." She tried not to let her anxiety show.

"I want to show her my new dress."

"We will find her after dinner and show it to her, okay?" Maya smiled at Sophia and she nodded and picked up her fork as the others began to eat.

"MARIAN, WHERE IS AVERY?" HOLDING A SLEEPING Nicholas against her shoulder, Maya cornered the older woman in the kitchen where she was cleaning the dishes from dinner.

Marian hesitated, wiping her wet hands nervously on her apron. "She is not feeling well, Maya."

"Not feeling well?" Maya frowned. "Avery is never sick."

"Mrs. Lanning sent her to her room before dinner and told us not to disturb her."

"Can you take Nicholas for me? I need to check on her."

Marian reached for the baby but before she could take him, Mrs. Lanning glided up behind them. "Your sister is fine. I took her some dinner earlier."

Maya stared at her. "Avery never gets sick. What is wrong with her?"

Mrs. Lanning shrugged. "I do not know. Perhaps the country air disagrees with her?"

Maya went to hand Nicholas to Marian, and Mrs. Lanning scowled at her. "You can check on her in the morning. Your first responsibility is the children, and Sophia is running around like a crazy child in the common room. Perhaps you should do what you were bought for."

Maya stalked back to the common room. She spotted Sophia sitting quietly with Marshall next to the fireplace. Tristan was sitting next to his mother on a sofa across from them. Maya chewed on her lower lip, smiling distractedly at Marshall when he glanced up and nodded to her, before making her decision.

"M'lord?" She stood in front of Tristan.

"What is it?" He glanced at Nicholas, still sleeping on her shoulder. "Is it Nicholas?"

"No, m'lord. Forgive me, Mrs. Williams. May I speak with lord Tristan alone for a moment?"

Tristan's mother nodded as Sophia scampered across the room and climbed into the woman's lap. "Will you sing me a song, grandmamma?"

"Of course, my darling girl." The woman smiled at her and brushed her hair back from her face.

Tristan stood and followed Maya a few steps away. "What's wrong, Maya?"

"It's Avery."

Tristan stiffened. "What about her?"

"She is sick, m'lord."

He frowned. "What do you mean she is sick? You told me she never gets sick."

"She doesn't." Maya was close to tears. "I was looking for her, and Marian and Mrs. Lanning said she was sick and resting in her room. They will not let me see her, m'lord."

Now the tears did begin to fall, dropping on to the top of Nicholas' head, and Tristan cursed under his breath.

"Come with me."

She followed him through the kitchen and into the slave quarters. Mrs. Lanning was just leaving one of the rooms and she stared at Tristan in surprise. "M'lord, why are you here?"

"Which room is Avery's?" He grunted at her.

"Sh-she is not feeling well, my lord," she stuttered. "She should not be disturbed."

"Tell me which room is hers," he snapped.

Her mouth pressed in a thin line, she pointed down the hallway to the door at the end. Tristan shouldered past her and walked quickly toward the room, Maya hurried behind him.

He opened the door without knocking. "Avery, are you -"

Maya gasped in shock. Avery was lying on her stomach on a thin blanket on the floor. Her top half was bare, and even in the rapidly-growing darkness she could see the dark bruises and wounds that covered her entire back.

"Gods!" Tristan knelt beside her and brushed a hand over her face. "Avery, wake up."

It was freezing in the room, and Maya could see the goose bumps that covered her body. Tristan stared up at her. "What the hell is going on? Where is her bed? Why is she not healing?"

"I do not know, my lord," Maya said. Awkwardly, still holding Nicholas against her, she knelt next to Tristan and squeezed Avery's hand. "Avery, can you hear me?"

Avery groaned and opened her eyes. She stared in confusion at Tristan, and then her eyes flickered to Maya. A look of relief crossed her face. "Maya, I've missed you so much."

She tried to sit up and cried out as a wound on her back split open and blood dripped down her back.

"Oh, honey," Maya said. "Why are you not healing?"

Avery fell back against the blanket. "I – I haven't been sleeping well. I'm so glad you're back, baby sister."

Her eyelids fluttered closed and Maya gave Tristan a frantic look. "Take Nicholas. I need to hold Avery."

She tried to hand the baby to him, and he shook his head. "No. I'm stronger and healthier than you. I'll take her to bed and hold her for a few hours. It worked before, it will work again."

"My lord, please. I need to be with her." Tears slipped down Maya's face as Nicholas woke up. He stared at her and burst into loud, wracking sobs.

Tristan stood and picked up Avery with a soft grunt. He held her to his chest, being careful not to touch her back and shook his head again. "Nicholas needs you. I will help Avery. I'll let you know how she is in a few hours."

He turned and left the room before she could argue.

CHAPTER 10

Avery opened her eyes. It was dark in the bedroom - the only light came from the glow of the embers in the fireplace across from the bed. She moved her upper body experimentally, groaning softly when it made her back throb and ache.

There was soft snoring above her, but she didn't need to look up to know that she was back in Tristan's bed and plastered against his naked body. He was lying on his back and she was sprawled naked across him on her chest and belly. His large thigh was wedged between hers, and his hard hands were resting on the backs of her thighs.

She licked her lips. Although her back was still burning, she thought that she might not feel as weary as she did before. She stared at the palm of her hand. The wound from the splinter had disappeared and she gave a small sigh of relief. Sleeping on Tristan was helping. It just hadn't healed her completely yet.

She put her hands on the bed beside him and lifted herself a little. She gasped sharply, tears coming to her eyes as another short but brutal burst of pain went down her back.

She could feel wetness on her back and knew that it was bleeding. She had felt very little pain since her monthlies had started, and her ability to withstand it had become nearly non-existent. Moaning, feeling stupid and weak, she let her head drop back onto Tristan's chest. Tears leaked from her eyes and her body trembled as her back ached and throbbed miserably.

She opened her eyes and stared at Tristan's chest. If she touched him, if she kissed and caressed his warm skin, it would help heal her faster.

"You cannot," she whispered. "You told him never again. You made him promise."

He doesn't have to know.

She stared blankly at the wall, her mind racing. Never before had she intentionally used another person's body without their permission or realization, to heal her own. Forget that she had told him she wouldn't sleep with him again. If she touched him now, while he slept and without his consent, she would be no better than the Lycans who purchased humans for their own breeding benefits.

Don't be foolish, she scolded herself fiercely. *Tristan wants you as much as you want him. Do you really think he's going to object to a little groping while he sleeps?*

She closed her eyes, trying to ignore the pain in her back as she warred within herself. She knew perfectly well that Tristan would sleep with her if she asked him to, but she wasn't sure she could bring herself to use him that way. Besides, her body was starting to heal. She would sleep, lie against Tristan for the rest of the night and in the morning, she would find Maya. Maya would help her heal completely.

Her mind made up, she decided to shift into a more comfortable position. She twisted her body to the right so that she could curl up next to Tristan on her side. The twisting brought on such a deep, intense pain between her shoulder blades that she began to cry helplessly, her hands clenching in the bed sheets.

Panting, trying to stop from crying, she collapsed back against Tristan. He slept on, oblivious to her struggles, and after a moment she moved one shaking hand and caressed his chest. Hating herself for being so weak but unable to stand the pain any longer, she nuzzled her face into his neck and kissed and licked his skin. She ran her hand down his abdomen, tracing the hard, ropy muscles with one trembling finger.

He moaned in his sleep and moved slightly under her, his hands tightening on her thighs. She held her breath but after a moment he relaxed, and she slipped her hand across his flat stomach to his hip. She ran her fingers lightly back and forth over his hip bone as she kissed and nuzzled his neck. It might have been her imagination but already the pain in her back felt less.

Wake him up. Wake him up and ask him to kiss you, touch you, make love to you.

She groaned softly, her stomach clenching with pleasure at the thought of Tristan's mouth on hers. No, she wouldn't – couldn't – do that. It was bad enough she was using him because she was weak. She would not humiliate herself further by begging him to fuck her. She would touch him for a while longer, just until the pain was not so bad, and then she would stop.

He shifted under her and she sucked in her breath when she felt his cock brush against her hip. He was hard and throbbing. She glanced up at him, expecting to see him awake, but his eyes were closed and his breathing deep and even.

A surge of warmth went through her at the realization that

her touch had aroused him even in his sleep. The warmth was starting to blot out the pain and quickly, before she could change her mind, she reached down and grasped his cock. She ran her hand lightly up and down the shaft, remembering the way it had felt when he had entered her. She was growing wet and she rubbed herself gently against his hard thigh. It brought a fleeting but delicious feeling of friction, and she clamped her mouth shut around the moan that wanted to escape.

Enough. Your back is not nearly as painful. Stop before he wakes up.

Her lower body was now the part of her that was throbbing, a slow and exciting aching need, but she forced herself to let go of his cock and move her mouth away from his skin.

"Don't stop now, girl." Tristan's deep voice, hoarse with desire, washed over her. She jerked against him in surprise, letting out a low moan as the pain in her back flared. She stared up at him, her eyes wide as he moved his big hands to her ass and squeezed.

AVERY WAS STARING WIDE-EYED AT HIM AND HE SQUEEZED her firm ass, relishing the feel of her smooth skin.

"I'm sorry," she whispered.

He bent his head to kiss her and she twisted her head so his lips glanced across her cheek. He growled low in his throat and cupped the back of her head, forcing her head still.

"Why do you stop?" He whispered against her mouth before licking her upper lip.

She hesitated. "I'm just using you, my lord. My back – it hurts and I cannot stand the pain. I was touching you as a way to feel better. I'm sorry. I should not have done that without your permission."

"And did it work?" He licked her mouth again, his hands threading through her long hair and she moaned and opened her mouth. Instead of kissing her, he took her lower lip into his mouth and sucked gently.

She dug her hands into his sides as he tugged her head back and kissed her throat. He licked his way down to the hollow of her throat and across to her collarbone. He nipped lightly at it and she jerked again.

"Well, did it?" he asked again.

"Aye," she moaned.

"Then why did you stop?"

She gasped as he reached between them, arching away from his chest so he could more easily cup her breast. "Because I'm just using you. It's not right, my lord."

"Tristan," he demanded as he tugged on her nipple, rolling it between his thumb and forefinger.

"It's not right, Tristan," she moaned again, her thighs clamping around his when he suddenly pinched her nipple.

"It is," he whispered. "I like making you feel good, Avery."

She arched her hips against him. "I don't want you to get the wrong idea that I'm going to – to have sex with you all the time. Do you understand?"

He nuzzled her throat. "I understand perfectly. You're hurting and fucking me will literally take the pain away." He kissed her mouth. "I'm willing to let you use my body tonight, but you have to make me dinner later."

She giggled and he grinned at her before falling solemn. "I want you, Avery. You have no idea how much. I don't care if you're just using me." He shifted her until she was straddling his waist and then sat up, threading his fingers through her hair and kissing her deeply on the mouth.

"In fact, whenever you're in the mood to use someone, you are to come to my bed and no other's. You belong to me and I will allow no other man to touch you." He ran his thumb across her bottom lip and stared at her.

"My bed and only mine – do you understand?" He raised one eyebrow at her.

She nodded. "Aye."

"Good."

He could hear the smug satisfaction in his voice, but before she could protest, he kissed her. She met his tongue with her own and they kissed hard for a few moments. He kissed down her chest until he could suck one throbbing nipple into his mouth. She arched her back and stared up at the ceiling as he pulled on her nipple. When he took her thighs in his hands and pulled her further into his lap, she thrust her hips eagerly at him.

He moved his hands to her hips, tilted her up easily, and entered her with one hard thrust. She cried out, her hands digging into the hard muscles of his shoulders as he pulled her flush against his chest. He moaned at the feel of her nipples rubbing against his chest and tugged on her legs.

"Cross your legs around my waist," he instructed.

She crossed her legs behind his back and cried out again when it opened her up even more to him, and he sunk his cock into her completely.

"So warm," he whispered.

With a small cry of excitement, she started to rock against him. He groaned and slid his arms around her. Being careful not to touch her back, he cupped her shoulders in his hands and holding her steady, thrust roughly in and out of her.

"Am I hurting your back?" he asked.

"No," she moaned breathlessly. "Please don't stop. Please..."

He leaned back and took her wrists, pulling her arms down straight until they were next to his legs. Holding her tightly, he rested against the headboard and continued to drive into her. She rode him helplessly, her legs squeezing his waist and loud moans of pleasure erupting from her throat. Her eyes were squeezed shut and her face flushed with colour as she bit her lip and panted and moaned.

Her full breasts bounced appealingly as he moved within her and he watched for a moment, feeling his groin tighten and his cock throb as her wet, tight core slid up and down him. With a small groan he looked down, his breath catching in his throat at the sight of his cock disappearing inside her warm body.

"Avery," he groaned. "Look at me."

She opened her eyes and stared at him. He knew his eyes were glowing, but no fear crossed her face as he reached between them and ran his fingers over her clit. At the feel of his fingers, she cried out and arched against him, coming immediately.

The same intense surge of pleasure roared through him and like before, he was helpless to stop from climaxing with her. He gave his own hoarse cry of pleasure, his hips bucking against hers and his fingers squeezing around her wrists as he came inside of her.

Gasping and panting, she collapsed against him. He stroked her back and allowed her to catch her breath before sitting her up.

"How's your back?" He rubbed her wrists, frowning at the red marks he had left there.

"I'm sure it's fine."

"Let me look at it."

She yawned. "I'm tired."

He grinned a little. "I know. I'll make it quick."

He lifted her off his lap and, muttering under her breath, she curled up on her side with her back to him. He scanned her back anxiously, frowning when he saw the bruises still on her skin.

"Avery, it's still bruised." He ran his hand lightly over her back.

"Not bleeding," she murmured sleepily.

He looked again. She was right. The bruising was still there but where the skin had been torn and split open was now completely healed.

He curled his body around hers, pulling the covers up around them before sliding his hand up to cup her breast and resting his chest carefully against her back.

"Good night, Avery."

Mostly asleep, she made a soft snorting noise in response. He sighed and kissed the back of her neck before closing his eyes and letting sleep overtake him.

CHAPTER 11

"Grandmamma, let's see if Tristan is awake."

Vivian smiled down at her granddaughter and squeezed her hand gently. "Sophia, Tristan is your father. You should call him papa."

Sophia shrugged, popping the last bit of bread into her mouth before scurrying ahead of her grandmother. "His room is down here."

Vivian sighed and followed Sophia down the hall.

AVERY SAT UP IN THE BED. BRIGHT SUNLIGHT FLOODED through the window and she looked beside her. She was alone in the bed and she sighed with relief. She didn't know what she would say to Tristan, and she was grateful that he had already risen and left. She stretched cautiously. There was no pain in her back, and she felt well-rested and better than she had in days. Sex with Tristan had sped up her healing as she had known it would.

She was just about to throw the covers back when the door to Tristan's bedroom popped open and Sophia came bounding in.

"Tristan – are you awake? Grandmamma and I are going for a walk. Will you come with -"

She skidded to a stop, staring at Avery in the bed who hurriedly tucked the bed sheet around her naked body.

"Hi, Avery!" She ran across the room and climbed up on to the bed, planting herself in Avery's lap. "What are you doing in Tristan's room?"

"Um," Avery could feel the blush rising on her face, "I was not feeling well and I don't have a bed in my room so Tristan let me sleep in his bed."

"That was nice of him." Sophia stroked her long red hair, rubbing a few strands of it between her fingers.

"Yes, it was. Your father is very kind." Avery kissed the girl's forehead. Sophia leaned against her companionably and Avery rested her chin on top of the girl's head.

"It always feels so nice to sit with you," the little girl said happily.

"Does it? I'm glad," Avery murmured. Sophia was wearing a dress and she could see a small bruise on her lower calf. She rested her hand on the bruise for a few moments and then lifted her hand, smiling with satisfaction as the bruise faded on Sophia's leg.

"Do you like my new dress?" Sophia asked suddenly.

"I do," Avery replied.

Sophia smoothed her hand over the fabric. "My grand-mamma bought it for me. She said I should wear pretty things. Tristan says I'm a country girl now and that I'll just get it dirty when I'm riding my new pony. He's going to start teaching me to ride soon."

She looked up at Avery. "Grandmamma says I should call Tristan papa."

Avery smiled at her. "Your grandmamma is right. He's your father and he loves you very much. I bet it would make him very happy if you called him papa."

"I could do that," Sophia said. She glanced towards the door. "Hi, Grandmamma."

Avery looked up. Her stomach dropped to her feet and her face turned bright red. There was a woman standing in the doorway watching them silently, her resemblance to Sophia so strong, she could only be Tristan's mother.

"Hello, Sophia." The woman walked slowly but steadily into the room. She stood next to the bed and looked Avery up and down, silently taking in her wild hair and obvious nudity under the sheet. Avery's face was so red she was starting to sweat but she made herself smile at the woman.

"And you are?" The woman said not unkindly.

Avery cleared her throat but before she could answer, Sophia piped up. "This is Avery. She's Maya's sister. Tristan," she paused looking at Avery, "I mean, *Papa*, bought her for me. She's a slave and I wanted her, so Papa bought her for me."

She announced this with the casual cruelty only capable by the very young and the very old.

She patted Avery's face and smiled happily at her grandmother. "She's very nice and she kissed my owie away."

The woman held a trembling hand out to Avery. "It's nice to meet you, Avery. I'm Tristan's mother, Vivian Williams."

Avery reached out and took her hand. "It's nice to meet you as well, Mrs. Williams."

Vivian frowned, staring down at their clasped hands. She pulled her hand free of Avery's grip and she flexed her hand gingerly and glanced up at Avery.

Avery bit her lower lip worriedly. Tristan's mother was ill. Very ill. Sophia stroked Avery's hair again and smiled at her grandmother. "Doesn't Avery have the most beautiful hair? I wish my hair was red."

Avery made a small choking noise in the back of her throat as Vivian smiled at her granddaughter. "Yes, my darling. Her hair is very lovely."

"Do you know where Papa is?" Sophia asked Avery.

Avery shook her head. "I do not. Perhaps he is already at breakfast?"

"I'm going to check." She kissed Avery's cheek and then slid off her lap. "Will you come for a walk with us after breakfast, Avery?"

Avery smiled. "That's very kind of you, Sophia, but I have work to do. But thank you for asking me."

Sophia nodded and held her hand out to Vivian. "Come with me, Grandmamma."

Vivian took her hand and nodded to Avery. They left the room, Sophia leading her grandmother by the hand. When the door closed behind them Avery groaned loudly and flopped back on the bed.

TRISTAN OPENED THE DOOR OF HIS BEDROOM AND STEPPED silently into the room. Avery was standing beside the bed, humming softly to herself as she gathered her clothes from where he had dropped them. She had obviously just finished having a bath. She was wrapped in his towel and her long red hair was wet.

He walked up behind her. "Feeling better this morning?"

Avery screamed softly and whirled around with her hand to her throat. "Gods, you scared me!"

"Sorry." He let his eyes drift down her body, grinning to himself when she flushed and turned away.

"Do you feel better?"

"Aye. Thank you for – for last night," she said.

"You're welcome." He stepped closer and she shivered when she felt his breath on her bare shoulder. She tightened the towel around her body.

"I should go. I have work to do," she whispered.

"Let me check your back first." He gathered her hair and draped it over her shoulder.

"It's fine, my lord," she replied.

"Let me check," he insisted. He pulled on the towel and after a moment, she let it loosen a bit so that he could peer at her back.

He stared at the smooth expanse of her back. It was perfectly healed, the skin returned to its milky colour, and he couldn't see a single blemish or bruise.

"See, it's fine. It doesn't hurt at all." She turned her head to look at her back and he gently pushed her head forward.

"Actually," he lied, "there's still some bruising."

"There is not," she protested.

"There is." He bent and kissed between her shoulder blades. "There's one right here." He kissed the back of her left shoulder. "And right here."

He kissed the curve of her spine. "Another here."

She shivered prettily. "It doesn't hurt."

He reached around her and cupped her breasts through the towel. "I think you'd better use me one more time - just to be on the safe side."

He kissed her neck, licking the droplets of water from her skin as she moaned and pressed her ass against his erection. He tugged on her hands until she let go of the towel and he unwrapped it quickly, pulling it free from her body. He dropped it to the floor and cupped her bare breasts, rubbing his thumbs over her nipples.

She moaned again, her hands coming up to grip the back of his head so that more of her breasts pushed into his hands. He grinned and plucked on her hardened nipples as he kissed the top of her shoulder with an open mouth and roving tongue.

He slid his hand down her flat abdomen, pausing at the curls between her legs, and smiling again when she immediately spread her legs. He kissed her neck while his left hand continued to rub and knead her breast.

"I love touching you. I love how soft and warm you are. I love the way you moan my name," he whispered into her ear.

"Please, my lord," she whispered. She reached down and tried to push his hand between her legs.

He brought his left hand up and turned her head to face him. He placed a warm kiss on her mouth as her hands squeezed the back of his head.

"Say my name," he demanded.

"Tristan," she breathed immediately.

He kissed her again as he slid his hand between her legs, swallowing her loud cry when he rubbed her clit roughly.

She shivered and moaned as Tristan explored her mouth with his tongue. He kissed his way up her jaw and then nipped her earlobe. She sighed at the feel of his hot breath and thrust her hips against his hand. He rubbed and circled her clit, pressing hard against the small pink nub and then circling gently around it again.

"Oh please," she cried.

"Say my name, girl," he whispered into her ear.

"Tristan," she moaned.

"Again," he demanded.

"Tristan."

"Again." He rubbed her clit furiously as she panted and moaned. Her body was starting to tense, signalling her orgasm, and he stopped touching her.

"Tristan, please, oh please," she begged.

"Avery," he whispered. He used the pad of his finger to rub her clit once again and then lightly pinched it between his thumb and finger.

"Tristan!" A surge of wetness covered his hand as she arched her back and came wildly.

HER HEART BEATING WILDLY, AVERY SLUMPED AGAINST Tristan as the last of her orgasm washed over her. He slipped his hand around her waist, holding her up as she stared at him. He kissed her urgently, his hands stroking her breasts and stomach and she reached down and took his cock in her hand. She stroked him firmly, watching his face as she stroked and rubbed and squeezed.

It was his turn to moan now, his hands squeezing her ass when she ran her thumb over the head of his cock. His nostrils flared and he stared down at her before roughly turning her around.

"Tristan, what -"

He lifted her and set her on the bed on her hands and knees. Before she could turn, he was standing against the edge of the bed, his hands around her hips and his cock pushing between her thighs. He put his cock against her wet opening and pushed hard, groaning as he watched his cock slide deep inside of her.

She gasped, her back arching and her ass slapping against

his pelvis. Holding her hips steady, he plunged in and out of her. He leaned over her, sweeping her hair up in one hand and tugging gently on it. She moaned low in her throat, and he placed a trail of hot kisses down her spine.

"Tristan, it feels so good," she moaned.

He kissed her spine again and then pushed gently on it. "Lift your hips, girl."

She buried her face in the bed and pushed her ass higher in the air, spreading her legs so that he could thrust more deeply into her. She could feel his hard hands rubbing her ass and hear his harsh panting as he pushed in and out of her.

She squeezed her muscles around him experimentally, smiling into the bed when he inhaled sharply and bucked his hips against her.

"Stop, girl. Don't do that," he muttered.

She lifted her head and looked over her shoulder at him. "Don't do what? This?" She squeezed again as hard as she could, and he cried out.

"Avery, please," he moaned.

"You don't like that?" she asked. "Maybe I'm doing it wrong." This time when she tightened her inner muscles, she pushed her hips back against him.

His fingers dug into her hips and she gasped a little.

"Avery, I…"

He made a long, low moan as she rocked her hips back and forth, pushing his cock in and out of her in a rapidly quickening rhythm.

"Oh gods," he groaned.

Avery's body tensed as the pleasure grew in her pelvis. She was so close. She pushed her hips at Tristan frantically, his groans of pleasure drowning out her own until with a loud cry she threw her head back and came violently. Vaguely she was aware of Tristan pumping frantically into her, of his own loud cry and then the warmth was flooding through her. She collapsed against the bed as Tristan lay down beside her and put his arm around her.

"You're mine," he whispered, kissing her temple.

CHAPTER 12

Avery listened to the solid beat of Tristan's heart beneath her ear. She rubbed her hand back and forth over his abdomen as he traced lazy circles on her bare back. She wanted to fall asleep, wanted to pretend that late mornings and hours of pleasure in Tristan's bed was her life now but she that wasn't reality.

"My lord -"

"Tristan," he said.

She propped herself up on her elbow. "You know I cannot call you Tristan. Please stop asking me to do so."

He opened his mouth to argue and she hurried on. "Sophia was here looking for you before breakfast."

He pushed a wayward piece of hair from her face. "Oh?"

"Your mother was with her."

She searched his face anxiously, but he just shrugged. "What did they want?"

"You don't understand, m'lord. I was – I was naked and in your bed." Her face burned at the memory.

"So? My mother is hardly a fragile flower. I don't think it would surprise her that her child has sex."

"With a human? And a Red at that? You don't think that she isn't a little alarmed at your choice of bedmate?"

"My mother has no say in who warms my bed," he replied arrogantly.

"It was humiliating to meet her that way," she said.

"I'll introduce you properly later today," he promised.

She shook her head. "Gods no – that's even more humiliating."

He laughed and kissed the tip of her nose. "You worry too much about what others think, girl. Now, what did they want? I was not at breakfast and haven't seen Sophia since last night."

"She wants you to go for a walk with her and your mother."

He smiled. "Then I will."

She slipped out of his embrace and sat on the edge of the bed, gathering her clothes from the floor. He sat up and kissed her back. "No more bruises."

"Aye," she said. "Back to normal."

He caught her hand, bringing it to his mouth and kissing the palm of it. "Come for a walk with us."

"I cannot. I have work to do." She finished dressing and reached for her leather boots, shoving her feet into them.

He frowned. "You forget that you belong to me. If I want you to go for a walk, then you will."

"My lord," she said, cupping his face with her hand. "Why do you deliberately try and make this difficult? How do you think it will look if the others see me out for a walk with you while they are forced to slave away?"

"I don't care what they think. And you're different from them. You're the daughter of one of the wealthiest families in the new world," he said.

"I was. Now my father is dead, my mother sold her own

flesh and blood for drugs, and I am nothing more than a slave without a cent to her name. All my life I have been different. My gift, my hair – it has set me apart from others. My father's wealth and status protected me, but I no longer have that luxury. All that matters to me now is keeping Maya safe. In order to do that, I need to blend in and avoid making enemies. Sleeping with you, receiving special treatment from you will not help me protect Maya. Do you understand that?
"

"No harm will come to you or your sister in my home," he said.

"Most of your other slaves already hate or fear me."

"It was Mrs. Lanning who beat you so badly, wasn't it? Tell me why she beat you."

"It was a misunderstanding, nothing more."

He grabbed her wrist. "Stop lying to me."

She glanced down at his hand and he let go of her. "Both you and your sister will be safe here. I promise. I would not have brought you to my home otherwise."

She laughed. "You brought me into your home because your seven-year-old child wanted me. If it had not been for Sophia, I would still be back at the slave house."

"What does it matter?" he said with growing frustration. "You're here now."

"And when your children are grown? What will become of Maya and me then?" she asked.

"Marshall is very fond of Maya. I have a feeling I will not have a nanny for much longer," he said.

She frowned a little. "Perhaps you are right."

"And there will always be a place in my home for you," he said.

"As your gardener?" She arched her eyebrow at him. "Perhaps now is the time to tell you that Maya was lying through her teeth about my gardening abilities. I have no luck with plants."

She patted his arm. "The best I can hope for is that you marry again. Find someone lovely who will bear you many more children that I can be a nanny to." Her chest tightened oddly at the thought of watching Tristan live his life with another woman.

"Avery, I -"

He looked at her helplessly and she smiled and patted his arm. "It does not matter, my lord. I am not sharing this with you to make you feel bad. My future is my own problem and not for you to worry about. But I can no longer afford to be different and I require your help with that. Will you help me?"

He sighed and nodded. She leaned forward and kissed him, not resisting when he cupped her face and deepened it.

After a moment she pulled away. "Thank you, my lord."

She stood and walked to the door, pausing before she opened it. "Your mother is sick."

"Aye, I know."

"Will her Lycan healing abilities not help her?"

"No. Our healing abilities do not kick in until we hit puberty, and as we age, they start to fade."

She looked back at him. "I can heal her, if you'd like."

"I did not bring her back here with the expectation that you would heal her. I wanted her to be with her grandchildren."

"I know." She slipped out the door.

———

AVERY KNOCKED ON THE DOOR TO THE NURSERY BEFORE opening it. "Maya, are you in here? I need -"

She stared in surprise as Marshall and Maya sprang apart guiltily.

"Avery! Are you feeling better?" Maya's eyes were over-bright, and her mouth was red and swollen.

"Aye, thank you." She frowned at the two of them as Marshall cleared his throat, nodded to her and left the room.

"You two seem close," Avery said. "Are you having sex with him?"

Maya gaped at her. "Avery!"

Avery shrugged. "If you're old enough to be sleeping with him, you're old enough to admit it."

"I am sleeping with him. We grew very close on our trip to Mrs. Williams' home."

Avery sighed. "Do you think it's wise to be sleeping with the best friend of the man who owns you?"

"No more than sleeping with the lord of the manor himself," Maya said defiantly.

"That's different. I slept with him only as a means to heal myself." She thought back to her earlier romp with Tristan and blushed a little. She had been perfectly healthy for that one, and both she and Tristan knew it.

Maya rolled her eyes. "Whatever, Avery."

Avery took her hands. "Maya, I only want what's best for you. I don't want you to get hurt and I'm not sure that Marshall is -"

"I love him!" Maya blurted out.

"Maya, you hardly know him," Avery said.

Maya pulled her hands free. "I know that he is sweet and gentle and treats me well. I know that the thought of not being with him makes me feel sick to my stomach. I know that I am old enough to know what or who I want."

"Maya -"

"I'm no longer a child, Avery. Please stop treating me like one."

"I suppose you're right." Avery kissed Maya on the forehead. "I'd better go. Just, please, be careful, all right? Do not give him your heart until you know for certain that his belongs to you."

"WHAT'S GOING ON?" AVERY GLANCED CURIOUSLY AT LAURA as she lined up with the other slaves in the kitchen. It had been two days since she had left Tristan's bed and her body was completely healed. She was thankful for that. Mrs. Lanning had sent her to the cellar the last two days to clean and prepare for the massive amounts of canning that would soon be taking place, and the work was physical and tiring. Even feeling as good as she did, she had collapsed each night into the small bed Tristan had ordered to be put in her room and fallen asleep almost immediately.

Laura shrugged. "I do not know."

Maya slipped into the kitchen and stood next to Avery.

"Why are we here?" she breathed into Avery's ear.

"I have no idea." Avery smiled at her as Maya took her hand and squeezed it.

Mrs. Lanning took out a large white envelope from her pocket. Without saying anything, she pulled a wad of bills from the envelope and handed a few to each person in the room. Avery stared at the bills in her hand, her brow creased. Beside her, Maya had an identical expression of confusion.

Mrs. Lanning folded her arms across her non-existent chest and cleared her throat. "The lord Tristan has decided to." she hesitated, "pay all of us wages."

There was a collective gasp of surprise before Renee gave

a small squeal of excitement. She clutched the bills to her chest and grinned at Laura. "Wages for slaves!"

"It's not much," Mrs. Lanning barked at her immediately. "But you must all make sure to search out and thank lord Tristan for being so generous. As long as you do your job and don't cause lord Tristan any trouble, you will continue to receive a weekly wage."

Maya squeezed her hand and put her mouth to her ear. "Did you have something to do with this?"

Avery shook her head. "No."

"Are you sure?"

Avery didn't reply, a small, pleased smile on her lips as she stared at the bills in her hand.

CHAPTER 13

Avery leaned the pitchfork against the stall and stripped off the sweater she was wearing. The days were cold now, but she had worked up a sweat cleaning out the stable. She was just picking up the pitchfork again when someone cleared their throat behind her.

She turned around, frowning when she saw Marshall standing there. It had been just over a week since she'd walked in on him and Maya, and she had a feeling that Marshall was avoiding her.

"Hello, Avery." Marshall smiled at her.

"Hello, m'lord." She stabbed the pitchfork in the wheelbarrow of clean hay and used it to transfer some of the hay into the stall.

"Please, call me Marshall."

She didn't answer, grunting softly as she transferred another pitchfork of sweet-smelling hay into the stall.

"I was hoping we could speak for a moment."

She sighed and stopped, leaning against the pitchfork and giving him an irritated look. "What is it?"

He stepped closer, cracking his knuckles. "I just wanted to tell you that I care for your sister very much. I love her in fact, and I'll die before I hurt her."

She stared silently at him and he blushed a little. "I love her, I do."

"I never thanked you for saving Maya's life," she said suddenly.

He blinked. "I – you're welcome?"

"Treat her well, Marshall. I don't want to have to cast a spell on you." She gave him a mock threatening look and he grinned like a schoolboy.

"I'm sorry I called you a witch. I know you're not."

She shrugged. "I'm used to it."

He moved forward until he was standing directly in front of her. "Maya is special. I just want you to know that I realize that, and I'll treat her well. I promise you."

She smiled. "Good. Because I'm not kidding – I'll kill you if you don't."

He stared at her thoughtfully. "Aye, I have no doubt of that."

He turned to go and then surprised her by turning back and hugging her. She dropped the pitchfork, wincing as it hit her foot.

"Thank you," he said sincerely. "Maya told me how you saved my life after the faerie attack, and I should have said thank you long before this."

She returned his hug. "You're welcome, Marshall."

"Am I interrupting something?"

They broke apart to see Tristan standing behind them and staring at them furiously.

Marshall shook his head. "No. Just talking."

He nodded to Avery and clapped Tristan on the shoulder

as he walked by. Tristan growled loudly, his eyes flashing green, and Marshall stepped back.

"Gods, Tristan. Relax." He held his hands up, rolling his eyes, and left the stable.

Tristan continued to stare at her, his nostrils flaring, and his hands rolled into tight fists at his sides.

Avery nodded to him. "M'lord."

She picked up her pitchfork and piled the last of the clean hay into the stall. Her stomach was churning nervously, and her palms were sweating. She had barely seen Tristan at all in the last week, never mind be alone with him. He had done as she asked and stayed away from her, barely acknowledging her existence when they were in the same room and spending most of his time with Sophia and his mother.

She refused to admit to herself how much she missed him. Every night she crawled into her cold bed and did her best not to think about Tristan and his warm mouth.

"What are you doing in here?" he asked.

"Cleaning the stalls."

"Where is Ian? He's in charge of the barn."

"I believe he's helping Leo in the west field. I accidentally killed Marian's herb garden she was growing in the window, and Mrs. Lanning thought it would be best if I took a break from gardening." She grinned and winked at him, trying to tease him out of his bad mood.

When he didn't laugh, she turned away from him, spreading the pile of hay in the stall across the floor. Tristan entered the stall and knocked the pitchfork from her hand.

"Hey!" She protested as he pushed her back against the wall of the stall and planted his hands on either side of her head.

"I thought you understood," he growled.

"Understood what?" She stared at him in confusion.

"I thought you understood what I told you." His voice was slow and deliberate.

"My lord, I have no idea what you're talking about."

"If you were in the mood to use someone, you were to come to my bed and my bed alone." His eyes glowed angrily. "Yet I come in here to find you touching Marshall – hugging him."

She gaped at him. "Are you kidding me? I wasn't in the mood to use anyone. Marshall is in love with my sister and you know that. He hugged me to say thank you for saving his life."

He appeared not to hear her. "I don't want you touching him again."

Her own temper flared, and she poked him hard in the chest. "Stop telling me who I can and cannot touch. And I told you – he was only saying thank you for saving his life."

"You've been naked with him before, kissing him, letting him touch you. Why should I believe you now?" Tristan leaned in until she could feel his hard chest brushing against her breasts. She stared at his mouth, feeling the slow heat rising in her belly.

"You asked me to do that."

"Bullshit."

"You did," she insisted. "You asked me to save his life and I did. How handy it must be for you to decide when I should and shouldn't touch your friends."

When he didn't respond, her anger got the best of her. "Ian seems like a nice enough man, and we've been spending quite a bit of time in the barn together. Perhaps we could arrange for him to be injured so that I'm allowed to touch him."

He cupped the back of her neck. "Stop deliberately provoking me, girl."

"Then stop acting like a spoiled child whose favourite toy is being played with by another," she said.

"You're mine," he growled. "You belong to me."

He kissed her roughly, thrusting his tongue deep into her mouth and shoving her back against the stall. She shivered, heat running through her stomach and into her pelvis before she pulled her mouth free and pushed him away with a hard shove. He staggered back, tripping over the pitchfork and landing on his back in the pile of fresh hay.

Before he could get up, she grabbed the pitchfork from the ground and pounced on him, sitting on him and holding the tines of the pitchfork to his throat. She stared down at him, panting harshly, and realized with a tingle of dismay that she wanted him desperately.

He stared silently at her, no fear in his eyes despite the pitchfork pressing against his throat, and she pushed her pelvis against the erection she could feel through his pants. She rubbed back and forth until a small moan escaped her throat and he gave her a predatory grin.

Still holding the pitchfork to his throat with one hand, she reached between them and unbuttoned his pants. She was wearing a long skirt and she tugged the fabric away from her body, letting it billow out around his hips, before pulling his cock free. His breath hissed between his teeth when she rubbed his cock against her and realized she wasn't wearing underwear. She was soaking wet, and it took just a small twist of her hips for his cock to slide deep within her.

He groaned and she tossed the pitchfork aside and leaned over him, taking his hands and pinning them above his head. She licked his mouth and then bit his bottom lip, making him cry out and jerk against her.

"Now you belong to me," she said before angling her mouth over his and shoving her tongue deep into his mouth. They kissed hungrily, their tongues battling against each other for control until they were both gasping and moaning. She released his hands but when he reached for her, she smacked them away.

"Don't move," she demanded.

He let his hands fall to the side and she yanked hard on his shirt. Buttons popped off as she ripped it open and leaned down to bite and kiss his chest. He groaned, his hands twisting into her hair as she licked her way to his flat nipple. She sucked it into her mouth, and he bucked against her. She bit it, pulling a hoarse cry from his throat before she licked away the sting of her bite.

She sat up, grinning down at him as she braced her palms against his chest and moved her hips. She lifted her hips until just the head of his cock was in her and then slowly plunged back down on him, rotating her hips in a clockwise motion as she did.

"The gods be damned, girl," he moaned, his hands sliding under her skirt to grip her bare thighs.

She grinned shark-like at him and repeated the movement, moaning a little herself at the feel of his hard cock rubbing against her soft walls.

"Please, girl," he moaned again.

She leaned down and kissed him on the mouth. "Say my name."

He stared at her and she grinned cheekily at him, lifting her hips until he slipped out of her. "Say my name."

"Avery, please," he groaned.

"Please what?" She reached between them and took his cock in her hand, holding it steady as she rubbed her clit against the head of it.

"Please fuck me," he begged.

"Soon," she panted. He groaned again as she continued to use his cock to rub her clit. She was panting, sweat trickling down her back, as she writhed and twisted against him.

He reached up and pulled the neckline of her blouse down until her breasts popped free. He kneaded her bare breasts roughly, tugging and pulling on her hard nipples as she rubbed herself against him.

She leaned over him, guiding her breast to his mouth and he sucked on her offered nipple eagerly, licking and nipping at it as she moaned above him. He cupped her breasts, pushing them together and running his tongue from one nipple to the other. She was incredibly close to coming and she forced herself to stop rubbing her clit against the smooth head of his cock.

She leaned back, staring down at him. "Should I fuck you now, Tristan?"

"Aye," he muttered.

"Aye what?" She cupped her own breast, running her thumb over the nipple and smiling when his eyes went from brown to green in an instant.

"Aye, please! Fuck me, Avery," he begged again.

"Since you asked so nicely." She grinned and sunk his cock deep inside of her.

He cried out, sliding his hands under her skirt to grab her thighs again. She moved against him in a relentlessly slow rhythm as he arched his hips up, nearly knocking her off of him.

"Slow," she whispered, pressing her weight down on him.

"Slow," he agreed as she rose up and down in a maddeningly slow pace.

"Look at me, Tristan," she demanded. He opened his eyes and sucked in his breath. She was cupping both her breasts, her hand squeezing and rubbing and her fingers tugging lightly on her nipples as she rode him.

"Faster?" she asked, arching her back and wiggling her pelvis against him.

"Oh Gods, yes," he groaned.

She rode him faster, her hips gyrating and thrusting, watching his face closely for signs that he was close. When his body tensed, she suddenly moving.

"Avery!" he gasped.

She went back to the previous slow rhythm she had set before. He made a groan of frustration and need.

"Slow," she moaned.

She was so close. The pleasure was building in her belly, her pelvis throbbed and pulsated with need, and when Tristan suddenly growled and grabbed her hips, she didn't object. With a loud guttural moan, he plunged roughly in and out of her, and she was suddenly and explosively having the best orgasm of her life.

She threw her head back, her back arching and her body shaking as her orgasm roared through her in a long, continuous bout of pure pleasure. Below her, Tristan, his eyes squeezed shut, was groaning loudly as he came inside of her.

She collapsed against him, breathing harshly, her body still vibrating from her orgasm. After a few moments, he kissed her on the top of her head. "That was incredible."

She sat up, pulling her shirt up and straightening her skirt. He frowned at the sight of her pale face and trembling lips. "What's wrong, girl?"

"I'm sorry, Tristan," she said. "I should not have done that."

He sat up, putting his arms around her waist and kissing her mouth. "Aye, you definitely should have."

She shook her head and struggled free from his arms. She

stood and paced in the stall as Tristan rose gracefully to his feet.

"No, I shouldn't have. I tell you to stay away from me, beg you not to touch me and then I attack you with a pitch-fork and force you to have sex with me the first time we're alone together."

"Avery -"

"I'm going crazy," she moaned, clutching her head.

He grabbed her arms and shook her lightly. "Listen to me, girl. You did not force me to have sex with you. I've been spending every moment since you left my bed a week ago, trying to figure out how to get you back into my bed. I swear to you."

"I can't keep doing this to you. I think it would be best if I left, Tristan. You could sell me to another or return me to the slave house."

"No." He shook her again. "You're not leaving my home."

"Please." She cupped his face. "We're both miserable. You know that -"

"No!" He gripped the back of her neck and rested his forehead against hers. "It doesn't have to be this way. Share my bed each night."

She didn't reply and he hurried on. "If the others know that it's your job to please me, they will not treat you differ-ently. If I make it clear that you're to be my companion -"

"You mean your whore."

He winced. "Avery, it would not be like that."

"Papa?" Sophia's voice echoed through the stable, and Avery pushed Tristan away from her. He stepped behind her, buttoning his pants as Sophia peeked into the open stable.

"Hi, Papa! Hi, Avery!" she said.

"Hello, my love." Avery smiled at her as Tristan buttoned the only two remaining buttons on his shirt.

"We are going riding today, aren't we?" Sophia swung on the stall door.

"Aye, little one. We are." He smiled at her.

"You have hay in your hair, Papa," she informed him solemnly.

"Do I?" He ran a hand through his long hair, as his mother appeared in the stall doorway.

"Tristan." She nodded to him; her steady gaze taking in Avery's flushed appearance and the hay in Tristan's hair and his haphazardly buttoned shirt.

"Hello, Mother." Tristan had the good grace to blush a little as Avery looked at the ground and prayed to the gods for it to open and swallow her whole.

Vivian held her hand out to Sophia. "Come, child. We will wait outside for your father."

"Okay." Sophia took her grandmother's hand and blew a kiss to Avery. "Bye Avery."

As soon as they were gone, Avery covered her burning face with her hands. "Gods be damned. Will I ever run into that woman when I haven't just finished fucking her son?"

Tristan laughed and she thumped him on the chest. "It's not funny, my lord."

"It's kind of funny." He grinned at her before sobering. "Avery, we need to finish talking about -"

"No." She shook her head. "Your child is waiting for you, and I have to get back to the house before Mrs. Lanning sends Renee looking for me."

She grabbed her sweater and gave him a pleading look. "Just promise me that you'll think about what I'm asking. You should send me away from here."

"You would leave your sister?" he said.

"She's not a child anymore and she can take care of herself. Besides, you won't let anything happen to her, will you?"

He shook his head. "No, I will not."

"Just consider it, my lord. Please."

She slipped out of the stall and as he watched her walk away, he shook his head again, muttering, "No, I will not."

CHAPTER 14

"Marshall is building a new home," Maya said dreamily. She was sitting in a chair in the corner of the room, feeding Nicholas his bottle.

Avery looked up from where she was scrubbing the floor. "Oh?"

"Yes." She smiled down at the baby. "He says he's building it for me. He says that once it's done, he'll buy me from Tristan, and we'll be married."

She kissed Nicholas' forehead. "It is a very small house. Only three bedrooms but Marshall says that's enough for us to have a boy and a girl. He says I'll have to learn to cook and clean. He cannot afford slaves, but I don't even mind the thought of that. Is that what love does to you, Avery? Does it make even the most menial tasks seem romantic?"

Avery laughed, scrubbing at a particularly dirty spot in front of the fireplace. "I wouldn't know."

Maya continued to stare dreamily at the baby. "I was so frightened when Mama sold us to the slave house. I used to lie awake at night and worry about what would happen to me. But look – I've fallen in love with a wonderful man who is building me a home of my own. We'll have babies and grow old together."

"Will his family object to him marrying a human?" Avery asked.

"He doesn't have any family. His parents died when he was very young, and Tristan's father took him in and raised him as his own. He thinks of Tristan as his brother." Maya smiled at her.

Avery returned her smile and dipped the wooden brush into the bucket of water. She scooted back and brushed the floor briskly. She'd had no experience with scrubbing floors until joining Tristan's home but, she reflected wryly, it was a skill easy enough to learn.

"I can't wait until I never have to look at that ugly old Mrs. Lanning again," Maya suddenly said. "She's a horrid old woman who makes both our lives miserable. The day I stop being a slave will be the happiest day of my life."

She suddenly gave Avery a look of shame.

"Avery, forgive me. I am being a complete idiot." Her mouth trembled and tears slipped down her cheeks.

"Maya, what are you talking about?"

"I've been going on and on about how happy I am, and I haven't once thought of your feelings."

When Avery only looked at her blankly, Maya swiped at the tears on her face. "I know you're miserable here, Avery. Mrs. Lanning and the others treat you horribly. You spend your days cleaning and scrubbing while I prance about cuddling babies, and -"

She paused and whispered, "You're in love with lord Tristan."

Avery dropped the brush and crossed the room to Maya. She crouched in front of her and took her hand in both of hers. "One, I am not in love with Tristan and two, your happiness makes me happy."

Maya looked at her doubtfully and Avery squeezed her hand. "It's true, Maya. You are the most precious thing in my life. To know that you're happy and loved is all I need to make my own heart happy."

Maya sniffed. "But what will become of you?"

"Stop worrying about that, Maya. I always make out just fine, do I not?"

"Perhaps in time lord Tristan will realize he loves you too and you will be married."

"Lord Tristan desires only one thing from me. What he feels is not love, Maya," Avery said.

"But I want you to be happy, to be married and to have children of your own," Maya said.

"With hair like this?" Avery tugged on her hair. "Even if Daddy hadn't died, we both know I would never have married anyway. I'm just lucky to have been bought by a man who doesn't believe that all Reds are witches and should be burned at the stake."

She leaned down and kissed Nicholas' head. She was actually feeling a little cheered by Maya's news. If Maya married Marshall and moved from Tristan's home, Avery would no longer need to worry about her safety. If she didn't have to fear that Maya would be labeled a witch along with her, she could breathe easier.

And, a voice deep inside of her whispered, *you could warm Tristan's bed and bring him pleasure.*

She frowned to herself. He called it being a companion, but it was nothing more than a fancy word for whore. A year ago, she would have been horrified at the thought of being sold to a man for the sole purpose of pleasuring him. Now she was considering it to be the better option for her life. She blinked back the sudden hot tears, deeply ashamed of herself.

"Avery?" Maya said, laying a timid hand on Avery's head. "Are you all right?"

"Good morning, Maya." Vivian entered the room.

Avery and Maya stood, and Maya smiled nervously at Tristan's mother. "Hello, m'lady. How are you feeling today?"

She shrugged. "I've had better days."

"I'm sorry to hear that," Maya said as Avery returned to her bucket and her floor scrubbing.

Vivian reached out to brush back a strand of Maya's hair. "My son tells me that you and Marshall will be married soon. Do you know he is like a son to me?"

Maya nodded. "He told me he loves you like his own mother."

"He's lucky that such a beautiful girl is so willing to marry him." Vivian frowned slightly. "I will not lie to you. I wish very strongly that you were a Lycan but since Marshall is only a half-breed himself, I can understand why he feels such a strong affection for you."

Maya flushed a little but remained silent. Vivian held her hands out for the baby and Maya carefully transferred him into her arms. She stared down at the blond-haired boy, smiling a little when he reached up and grabbed her chin. "He's a handsome child, is he not?"

"Aye," Maya said.

"I thought my son was foolish for taking in a bastard child, but Sophia loves him very much. I understand why he did it."

She handed Nicholas back to Maya who nestled him against her shoulder and patted his back gently. "If you're looking for lord Tristan, he has taken Sophia riding. They should return soon."

"Actually, it is your sister I wish to speak with."

Avery looked up in surprise as Maya glanced at her. "Very well, m'lady. I will leave you with her."

"I had a sister once. She died many years ago. You and your sister remind me of the way we were." Vivian paused, smiling dryly at Maya. "I imagine that whatever I say to your sister will be repeated to you anyway. You might as well stay and hear it now."

She turned and motioned to Avery. "Come here, girl."

Avery stood in front of Tristan's mother. Vivian reached out and pulled a strand of her hair free from her braid, rubbing it between her fingers. "Sophia is right, you know. Your hair is very beautiful."

"Thank you, m'lady."

"I imagine it has brought you nothing but trouble and sorrow your entire life, has it not?"

Avery didn't reply as Vivian continued to study her hair in the sunlight. "Yet you wear it proudly. You choose not to cover it or perhaps cut it short so that the red is not as noticeable. I admire that. I do."

She smiled and released Avery's hair. "My son is very taken with you. Tell me, was Sophia telling the truth? Did he buy you because she wanted you, or did he buy you as a companion for himself?"

"He bought me because of Sophia," Avery said.

"So, you seduced him then. Do you believe that you may one day be his wife?"

"No, m'lady. I am not so foolish that I would believe your son has any interest in me other than his own physical pleasure."

Vivian regarded her solemnly. "You're a very wise girl. There is something about you that makes you quite unlike any slave I've ever seen. I can see why my son is so taken with you."

Vivian crossed her arms over her chest. "I love my son very much and I want nothing more than for him to be happy. I want him to marry and give Sophia many more siblings. I want him to live to an old age with someone who loves him. It's what all mothers want for their children, is it not?"

"Aye," Avery said.

"Tristan is a Lycan. He should love and take a Lycan as his mate. Only a Lycan can truly understand how to make him happy."

"From what I hear that didn't work out so well for your son the first time around," Avery said as Maya gasped in horror behind her.

Vivian gave her an almost admiring glance. "Aye, but she was a city Lycan. Just between you and me, I had my reservations about her from the start. I've arranged for the children of some very old friends to come for a visit. Victoria is a lovely girl and has many pleasing qualities. She remembers my son and is quite eager to see him again. I have high hopes that sometime in the near future our families will be joined together."

She smiled at Avery. "In order for that to happen, I need you to stay away from my son. Do you understand?"

Avery nodded. "Perfectly, m'lady."

"You think me cruel, do you not? To ask you to do this favour for me when you hardly know me? To ask you to do this when you're in love with my son?"

Avery swallowed hard. "I am not in love with your son, m'lady."

Vivian laughed. "Do you think me stupid, girl? I see it on your face every time you look at him. I bear you no personal

140

ill-will, child. I want only the best for my son. A human, and a Red at that, is not what he needs. Will you stay away from him?"

"Aye, I will," Avery said.

Vivian studied her closely for a moment and then, satisfied by what she saw in Avery's eyes, walked out of the room.

Avery turned away and dropped to her knees by the bucket of water. She scrubbed the floor with hard and savage strokes, blinking the tears away.

Maya's cool hand dropped onto her shoulder. "Avery, are you okay?"

"I'm fine," she said.

"Please stop and look at me," Maya said.

Avery pulled away from her. "Maya, go. I wish to be left alone for a while."

"No. Avery, we should talk."

"Maya, leave me be!" Avery shouted.

Maya stumbled back with a frightened squeak as Nicholas woke and began to cry lustily. She turned and fled the room, holding Nicolas tightly against her. The minute the door shut, Avery dropped the brush and wept bitterly into her cupped hands.

CHAPTER 15

Avery lugged in an armful of wood as Laura held the door open for her. The weather had turned cold two days ago and she stepped gratefully into the warmth of the kitchen, dropping the wood into the box with a loud clatter.

"Gods be damned, it's freezing out there tonight." Laura rubbed her arms as Avery stood next to the stove, holding her cold hands over it for warmth.

"Aye. I'll be taking a warming rock to my bed tonight," Avery said.

She had spent the first night of the cold snap in her small room huddled under multiple blankets and still shivering uncontrollably. Without a fireplace, her room was as cold as a crypt. Laura had taught her the warm rock trick, showing Avery how to warm it in the oven and then carefully wrap it in cloth and transfer it to her small bed. The room was still freezing cold, but Avery could at least curl up around the rock and enjoy its heat.

She glanced around. "Where is everyone? It seems quiet tonight."

It had been two days since her discussion with Tristan's

mother, and since then she had done everything in her power to avoid Tristan. Mrs. Lanning had been all too willing to send her off to the less-used rooms of the house to clean, and she had eaten her meals standing in the kitchen, rather than at the slave's table in the dining room.

"Haven't you heard? Mrs. Williams collapsed just after supper. Mrs. Lanning does not believe she will make it through the night," Laura said.

"What?" Avery stared wide-eyed at her.

Laura nodded. "It's true. Lord Tristan carried her to her room and has been keeping watch over her since then. Marian went to gather his supper dishes, and she said he hadn't eaten a bite and would not speak a word to her when she spoke to him. She said he is very distraught over his mother's condition."

"How is Sophia?" Avery asked.

Laura sighed. "She's been in her room crying. Maya is with her and trying to comfort her, but I guess the little one has become quite taken with her grandmother. It's terribly sad, it is. Mrs. Williams is not that old."

"Did Tristan, I mean, lord Tristan, ask for me to come see his mother?" she asked.

Laura gave her a strange look. "No. Why would he?"

Avery shook her head. "Never mind. He wouldn't."

Using long metal tongs, Laura pulled the large rock out of the oven and wrapped it carefully in a large piece of flannel. "Here - take this to bed with you."

Avery took the rock, slipping quietly down the hallway and into her cold, dark bedroom. She climbed into her bed, sliding the rock in after her, and curled her body around it, staring thoughtfully up at the ceiling.

AVERY, DRESSED ONLY IN HER NIGHTGOWN, WALKED barefoot through the house. She had lain in bed for almost an hour before easing out of her room and creeping out of the slave's quarters. She knew which room was Vivian's, had scrubbed the floor and changed the sheets of her bed, and she made her way silently through the hallways toward it.

She opened the door and slipped into the room, wincing a little when the door clicked shut loudly behind her. She could just make out Tristan sitting in an armchair next to the bed. His head was back, and his arms folded across his chest. He was snoring softly, and she crept carefully past him and looked down at the bed.

Mrs. Williams was lying on her back, breathing harshly through her mouth. Her usual tanned face was pale, and her mouth trembled with every breath she took. Quickly, before she could change her mind, Avery slipped into the bed beside the woman and molded her body to hers. She kissed Vivian's cheek and then rested her head against hers. She closed her eyes and waited.

"MAYA! LET ME IN. MAYA!"

Maya woke with a start and stared at the door as there was another soft knock. "Maya, please let me in."

Maya climbed out of bed, glancing across the room at Sophia asleep in her small bed and at Nicholas in his crib, as she crossed the room. It was only a few hours until dawn and she frowned as she unlocked the door and pulled it open. "Avery, what's wrong?"

Her face pinched with worry as Avery, her skin pale and her legs trembling violently, crashed against her. "Maya, can I lie with you in your bed for a while?"

"Of course." Maya helped her to the bed and tucked her in, climbing in next to her and hugging Avery close to her small body.

"Avery, what happened?"

Avery shook her head, "Later, please, Maya. I need to sleep."

Maya nodded and stroked her back as Avery slipped into sleep.

———

Tristan woke with a start. Sunlight was streaming through the window and dread filled his body when he realized he could no longer hear his mother's harsh breathing. Slowly, the muscles in his neck creaking, he looked at the bed.

Vivian, her cheeks rosy and her dark eyes sparkling, was sitting up in the bed staring at him. "Good morning, Tristan."

"Mother?" He stared in shock at her. "What happened?"

She smiled. "I do not know. I woke up this morning feeling much better than I have in a long time."

He sat beside her on the bed and took her hand in his. "Do you remember what happened last night?"

She shook her head. "No. I remember I felt very poorly after supper."

"You collapsed, Mother. I carried you to your bed."

"Did I?" she said. "I don't remember that. In fact, I don't remember a night where I have slept so well. Perhaps that was all I needed – a good night's rest."

"Perhaps." He leaned forward and kissed her cheek. "I'm going to find Sophia and tell her you're feeling better. She was very worried about you last night and will want to see you."

"I'd like that," Vivian replied. "I'll ask her to go for a walk with me this afternoon."

As Tristan walked to the door, she called out to him. "Could you have them bring me something from the kitchen? I'm starving."

He smiled. "Aye, of course."

He left his mother's room but instead of heading to the nursery, he turned right and hurried to the slave's quarters. By the time he reached the hallway he was almost running, and he burst into Avery's room without knocking.

"Avery, did you

He stopped, staring at her empty bed with disappointment.

"Maya," he said, and bolted for the nursery.

AVERY SIGHED AND SNUGGLED CLOSER TO MAYA. HER SISTER kissed the top of her head. "Do you feel better?"

"Aye." She smiled at Maya and nestled her head back on her shoulder.

"Avery, did you heal Tristan's mother last night?" Maya asked.

Avery nodded and Maya sighed harshly. "Why did you do that? After what she said to you – you should have let her die."

Avery sat up and stared at her in shock. "Maya – I had to."

Maya shook her head angrily. "No, you didn't, Avery. He did not ask you to heal his mother. You could have - should have - let her die. With his mother dead, you may have had a chance with Tristan. Why did you heal her?" She smacked Avery repeatedly on the arms.

"Maya, stop it." She grabbed her sister's hands and squeezed them tightly. "I had to. Don't you get that? I could not stand to watch Tristan or Sophia suffer the way we did after our father died. Not when I could save her."

"Oh, Avery." Maya began to cry, and Avery wiped away her tears.

"Stop crying, Maya. Everything will be fine."

The door to the nursery opened and Tristan stepped into the room. He stared at Avery. "Did you – you healed her, didn't you?"

Before Avery could reply, Sophia sat up in her small bed. "Papa?"

She looked at him with alarm, tears beginning to slide down her cheeks. "Is Grandmamma dead?"

He shook his head. "No, my love. Your grandmother is feeling much better today."

She grinned through her tears and then held her arms out to him. "Take me to see her, Papa."

He picked her up and she flung one thin arm around his neck. He looked at Avery and Maya still huddled together in Maya's bed.

"Thank you," he said hoarsely before carrying Sophia from the room.

AVERY CRAWLED INTO HER BED. SHE PUSHED THE ROCK TO the far side of the bed and curled up close to it. After Tristan had left the nursery, she had dressed quickly and left for the west field with Laura and Leo, digging potatoes from the cold ground for most of the day. It was cold and unpleasant work, but it had kept her out of the house and away from Tristan.

She stared at the wall, shivering despite her hot bath

before bed and the heat radiating from the rock next to her. Leo and Laura had spent the entire day giggling and flirting, and she had found it both amusing and irritating.

She realized she was jealous of their obvious affection for each other and rolled her eyes at herself. Being jealous of something she would never have was a ridiculous waste of energy. She closed her eyes and moved closer to the rock, resting it against her midsection and ignoring the voice that called her a fool when she pretended it was Tristan's warm body.

She woke in the dark a few hours later. Someone or some-thing was in her room and she clutched the rock in her bed nervously.

"Who's there?" she demanded, trying to keep her voice steady.

"Gods be damned, it's cold in your room." Tristan's voice came floating out of the darkness and she let her breath out in a harsh rush. She could hear the rustle of clothing and then Tristan was pulling back the bedcovers, letting the cold air rush in.

She gasped as her body broke out in goose bumps. "What are you doing?"

"Getting into bed before I freeze to death," he grumbled. He shoved her over until she and the rock were pressed against the wall. "Gods, girl, your bed is small."

"It's meant for one person," she said pointedly as he pressed his naked body against her back and wrapped his arm around her waist.

His hand brushed against the flannel-covered rock and he touched it curiously. "Why do you have a rock in your bed?"

She started to giggle as he picked up the rock and dropped it onto the floor behind him. It hit the floor with a loud thud, and she smacked his arm. "Hey, that's keeping me warm."

"You use a rock to keep you warm?" he asked with amusement in his voice.

"Aye. Some of us don't have fireplaces in our bedrooms," she replied.

He slipped his hand into the front of her nightgown and cupped her bare breast. "You don't need the rock. I'll keep you warm."

"The rock is probably a better idea," she said breathlessly, trying not to arch her back as he rubbed her nipple with the tip of his finger.

"The rock won't help you heal," he murmured before he switched to her other breast and squeezed it gently.

This time she was helpless to stop her back from arching and he groaned appreciatively when her ass pressed against his cock.

"I don't need to heal," she gasped.

"I know you healed my mother last night while we slept. Do not try and lie." He plucked on her nipple and she grabbed his wrist, her fingers squeezing tightly as he circled and rubbed her nipple.

"I went to Maya afterward." She cleared her throat, trying to ignore the pleasure radiating from her breasts down to her pelvis. "She helped heal me."

"Are you sure?" he whispered. He slid his arm further into the loose neckline of her nightgown, circling her belly button with his warm fingers before tracing them back and forth from one hip bone to the other. "You seem a little pale to me."

She turned her head to face him. "Now you're just -"

He caught her mouth in a kiss, his tongue stroking against hers, and at his familiar taste she moaned and gave up protesting.

He pushed back the covers and pulled her nightgown up

and over her head. She shivered as the cold air hit her body and he quickly pulled the bedcovers back up over them. He kissed her chest and throat before kissing his way down her body. He nipped and licked the sensitive undersides of her breasts as she clutched his head in her hands and moaned encouragingly.

He moved his body to the bottom of the bed, cursing a little when he nearly fell off the end of it. She giggled as he wedged his upper body between her thighs and muttered, "This would be much easier in my bed."

She lifted the covers and peered under them, snorting back the laughter as he stared at her, his eyes glowing in the faint light.

"What on earth are you trying to do?" She giggled again.

The laughter quickly turned into a moan when he bent his head and kissed her flat abdomen before licking her hipbone and the tops of her thighs. He moved further down until she could feel his warm breath on her core, and she inhaled sharply when he licked her with his warm tongue.

"Tristan, what are you doing?" she moaned, her hands gripping the bed sheets.

"Open your legs, girl."

He kissed the inside of one smooth thigh and with another soft moan she shifted her legs apart until she was completely open to him. He licked her clit with wide, flat strokes of his tongue until she was twisting and moaning under him.

"Tristan, oh, Tristan." She reached for his head, groaning in frustration when she felt nothing but the covers. She shoved them back, not caring about the coldness of the room. She looked down and a spasm of pleasure rocketed through her belly at the sight of his head between her legs.

She clutched his head in her hands, pushing him further into her as she braced her feet on the bed and arched her pelvis against his mouth. He sucked hard on her clit and she cried out and came immediately, her body thrashing under his mouth.

Before she had finished climaxing, he was sliding up her body, his hot mouth everywhere and his hands rubbing and squeezing her soft flesh. He drove his cock deep inside of her, both of them crying out as her warm, smooth core squeezed involuntarily.

"You're so warm, so wet, Avery," he moaned before kissing her. She could taste herself on his mouth, and it sent a new spasm of excitement through her.

He lifted her leg, pushing it straight up until it was draped over his shoulder, and propped himself up on his hands above her. He plunged in and out as she wrapped her other leg around his hips and met each of his thrusts.

"Touch yourself," he whispered.

She hesitated and then, her face pink, reached between them and slipped her fingers between her legs. She rubbed delicately at her clit, moaning a little, and he slowed down his wild thrusting.

"Does that feel good, girl?" he murmured.

"Aye," she moaned. "So good."

He increased the pace, watching as she rubbed and circled and found the spots that gave her the most pleasure. Her fingers were speeding up, and she rubbed and touched herself furiously. She stiffened beneath him, her fingers pressing down as she arched her body upward.

He moaned her name as he came inside of her. She could feel his body tensing as the pleasure rushed through him, until he finally collapsed against her soft body. He buried his face in her neck, breathing in her scent as she hugged him with her arms and legs, rubbing his back and stroking his long hair.

She loved the feel of his body on top of hers, but after a

while she shifted slightly under him. He was starting to get too heavy for her, and she tapped him on the back. He pushed away from her warm body before pulling the covers up and lying on his back. Her bed was so small, and he was so wide that she was left with no choice but to sprawl mostly on top of him, their limbs entwined and her head resting on his chest.

He stroked her bare back, running his fingers up and down her spine. "Are you warmer now, girl?"

"Aye, thank you."

"Better than a rock?"

She could hear the amusement in his voice, and she lifted her head and smiled at him. "Well, the rock was probably harder but you're definitely warmer."

He growled and slapped her playfully on the ass, making her giggle and squirm against him.

He suddenly sobered. "Thank you for healing her, Avery. I owe you a debt."

"You're welcome."

She rested her head back against his chest. At the mention of his mother, her good mood had deflated like a balloon. Despite what Tristan said, it was obvious that his mother's opinion mattered to him. His mother would never accept her as Tristan's mate, and by healing her she had ruined even a small chance of a life with Tristan. She was horrified to realize she was close to tears, and she took a deep, calming breath as Tristan traced the curve of her spine again.

"Tristan?"

"Hmm?"

"Have you – have you thought anymore about our earlier discussion? About selling me to someone else?"

He stiffened beneath her. His hand which had moved to

trace lazy circles on her hip tightened painfully on her soft skin.

"No, I have not," he admitted.

She sighed. "I wish you would."

"Now is not a good time," he said. "My mother told me this afternoon that she has arranged to have house guests visit us. Victoria and Hendrick are old friends from when I was a child. They'll be here before the end of the week and if I remember correctly, the Sanders like to travel with nearly their entire household."

He gave her a teasing smile. "Mrs. Lanning will need all the help she can get. Even from a Red."

She didn't return his smile. "My lord, please. You know we cannot continue to -"

"Enough, girl." His smile disappeared. "Can we not have just one time where our lovemaking does not end with you listing all the reasons why we shouldn't have done this?"

"Aye, but you can't be comfortable in this small bed. I'll understand if you want to return to your own."

He sighed impatiently and twisted onto his side. He pressed her up against the wall and slid her leg over his hip, pushing his leg between hers and burying his face in her neck as he tucked the covers firmly around them. He placed a gentle kiss on her throat.

"I threw your rock out of the bed. You'll freeze to death if I go back to my own bed."

She smiled and he kissed her throat again. "I would rather be here with you in your freezing room and your small bed then alone in my own. Do not ask me to leave, girl."

She kissed the top of his head. "Good night, Tristan."

"Good night, Avery."

CHAPTER 16

"Laura!" Mrs. Lanning barked out.

Laura hurriedly set down the dish on the dining table and ran into the kitchen. "Aye?"

"Where is the Red? Gods be damned, it's nearly seven and I need her to run and fetch more wood for the cook stove. It's like an icebox in here."

"Perhaps she's still sleeping. Should I check her room?"

Mrs. Lanning rolled her eyes. "Aye, you idiot." She sighed as Laura ran out of the kitchen and down the hallway towards Avery's room.

She knocked lightly on Avery's door. When there was no answer she knocked again and waited a few moments before opening the door.

"Avery, Mrs. -" She squeaked to a stop, her face turning a bright red and her mouth dropping open.

Tristan, his back to her, was sitting naked on the end of Avery's small bed with an equally naked Avery straddling him. Her slender torso was hidden behind Tristan's broad back, and her hands were clutching his shoulders tightly as she moaned. Her knees were planted firmly on either side of his hips and he was kissing her throat, his hands tangled in her long red hair, as she rode him enthusiastically.

At the sound of Laura's small squeak, Tristan looked behind him. Avery stopped bouncing on his lap and buried her face in his neck with embarrassment. Her hands dug into his broad shoulders as he raised one eyebrow at Laura.

"Can we help you?"

"Mrs. Lanning," Laura whispered. "She's looking for her. She needs her to fetch more wood for the cook stove."

Tristan winked at her. "Tell Mrs. Lanning I'll send Avery out when she's done with *my* wood."

Laura's face turned nearly purple with embarrassment and she stared slack-jawed at them for a few more seconds.

"Go on, Laura. Shut the door behind you," Tristan said.

Laura fled the room, slamming the door behind her.

———

As Laura ran from the room, Avery lifted her head from Tristan's shoulder. She wanted to sink into the floor with shame.

Tristan grinned wickedly at her. "Where were we?"

She gave him a look of horror. "Are you crazy? I have to go, and I have to go right now. I knew I should have made you leave earlier."

She tried to climb off his lap, and he cupped her shoulders, holding her on his lap and keeping his cock planted firmly inside of her.

"We are not stopping now," he growled before kissing her collarbone.

She shivered and shoved at his shoulders. "Tristan, the others - Laura will tell them you're with me. We should not be doing this."

He shrugged and held her around the waist, easily lifting her slender body up and down his cock, smiling when she couldn't stop the low moan in her throat.

"Like they didn't already know, girl. Nothing is a secret in this household."

She gave him a look of panic-stricken worry and his face sobered. He brought her mouth down to his and sucked gently on her upper lip.

"Stop worrying, my love," he whispered. "No harm will come to you."

———

"WE HAVE AN AGREEMENT DO WE NOT, AVERY?"

Avery gathered the bed sheets from the room she was cleaning. Their houseguests were arriving later today, and Mrs. Lanning had sent her to clean the room Victoria would be staying in. She had been trying very hard not to think about the fact that Victoria's room was directly across from Tristan's, when Vivian's soft voice had interrupted her.

"Aye, m'lady. We do."

She brushed past Vivian with the armful of sheets, stumbling to a stop when Vivian said, "And yet I find out that my son was seen leaving the slave quarters, leaving *your* room, this morning."

Avery's back stiffened as Vivian said, "You disappoint me, Avery."

Avery whirled around and glared at her. "What would you have me do when your son climbs into my bed in the night? When he tells me that I belong to him and he will do with me what he wishes?"

When Vivian only stared at her with her dark eyes, Avery

snorted. "Perhaps it is your son you should be making an agreement with."

Vivian smiled. "My son is like all men when it comes to women. They are weak and easily seduced by -"

"I did not seduce your son!" Avery shouted. "Do you believe me proud to be a slave? To know that my choices are no longer my own, and that I can no longer act of my own free will?"

She held the bed sheets tightly against her chest, her cheeks flushed and her eyes flashing. "Do you think it pleases me to be in love with your son, and know that I am nothing more to him than the whore who warms his bed? Do you think I enjoy constantly wondering when he will grow tired of me and what will become of me then?"

Her voice caught in her throat, but she stared dry-eyed at Tristan's mother. "I have no doubt that Tristan will bend to your wishes and marry Victoria. He will abandon my bed for hers, but I guess I should be happy that he will likely keep me on as a nanny to the children she will bear for him."

She gave Vivian a pleading look. "I have no desire to watch the man I love grow old with another. I have begged him to let me leave his home, to sell me to another, but he refuses. He will listen to you, I know it. Will you not speak with him? Ask him to - "

Vivian's eyes flickered to the left and widened. Avery, dread filling her belly, turned around slowly. Tristan was standing in the doorway. She groaned, the colour dropping from her face, as he started towards her.

"Avery -"

"Leave me alone, my lord. Please." Still holding the bed sheets, Avery ran from the room.

TRISTAN TURNED TO GO AFTER AVERY, BUT VIVIAN CAUGHT his arm. "Tristan, wait."

"Is it true?" Tristan stared at his mother.

"What?" she asked.

He scowled at her. "What Avery said. Are you bringing Victoria here in order to marry me off?"

"Tristan, my darling, do not be angry with me. I wish only for your happiness, and Victoria would be an excellent match for you. You were such good friends as children. Are you not the least bit interested in seeing the Lycan she has become?"

"What prompted this sudden desire to have me married?"

Vivian smiled at him. "Sophia deserves a stable home with a mother who loves her. You are an excellent father, but every child needs the gentle touch of a mother."

"She has Maya," Tristan said.

Vivian laughed. "For what - another three months perhaps? You know that Marshall will spirit her away as soon as he can. And then what?"

"Sophia loves Avery just as much as she loves Maya," Tristan said. "She can take over the nanny duties."

"You would have a human raise your Lycan daughter? And not just a human but a Red at that? Sophia is already too attached to her. She believes her to be beautiful. She believes that she has some kind of," Vivian waved her hands vaguely in the air, "magical healing power. She asked me the other day if she could have red hair like Avery's when she grew up."

Tristan grinned a little and she gave him a look of disapproval. "This is not funny, Tristan. The Reds are widely regarded as witches by the humans. There are even many Lycans who believe it. And who is to say they aren't right? Avery will not make a good mother for your children, or a good mate for you. If you were not so blinded by your lust for her, you would see that."

"Why do you dislike her so much?" Tristan asked. "How has she offended you?"

"She has not," Vivian said. "In fact, I find her to be surprisingly charming and I'm impressed with her intelligence. She is quite unlike any slave I've ever seen before. If she was not trying to trap and seduce my son into a life he would soon regret, I would find her to be pleasant company."

"She is not trying to seduce me," Tristan said. "She would not have gone anywhere near me if I had not pursued her."

Vivian gave him a pitying look. "I know you want to believe that, my darling, but for a slave she's extraordinarily clever. You cannot put it past her to -"

"She's the oldest daughter of James Hendrin," Tristan said.

Vivian stared at him. "The gods be damned... how on earth did she become a slave?"

"Her father died, her mother turned to drugs – it is a long story. But she is more than just a slave. She is unique."

"No wonder she does not carry herself like a slave. To go from living the life she did to this... it explains why she is so miserable here," Vivian said.

"She's not miserable here," Tristan said.

"She is, my darling. Someone like her was never meant to be a slave. You cannot help her with that – life has struck her a cruel blow and she must endure it as best she can. But you can ease her life a little by sending her away. You heard her earlier. She is in love with a man she can never have."

He opened his mouth to protest and she squeezed his arm gently. "No Lycan in the history of our family has ever married a human. You know that. You will marry again, if not Victoria, then another Lycan. The most you will ever be able to give Avery is a safe place to live out her days. I understand that you are – are very fond of the girl, but you must think of Sophia now and what is best for her. Sophia is young and impulsive and can barely control her shifting. She needs a Lycan mother to help her become a strong and courageous woman."

She pulled Tristan into her arms and hugged him hard. "The girl loves you. Will you force her to watch you live your life with another? Do as she asks and sell her to another. Sell her to Marshall. She would be happy to live with her sister, would she not?"

"Marshall will barely be able to afford to feed himself and Maya," Tristan said.

She sighed. "Then sell her to someone you know and trust - someone who will treat her well. You know of other Lycans who do not believe the human's fairy tales about the Reds."

She cupped his face. "She is desperately unhappy, my darling. Do the right thing for the both of you and for Sophia and send her away from here. Will you?"

He pulled away, rubbing his forehead wearily. "I will find her a more suitable home after our guests have left."

"You are making the right choice, Tristan."

"Stop it, Mother. I am in no mood to be placated." He pulled free of Vivian's grip and stormed out of the room.

CHAPTER 17

Tristan stepped silently into the kitchen. After his discussion with his mother, he had walked deep into the forest before stripping off his clothes and shifting. He had run for a few hours, not thinking, just working off the restless energy within him.

Now, he stared quietly at Avery. She was standing at the sink with her back to him, scrubbing potatoes while Laura chopped vegetables and chattered away to her. Her body stiffened but she did not turn when he stepped behind them and cleared his throat.

"Leave us," he said to Laura who bowed and left the kitchen quickly.

"Hello, girl."

"Hello, my lord." Avery continued to scrub the potatoes.

"How are you?"

"Very well, thank you. And you? I imagine you are looking forward to having your friends visit."

"Avery," he said, "will you not turn and look at me?"

She shook her head. "No, my lord. Please do not make me. I have humiliated myself enough for one day."

Her hair was in a high ponytail and he rested one warm hand on the back of her bare neck. She froze, her hands squeezing the potato she was holding, and he sighed. "There is nothing to be embarrassed about, girl. "

She barked a short and bitter laugh. "Aye, of course there is not."

"There isn't," he insisted. He rested his lips on the warm curve of her neck, breathing deeply of her scent and she shivered.

"Please, Tristan. Do not torment me this way."

"I'm sorry, girl," he whispered against her skin. "It was never my intention to hurt you."

"I know."

He put his arms around her waist and leaned against her, staring moodily out the window in front of her. She was trembling against him, but she continued to scrub the potatoes and her voice was light and cheerful when she spoke.

"How many years has it been since you've seen your friends?"

"Many," he replied. "After our houseguests have left, I will search for a more suitable home for you. I know of a few Lycan households who would be willing to take a Red. They would be no more than a few hours ride from your sister so you will be able to see her from time to time."

She dropped the potato she was holding and gripped the sides of the sink, her fingers turning white.

"Thank you, Tristan," she said.

"Aye," he grunted. His hand tightened around her waist. "Are you that unhappy, Avery? I am not married yet. Is there no part of you that wishes to stay here with me for a little longer?"

"Tristan, I -"

There was the sound of horses and a large, black carriage

pulled into the yard. A horse-drawn wagon was behind it, filled with slaves. There were shouts of greetings and laughter, and she patted the arm around his waist.

"Your guests have arrived. You must go and greet them."

He kissed her throat. "I have agreed to sell you to another. Will you agree to share my bed until you leave?"

She hesitated. "If that is what you want, my lord."

He was suddenly angry with her. "I want you in my bed only because you choose to do so. Make your decision, girl."

"Then my answer is no," she replied.

His anger disappeared, leaving him feeling tired and depressed. He sighed and she squeezed his arm around her waist.

"I'm sorry but it will only make it more difficult."

"Aye. It was selfish of me to ask that of you."

"Go to your guests, Tristan," she replied. "And thank you again."

AVERY BLINKED BACK TEARS AS TRISTAN KISSED HER THROAT once more, resting his mouth against her skin for nearly half a minute before he left the kitchen. She watched out the window as he approached the carriage. The door opened and a young man, his hair so blond it was nearly white, bounded from the carriage. He hugged Tristan, clapping him roughly on the back before turning and helping a young woman climb carefully out of the carriage.

She was as blonde as her brother but shorter with a lean and muscular build. Even from the kitchen window Avery could see the brilliant blue of her eyes. She smiled at Tristan, her eyes traveling down his body and back to his face before she gave him a warm and inviting hug, pressing her entire body against his.

Jealousy flowed through Avery and she gripped the side of the sink as the woman who could only be Victoria, placed a soft kiss on the corner of Tristan's mouth. He smiled at her and said something that made her laugh and place her hand on his arm.

"She is very beautiful." Laura was standing at her elbow, and Avery glanced at her before looking back out the window.

"Aye. She carries herself well."

She stared at the woman's skin. Even in the cold weather, she was tanned, and her skin glowed in the sunlight. Avery glanced at her own pale arms. She had always enjoyed the contrast of her paleness against Tristan's tanned skin but now, watching the woman hook her arm familiarly around Tristan's and walk with him towards the house, she wished bitterly that her skin was tanned and glowing like Victoria's.

As they disappeared from her sight, she sighed and turned back to her sink of potatoes. Tristan had promised he would sell her to another. She should be happy, but she was more miserable now than ever.

"GODS BE DAMNED, TRISTAN! I DID NOT KNOW YOU HAD A Red in the house!" Hendrick stared at Avery when she entered the room. She ignored his look and gathered their dessert dishes. Tristan, Vivian, Hendrick and Victoria had retired to the common room after dinner where Maya had brought Sophia and Nicholas in to meet them.

Victoria was sitting between Vivian and Tristan on the couch and holding a sleeping Nicholas. She looked Avery up and down, her nose wrinkling. "I saw a Red once. She was older and had her hair cut short so as not to bring attention to herself."

She glanced at Avery's long ponytail and then at Vivian. "Why do you not cut her hair short? I have some skill with scissors – I will cut it tomorrow."

Maya gave Avery a look of horror as Sophia, leaning on Tristan's knee, frowned, "Papa, I don't want her to cut Avery's hair."

He ran his hand over her dark hair. "Then she will not cut it, my love."

Victoria frowned. "Tristan, it's bad enough to have a Red in the house. Why would you allow her to flaunt her hair in such a way? Do you really think a child, even one as smart as Sophia, should be allowed to make such demands?"

Avery could hear the irritation in Tristan's voice when he said, "This is my home and I am glad to have you here, but I do not take kindly to having my decisions questioned. The girl's hair is not to be touched, Victoria. Have I made myself clear?"

Victoria nodded contritely. "Of course, Tristan. I'm sorry. I did not mean to offend."

He grunted in reply and Hendrick stepped in smoothly. "Well, I've never seen a Red." He waved his arm at Avery. "Come closer, girl. I wish to see you."

Avery hesitated and then set the tray of dishes on the side table. She smoothed her skirt and approached Hendrick. She stood in front of him, staring at a spot on the wall as he smiled and patted his knee.

"Have a seat, girl. I don't bite." He winked at her and she sat down gingerly on the edge of his knee, staring across the room at Maya. He ran his hand over her ponytail and then grasped her chin gently. He turned her face towards his and smiled at her.

"For a Red, you're a pretty little thing."

"Thank you, my lord," Avery said as she studied his face. His eyes were as blue as his sister's, and his teeth were very white against his tanned skin and blond beard.

He stared at her for a moment before he cupped her face and drew her closer to him.

"Touching you is very pleasant." His voice was strained, and she watched nervously as his eyes turned a pale yellow.

"Warm," he growled. He shook his head and took a deep breath. "What did you say your name was again, girl?"

"Her name is Avery." Sophia had appeared next to them, and she leaned against Hendrick's other knee and rested her head on Avery's leg.

"She's a slave and she belongs to me. Papa bought her for me." She smiled at Avery who returned her smile as Hendrick released her chin and rested his hand high on her leg. He moved his hand almost lazily, letting his fingers brush against her tightly closed thighs as he smiled at Sophia.

"Belongs to you does she now?" He ruffled Sophia's hair with his other hand, and she giggled.

"Aye. She makes my owie's better."

Avery could hear low growling and she glanced at Tristan. He was staring angrily at the younger Lycan and Victoria touched his arm. "Tristan, are you all right?"

"Fine," he grunted.

"It feels nice to touch her doesn't it?" Sophia said to Hendrick.

"Indeed it does, little one." He smiled again at Avery and squeezed her thigh.

"I want to sit in her lap," Sophia said.

"Excuse me, my lord," Avery murmured.

Before she could stand, Hendrick pulled her further into his lap and then grinned at Sophia. "Come up, little one. The more the merrier I say! We'll build a tower."

Sophia laughed and clapped her hands before scaling Hendrick's lap and crawling into Avery's. Avery squirmed a bit. Hendrick had moved his hand from her leg and slipped it around her waist. He was resting his hand against her hip and rubbing slow circles, and she gave him a nervous smile.

Sophia leaned against Avery's chest and pursed her lips. "Give me a kiss, Avery."

Avery pressed her lips to Sophia's as Hendrick stroked her long pony tail. He smiled and slid his hand around the back of Avery's neck as Sophia leaned her head on Avery's chest and closed her eyes.

"Aye, give us a kiss, Avery," he murmured and pulled her head down toward his.

"Avery!"

Hendrick released her at Tristan's angry shout. She turned to look at him, her stomach fluttering nervously at the pure fury in his gaze.

"Our guests require more wine. Bring it from the kitchen. Now, girl."

She picked up Sophia, sliding off of Hendrick's lap and plopping the little girl down onto his lap. Sophia leaned companionably against Hendrick who kissed the top of her head and she smiled up at him. "I like touching Avery."

"Well, that makes two of us!" He winked at Avery

She blushed and headed for the doorway as Victoria rolled her eyes and said, "Gods be damned, Hendrick. Try and control yourself, would you?"

"HENDRICK SEEMS QUITE FOND OF YOU," MAYA SAID. SHE was sitting in the rocking chair in the nursery, rocking Nicholas who was drinking a bottle.

Avery, who was sitting on Sophia's bed and stroking the sleeping girl's hair, nodded. "Aye."

"Do you find him good looking?"

"He is handsome enough." She tucked the covers around Sophia and sat on the floor next to the rocking chair.

Maya grinned at her. "I have to admit it was amusing to see you turn so red when he made you sit on his lap."

Avery smacked her lightly on the leg. "Amusing for you perhaps."

"Not so amusing for lord Tristan either. I thought he was going to leap from the couch and rip you from Hendrick's lap himself."

Avery rubbed her forehead. "It's getting late and I'm tired. Good night, Maya."

She stood, kissed Maya's cheek, and walked to the door. She opened it and started to leave before she froze and slipped back into the room. Her face pale, she closed the door quietly and stared at Maya.

"Avery, what's wrong?" Maya said.

"Tristan and Victoria are in the hallway. They're kissing," Avery whispered.

"THANK YOU AGAIN FOR INVITING US INTO YOUR HOME, Tristan." Victoria smiled up at him and squeezed his arm.

"You're welcome. It is nice for my mother and for Sophia to have visitors."

"Sophia is a lovely little girl. It's a pity she has had to

grow up with a mother who was not there for her," Victoria said.

"Aye, a pity." He stopped in front of her bedroom door. "Good night, Victoria."

"Good night, Tristan." She smiled sweetly at him but did not let go of his arm. She looked down the hallway. "Which room is yours?"

He pointed to the one across the hall. "This one right here."

"I like knowing you are close."

He cleared his throat. "It is getting late."

Before he could pull away, she had pushed him back against her door with surprising force and, standing on her tiptoes, pressed her mouth against his. She kissed him slowly and pushed at his closed lips with her tongue, urging him to open his mouth.

There was a noise to his left and he pushed her back gently. He had thought he heard a door shutting but the hallway was empty.

"Tristan," Victoria draped her arms around his neck, "will you not kiss me?"

"It is late, and I'm sure you're tired from your travels. Perhaps it's best if you retire for the night."

She cocked her head at him before smiling. "You think me too forward, do you not, Tristan?"

"No, I just think -"

She pressed her body against his. "I have found you attractive since I was a young girl. Your mother says you have not been with a Lycan since your wife left you." She ran her hand over his shirt-covered chest. "I know of men's needs."

She reached for his crotch and he stepped away, holding her hands away from him. "I am flattered, Victoria, but right now my concern is for Sophia and ensuring she feels safe and happy."

She smiled. "Of course, Tristan. That's part of the reason I am here – to help you with Sophia. She could use a strong Lycan female as a role model."

"Thank you. Your help is appreciated." He crossed the hallway and opened the door to his bedroom.

"Good night, Victoria. I will see you in the morning."

"Good night, Tristan." She gave him one last slow and inviting smile before he slipped into his room and shut the door.

He leaned against the closed door and stared into the darkness, wondering if Avery was still awake. He had felt nothing when Victoria had kissed him. He couldn't stop thinking about Avery and the way Hendrick groped her earlier. Although the rational part of him knew that Avery would be in her room by herself and not in Hendrick's room, he wouldn't be able to sleep until he confirmed it for himself. He waited a few moments before opening his door and checking the hallway. It was empty and he moved silently toward the kitchen.

AVERY PEEKED INTO THE HALLWAY. IT WAS EMPTY AND SHE sighed with relief. "They're gone. Good night, Maya."

She blew a kiss to Maya who gave her a look of sympathy as she left. Avery walked quietly past Tristan's bedroom door. She was unable to resist from stopping in front of his door and listening for a moment. There were no sounds emitting from his bedroom, and she said a brief prayer of thanks to the gods before she glanced at Victoria's closed door.

He's probably in her room, her mind whispered viciously

at her and she muzzled it savagely. Trying hard not to think about Tristan touching and kissing Victoria, she walked quickly through the dark house toward the slave quarters.

As she crossed the kitchen in the dark, a low, angry voice stopped her in her tracks and sent her pulse racing.

"Where have you been?"

Frowning, she stared into the darkness. "Is that you, my lord?"

He stepped into the dim light from the window and she squinted at him. "Why are you hiding in the kitchen?"

He stepped closer and she backed up until her ass hit the counter. He stared down at her. "Where have you been, girl?"

"With Maya," she replied.

"It's late to be visiting with your sister. You need to be up early in the morning, do you not?"

"You're right, it is late. If you'll excuse me, I'm going to bed."

"Did you enjoy Hendrick's touch earlier this evening?" He asked.

"What?"

"Did you enjoy sitting on Hendrick's lap? It appeared so," he said sulkily.

"He is your guest, my lord. What would you have me do? Should I have refused him? He was only being friendly. It was a nice change from how people normally react to me."

"You seemed to enjoy his friendliness," he grunted.

"You seemed to enjoy Victoria's kisses," she said.

He twitched guiltily and glared at him. "That's right, my lord. I'm late because I was trapped in my sister's room, waiting for you and Victoria to finish your goodnight in the hallway. You seemed very... pleased to see your childhood friend."

He grinned. "You're jealous."

"I am not jealous," she said.

"You are." He stroked her cheek, making her shiver. "Now you know how I felt watching Hendrick fondle you after dinner."

"I had no choice," she muttered.

"Neither did I."

She snorted. "Of course, you didn't."

"She kissed me. I had no idea she was going to do that. In fact, I pushed her away."

"Fine," she replied. "We both were innocent. Good night, my lord."

He blocked her from stepping around him and frowned. "Stay away from him, girl."

"How do you suggest I do that, my lord? He is a guest in your home. If he wants to spend time with me, I cannot say no."

He growled in frustration. "If he touches you again, I'll kill him."

She laughed and couldn't resist teasing him. "That seems a bit extreme. Perhaps you could start with punching him and work your way up to killing him?"

He grinned in spite of his anger and she smiled delightedly at him. He stared at her mouth, and when he spoke his voice was low and filled with need. "I would very much like to kiss you, Avery."

She stiffened and pulled her head back. "Please don't, Tristan."

His nostrils flared with anger, but he stepped back, allowing her to slip around him and head toward the slave quarters.

CHAPTER 18

"What household owned you before this, Avery?" Victoria asked.

Avery paused in her brushing of Victoria's long blonde hair. Victoria was a late riser and Mrs. Lanning had sent her to Victoria's room with a breakfast tray after the others had finished eating. Victoria had demanded she wait in her room while she ate breakfast, and Vivian and Sophia had shown up just as she was finishing.

Vivian poured herself a cup of tea and the women chatted familiarly. Avery made Victoria's bed and folded her clothes from the night before, while Sophia followed her around the room and chattered happily to her. She was about to leave when Victoria handed her the brush.

Sighing inwardly, Avery had begun to brush the woman's soft, blonde hair as Sophia watched. Now, she glanced at Victoria in the mirror and gave her a small smile. "I was in a slave house, m'lady. Lord Tristan purchased me and my sister on his way home from the city."

"And before that?" Victoria prompted.

Vivian, drinking a cup of tea in a chair by the window,

said, "They were owned by a family in the city who had to sell them when they ran out of money."

Avery glanced at Vivian who returned her gaze steadily.

"I'll have it braided." Victoria slapped Avery's hand. Avery gritted her teeth and started to braid Victoria's hair.

"You know," Victoria stared at her thoughtfully in the mirror, "you're not as ugly as I first thought. I mean, the red hair obviously is awful, and your skin is so pale you look like a leech, but I can see why my brother fancies you."

Avery bit her tongue and continued to braid as Victoria looked at Vivian. "I would never have thought I would have a Red in my household, but this one seems pleasant enough. I could see me keeping her on here as my personal slave. She couldn't go near the children of course. I shudder to think what ideas she's put in Sophia's head already."

Vivian frowned. "Avery is actually very good with Sophia."

Victoria shrugged. "I will talk with Tristan about it. And I will work on convincing him to cut off her dreadful hair."

Wrapping a piece of leather around the end of Victoria's braid, Avery said, "Actually Tristan has arranged to sell

She cried out when Victoria whirled around and struck her viciously across the face, knocking her to the ground. She was wearing a large ring on her hand and it cut Avery's cheek open. The blood flowed freely as Vivian gasped and Sophia ran to Avery.

"Avery," she cried. "You're bleeding!"

"It's all right, my love. I'm fine." Avery reassured her as Victoria rose to her feet and stood over her.

"You are a slave and you will refer to Tristan as lord Tristan or my lord. Do you understand me, slave?" She snapped.

Avery stood and stared at the floor, trying to tamp down

the anger in her voice. "Forgive me, my lady. It will not happen again."

"See that it does not." Victoria turned to Vivian. "Gods be damned, Vivian. Does Tristan have any control over his slaves at all?"

When Vivian didn't reply, she turned back to Avery. "Leave, girl. I am tired of your ugly face."

"Avery?" Sophia whispered.

"Sophia, go to your grandmother," Victoria demanded.

Sophia hesitated and Avery pushed her gently toward Vivian. "Go, my love. I will see you later."

She left the room as Sophia fled to her grandmother.

"AVERY! WHAT HAPPENED TO YOUR CHEEK?" MAYA LAID Nicholas in his crib and rushed to her.

"Victoria slapped me," Avery said.

"What? Why would she do that?"

"Because she's a bitch." Avery grimaced as she touched her cheek.

"Here, give me your hand." Maya reached for her.

The door opened and Tristan stuck his head into the room. "Maya, have you seen Sophia? I want to take her riding this morning."

He stared Avery, cursing loudly before entering the room and striding toward her, He took her chin in his hand. "What happened to your cheek?"

"I tripped," she said.

He frowned. "Tripped on what?"

"My own feet." She smiled at him, but he didn't return her smile.

She pulled her chin free of his grip and he gave Maya a hard look. "Why are you not helping her heal?"

"She was just about to, my lord," Avery said.

He grunted in reply and then suddenly picked her up and carried her to the overstuffed chair near Sophia's bed. He sat down and settled her on his lap, wrapping his arms around her and pushing her head down on his chest.

"My lord, this is not necessary. Maya will help me." She tried to sit up and he tightened his arms around her.

"Quiet, girl."

She gave up struggling and relaxed against him. He slipped his hand under her hair and cupped the back of her neck, kneading the muscles lightly. She watched as Maya lifted Nicholas from the crib and carried him to the window on the far side of the room. She stared out the window, swaying back and forth and singing to Nicholas.

"How is your morning?" Tristan asked suddenly.

"Fine, my lord. And yours?"

"Good."

"You're taking Sophia riding?" she asked.

"Aye," he paused. "She asked me last night if I would take her to a party."

"Really?" Avery rested her hand on his chest, resisting the urge to slip her hand between the buttons of his shirt and rest her palm against his warm skin.

"Aye. She remembers the other girl, Renee maybe, talking about dancing and parties that day in the wagon. She's had it in her head ever since."

"Are you going to take her to one?"

"No. But I thought maybe I would throw her one here. What do you think?"

She sat up and smiled down at him. "I think that's a wonderful idea."

He grinned. "Good. Then I'll do it."

Behind them, Nicholas let out a short wail and they could hear Maya soothing him.

"Maya loves to dance. She'll be very excited," Avery said.

"And you? Do you love to dance?" He asked.

"Aye, I suppose I do."

He cocked his head and studied her. "What is it?"

"It's hard to find many who are willing to dance with a Red." She wiggled her eyebrows at him, and he tightened his hand around her neck.

"I'll dance with you," he said.

Her breath caught in her throat as his eyes darkened and dropped to her mouth. She could feel him growing hard underneath her and it took all of her willpower not to rub her ass against him. "Tristan, my cheek is healed."

She didn't want to leave his lap. She wanted to sit with him forever and pretend that he loved her the way she loved him. Suddenly feeling depressed and angry for torturing herself, she tried to struggle from his lap.

He refused to let her go. "Let me see."

She turned her face obediently so he could examine her cheek. He wiped the smears of drying blood away, a satisfied look crossing his face when it revealed her smooth cheek with no trace of the cut that had marred it.

"It's almost healed," he said before staring at her mouth again. "One kiss should do it."

"Tristan…"

"Just one small kiss, my love, and I'll let you go," he whispered.

Still holding her neck, he tugged her face down toward his and she gave up protesting and pressed her lips against his. He kissed her softly, his mouth warm against hers, and she sighed with pleasure.

After a moment he pushed his tongue against her lips, and she pulled back a little.

"Tristan, this is not a good idea."

"Please," he whispered against her mouth. She kissed him again, powerless to resist his plea. He sighed into her mouth as she parted her lips and he pushed his tongue eagerly into her mouth. She cupped his face, stroking his cheekbone with her thumb as he rubbed her back with his warm hand.

The door to the nursery opened and Victoria entered. She studied Maya at the window. "You there, have you seen Tristan?"

Avery had slipped off of Tristan's lap the moment the door opened. She stood a few feet from the chair, staring at the floor with flushed cheeks as Tristan cleared his throat.

"Tristan." Victoria smiled sweetly and crossed the room as Vivian and Sophia entered the nursery. She sat down on his lap before he could stand and put her arms around his shoulders. "Good morning."

"Good morning, Victoria."

He glanced at Avery and Victoria followed his gaze. She scowled. "Leave us, slave."

Avery started towards Maya. Sophia met her in the middle of the room and gave her a unhappy look. "Are you still hurt, Avery?"

Avery bent and picked her up, rubbing the girl's small back. "Hello, my love. Come, we'll stand with Maya and your grandmamma."

She joined Maya and Vivian at the window. Vivian had taken Nicholas from Maya and was kissing his warm, round head. She gave Avery a troubled look as Maya took a cloth and wiped the blood from Avery's cheek.

"Is your cheek okay, Avery?" Sophia whispered.

She nodded. "Aye, Sophia. It is perfectly fine."

"Shall I kiss it better for you?"

"There is no need, my love," she said to the girl. "Maya kissed it better for me. Look." She showed the girl her smooth cheek and Sophia's face relaxed.

Vivian frowned and took Avery's chin in her hand. She examined Avery's cheek closely. "How is this possible?"

Avery tugged free of her gentle grip. "It was not nearly as bad as it seemed, m'lady."

"I saw the blood," Vivian said sharply.

When Avery didn't respond, she said, "I will speak with my son about this."

"No, do not," Avery said in a low, urgent tone. She glanced at Sophia and lowered her voice even further. "He believes I tripped. Do not tell him otherwise."

———

"How did you sleep, Victoria?" Tristan asked.

She smiled. "Very well, Tristan. Although it was cold in my bed."

"I'll have more blankets brought to your room tonight." He shifted uncomfortably under her. He was still hard from kissing Avery, and he was frustrated with Victoria for interrupting them.

"That's very kind of you but perhaps we can think of another way to warm my bed. I have many ideas for -"

She paused as she registered the hardness under her lap.

"Lord Tristan," she purred, "it would seem you have ideas of how to warm my bed as well."

He stood up abruptly, catching her arm when she nearly

fell and gave her a look of apology. "Forgive me, but I have promised Sophia I would take her riding this morning."

She smiled at him and linked her arm around his as he started towards Sophia and the others. "I would very much like to join you. May I?"

"Of course." He allowed no trace of the dismay he was feeling to show on his face. His mother believed that Sophia needed a Lycan mother and since the moment Victoria had arrived, he had been torn between his feelings for Avery and his desire to do the right thing for Sophia.

They joined the others at the window and Sophia reached for him from Avery's arms. He took her, his hand brushing against Avery's breast.

"Sorry," he muttered as he settled Sophia in the crook of his arm. "Are you ready to go riding, my love?" He smiled, feeling a wave of love for the little girl, as she stroked his long ponytail.

"Aye." She gave him an I-want-something grin. "Can Avery come with us, Papa? Please?"

"I'm going to be joining you, sweet girl." Victoria patted her leg. "Won't that be fun?"

"I want Avery," Sophia muttered and buried her face in her father's neck.

Avery squeezed her thin shoulder. "I cannot, my love. I have work to do. You will have fun with your father and Lady Victoria."

Maya held out her hand to Avery. "Walk with me to the common room, Avery. Marshall is waiting for me." She looked to Vivian. "Shall I take Nicholas, my lady?"

Vivian shook her head. "No. I will keep him with me a while longer."

CHAPTER 19

"How long have you owned the Red?" Victoria asked Tristan. They were riding through the forest. Sophia, on her small pony, was a few feet ahead of them, chattering animatedly to the animal as it picked its way through the trees.

"Just over a moon or so. Why?"

"Just curious. Your mother said she and her sister were owned by a family in the city who had to sell them. Which family was it? Were they Lycans?"

"I never asked," he grunted.

"They must have been. No human family, with their silly superstitions, would have allowed her in their home," she mused. She reached across and stroked his arm. "It was kind of you to take her in."

He grunted again and they rode in silence for a few moments. Victoria sighed. "Although I do not believe the humans and their stories of the Reds being witches, I do worry about her influence on your Sophia."

"She would never harm Sophia," Tristan said.

"No, of course not, my lord. She is obviously very fond of the girl - and her father." Victoria glanced at him.

When he didn't reply, she continued. "I just think that Sophia has an unnatural attachment to her. It does not seem proper for a Lycan child to spend so much of her time with a human. As nice as the Red seems to be, we all know that humans can never fully be trusted. Do you not worry that she will use Sophia as a way to better her situation? Perhaps you should begin to think of separating Sophia from her. I would be glad to help you transfer Sophia's affections to someone more suitable. Perhaps -"

"It does not matter," Tristan said. "I am selling her to another."

"You are?" Tristan could hear the obvious relief in Victoria's voice.

He nodded and she gazed thoughtfully at him for a moment. "You should speak with my brother. He seems to fancy her and would buy her from you. I'm most certain of it."

"Your brother lives too far away. I promised Avery I would sell her to someone who lives close to her sister."

Victoria stared at him. "Since when do we care what the slaves want, Tristan?"

"They are still people, Victoria. They have thoughts and feelings like everyone else."

"Aye, I suppose you are right," she said. "Still, I think you should consider it. She seems to have a connection with Hendrick, and he would treat her well, I can assure you of that."

"Sophia, you are too far ahead." Tristan urged his horse forward, ending their conversation.

"LORD TRISTAN HAS GONE MAD." MRS. LANNING FUMED. "Four days to plan a party and all because a child demands it. The party guests will be here tonight, and we still haven't fully cleaned the east wing, nor do we have enough food."

Marian smiled timidly at her. "There is not much left to clean in the east wing. Avery, Laura and Nadine are there now and will be finished it by mid-afternoon. As for food, lord Tristan sent Jeffrey and Marshall to the village yesterday for more groceries. They will be back any time now."

"Besides," Renee piped up from where she was scrubbing the top of the large black cook stove, "think of how much fun it will be. There will be music and dancing, and lord Tristan's guests are sure to bring their slaves with them. Some of them may even be young men who will fall over themselves to dance with me."

Mrs. Lanning scowled at her. "You will not be enjoying yourself as much when you are cleaning up after this party, will you, Renee?"

When Renee only shrugged and continued to clean the cook stove, Mrs. Lanning rolled her eyes. "It is a huge waste of electricity. We are forced to use candles and lanterns for most of the year, yet he will undoubtedly use up a year's supply of electricity on the lights in the common room alone."

She stormed out of the kitchen, still muttering to herself and Marian grinned at Renee. "I swear, Mrs. Lanning is only happy when she has something to be unhappy about."

———

"AVERY — LAURA AND I ARE GOING TO START CLEANING THE last bedroom. Are you almost done in here?" Nadine stuck her head in the doorway of the bedroom.

"Aye." Avery nodded as she unfolded the sheet in her hand. "I just need to finish making the bed and I'll join you."

She snapped the sheet over the bed and tucked it in firmly around the mattress. Tristan was a constant thought in her head, and her stomach twisted a little. She had seen very little of him for the last five days. The first few nights she had lain awake for hours in her cold bed, wondering if he would come to her and knowing she would not turn him away if he did. He had honoured her decision though and kept away from her. She alternated between cursing herself for telling him no when he had asked her to share his bed and reminding herself it would only have made it more difficult when the time came that he sold her to another.

He had been spending his days with Sophia, Victoria and his mother, and Avery couldn't help the thread of jealousy that shot through her veins.

"Stop it, girl," she scolded herself fiercely. "He will marry Victoria and that's the end of it." She tucked the bed sheets in with renewed vigor.

"Hello, Avery."

She jumped and whirled around, her hand clutching nervously at the low neckline of her blouse as she stared at Hendrick. "My lord, you scared me."

He smiled easily at her, his teeth flashing, and stood in front of her. "Forgive me, I did not mean to startle you."

She folded her arms across her torso. His eyes drifted down to her full breasts and he grinned again when she moved her arms over her chest.

"You're really very lovely. Did you know that, Red?" He reached out and brushed his thumb across her mouth.

She backed away, picking up the top sheet and shaking it out in front of her. "Thank you, my lord."

She placed the sheet on the bed as he stepped closer and took her arm. "Stop please, I wish to speak with you."

She turned back to him, plastering a polite smile on her face. "Yes, m'lord?"

He smiled and pulled her into his arms, putting one hand firmly against the small of her back and stroking her long hair with the other. He was the exact same height as her and she squirmed nervously as he tipped his head toward hers.

He ran his hand over her cheek and then traced her collarbone with the tips of his fingers. "Touching you is very pleasant. I wonder what it feels like to kiss you."

He dipped his head and placed a soft kiss on her mouth. He released her mouth and stared at her. He was breathing heavily and there was a dazed look in his eyes.

"Gods, I've never felt anything like it," he muttered and then kissed her again.

He probed her closed lips with his tongue, but she refused to open them. After a moment, he murmured, "Open your mouth, Red."

She shook her head and then shrank back at the fleeting look of anger in his eyes.

"Open your mouth," he repeated, his hand tightening painfully on her long hair.

She stared silently at him and his brow darkened with anger. "I will not ask you again, Red. Open your mouth."

"Gods be damned, Avery. What's taking you so long to make the bed?" Laura stuck her head into the bedroom.

Avery yanked free of Hendrick's grip and ran to the door. "Sorry, Laura. I'm finished here." Without looking at Hendrick she took Laura's arm and dragged her from the room.

"MAYA?" AVERY KNOCKED ON THE DOOR OF THE NURSERY and then peeked inside. "Marian said you were looking for me."

Maya grinned at her. "Aye. You must braid and pin my hair for me and then I'll do the same for you." She pulled Avery into the room and danced around excitedly in her white nightgown. "Oh, Avery, I'm so excited! A party with music and dancing – it's been so long."

Sophia giggled and wrapped her small frame around Avery's leg. "Do I look pretty, Avery? Papa bought me a new dress."

"Let me see." She stood back and examined the little girl carefully. She was wearing a soft pink dress with lace on the collar and cuffs, and Maya had pinned the sides of her hair back. It fell to the middle of her back in a long dark cascade and her dark eyes were sparkling.

"You will be the prettiest girl in the room." She smiled down at the little girl.

"I know," Sophia said and both Maya and Avery laughed.

Avery braided Maya's hair and Maya smiled at her in the mirror. "Have you met the Tomlins yet, Avery?"

Avery shook her head. "No. Mrs. Lanning had us scrubbing and cleaning right up until the last moment. I had just finished my bath when Marian told me you were looking for me." She wound Maya's braid around her head and carefully pinned it. "Have you met them?"

Maya nodded. "Aye, and the Bartons as well."

"What were they like?"

"The Tomlins were a rowdy bunch. They have three teenage boys and two younger daughters. Mrs. Tomlin looks," she hesitated, "very tired."

Avery grinned at her as Maya stood and pushed Avery

into the chair. "Your turn." She brushed through Avery's damp hair and braided it carefully.

"What about the Bartons?"

Sophia leaned against Avery's knee and watched fascinated as Maya braided. "They're an older couple. They have a son who is about my age I believe. Mrs. Barton was very kind. She spoke to me almost as an equal."

"They are Lycans?" Avery stroked Sophia's soft hair.

"Aye. I guess lord Tristan has known them for many years. In fact, the Bartons live not ten miles from here and the Tomlins are only half a day's ride."

Avery stiffened a little. They were the Lycan families Tristan had mentioned to her. She took a deep breath and vowed to make a good impression.

Maya finished pinning her hair and squeezed her shoulders. "There. Now, let's get dressed."

Avery looked down at her plain white blouse and black skirt. Many of the other slaves, especially those who had been in Tristan's household for years, had acquired nicer clothing over the years. Avery had nothing to wear but what had been bought for her by Marian and Mrs. Lanning at the village close to Tristan's home. She had washed and pressed her outfit carefully and although it fit her well enough, it was a far cry from the expensive silk dresses she had worn to parties thrown by her father. Still, they were the nicest pieces of clothing she owned, and it felt good to be in something other than her work clothes.

"Maya, I am already dressed," she said as her baby sister skipped to the door that led to the large closet in the nursery. She disappeared inside and returned carrying two long, black bags. She laid them carefully across her bed and motioned for Avery to join her.

She pulled the zipper down on the closest bag and slipped

the dress out. Avery sucked in her breath. The bodice was a dark green that gradually faded in colour, leaving the long, full skirt a shimmering light green. Avery reached out and ran her fingers along the fabric. It was silky soft, and she smiled delightedly at Maya.

"It's beautiful. Here, I'll help you put it on."

Maya grinned. "Oh, it's not for me. It's for you. Marshall bought me this one." She pointed to the other bag.

Avery gaped at her. "What?"

Maya lifted the dress carefully from the bag. "It's for you. Marshall picked it up in town when he and Leo went for the groceries."

"Where on earth would Marshall get that kind of money? This dress had to have cost a fortune."

Maya laughed. "Marshall didn't buy it, silly. Lord Tristan did."

Avery sat down on the bed, staring at Maya in stunned silence.

"Before they left, lord Tristan gave Marshall some money and told him to buy a dress for you. A dress that would match your eyes, he said. Marshall asked me for your dress size."

Sophia ran her small hand over the fabric as Maya beckoned to Avery. "Come, let's get you into it."

"Maya, I cannot wear that. You know I cannot. If the others see me in this dress they will -"

"Gods be damned, Avery!" Maya suddenly burst out impatiently. "Who cares what the others think? Lord Tristan wants you to wear this dress and you will. Now take off that dreadful shirt and skirt."

CHAPTER 20

Marshall tugged irritably at his tie. "Gods, I hate these things."

Tristan grinned and straightened his own tie. "Aye, but you look very handsome."

Marshall punched him in the arm. "Shut up."

Tristan sucked in his breath. He was staring at the door to the common room and Marshall followed his gaze.

"Gods be damned," Marshall breathed.

Maya, gorgeous in a soft blue dress and her blonde hair glinting in the hundreds of twinkling lights that had been strung to the ceiling, had entered the common room, carrying Nicholas and holding Sophia's hand.

But it was not Maya that had Tristan's attention so riveted. Behind her, smiling and clasping her hands nervously in front of her waist, was Avery. Her red hair was braided and wound around her head with a few soft curls pulled down and framing her pale face. The dress Marshall had picked out for her fit her perfectly. The bodice clung to her full breasts and small waist, and her skin glowed against the dark green material.

He couldn't stop staring at her as Marshall crossed the room and kissed Maya on the cheek. Sophia leaned against Avery's leg, and she smiled down at her and stroked the small girl's hair. Tristan, his stomach churning with sudden nerves, smoothed his jacket and started toward her. Victoria, wearing a dress the colour of blood, stepped in front of him.

"Good evening, Tristan."

"Hello, Victoria." He strained to look around her as Avery, holding Sophia's hand, was approached by the lord and lady Barton.

Victoria tucked her hand into the crook of his arm and led him towards the long table that was laden with food. "Will you join me for a bite to eat, Tristan?"

He forced himself to smile at her. "Of course."

AVERY WATCHED AS TRISTAN DANCED WITH VICTORIA. ONCE everyone had eaten their fill, the tables had been pushed against the wall and the music had begun for dancing. The Lycan looked gorgeous. Her blonde hair and tanned skin were a startling contrast to her deep red dress, and Avery swallowed hard as Tristan said something to her and she laughed up at him.

She sighed and forced herself to look away. The evening was the best night she'd had since her father died, and she refused to spend it feeling sorry for herself. She heard Sophia laugh and smiled as the little girl, holding Maya's hands and dancing around the room, waved at her.

"Would you like to dance?"

She glanced up to see the Barton boy, she thought his name was Rory, standing in front of her.

She smiled. "I would love to."

She took his offered hand and let him lead her to the dance floor.

TRISTAN LEANED AGAINST THE WALL AND WATCHED AS THE others danced. The music, a fast and furious beat, throbbed through the room and he grinned as the people twirled and spun around the room. Avery, her face flushed and glowing, was in the middle of the room dancing with Maya and the Tomlin brothers. She stomped her feet and wiggled her hips, laughing and giggling.

"It's a fine party." The lord Barton stood next to him and Tristan forced himself to stop looking at Avery and concentrate on the older man.

"Thank you for joining us, Thomas."

"Thank you for inviting us," Thomas replied.

Tristan's gaze turned to Avery again. Her red hair gleamed like fire under the lights, and he stiffened a little when Hendrick took her hands and spun her around in a rapid circle.

"I spoke with Miranda. She's open to the idea of taking the Red. She spoke at length with her earlier and is quite taken with the girl," Thomas said. "What's her background? She's not like any slave I've ever met before."

"I'm not sure," Tristan said. "I haven't asked her."

"She's a hard worker, is she?"

"Aye, she is."

"Well, we'll take her then. Miranda could use some help around the house."

Tristan nodded stiffly. He had already spoken with Lord

Tomlin and he too, had expressed interest in taking Avery. He knew he would prefer that Avery go with the Bartons. Not only because she would be closer to him, but he didn't care for the way Paul, the oldest Tomlin boy, was looking at Avery.

"If you'd like, we'll take her back with us when we leave tomorrow afternoon. It will save you a trip bringing her to us."

Tristan shook his head immediately. "No, I'll need her until after our houseguests have left."

Thomas smiled. "Are you sure? With yours and the Sanders slaves, you seem to have more than enough help at the moment."

"I will bring her to you in a few weeks, Thomas," Tristan said harshly.

His stomach had clenched painfully when Thomas had offered to take her with them and he wondered, not for the first time, if he would even be able to honor his promise to Avery. The thought of not seeing her every day, of not hearing her voice or touching her soft skin, made him feel nearly mad.

Thomas held up his hands. "That's fine, Tristan, Are you sure you want to sell her to me? You don't seem keen on giving her up."

Tristan didn't reply. The music ended and another song began, a slow and soft one this time. He watched as the dancers broke off into couples and Avery wandered to the edge of the dance floor. She leaned against the wall and watched the couples dancing.

Tristan pushed away from the wall. A flash of red caught his eye and he groaned inwardly as Victoria weaved her way through the dancers towards him. As she approached, he turned to Thomas. "Do me a favour, Thomas?"

The old man raised his eyebrows at him.

"Ask Victoria to dance."

Thomas glanced at her and then back at Tristan who was staring at Avery again. "Aye, I can do that, Tristan."

Victoria stopped in front of them. Before she could speak, Thomas smiled at her and held out his hand. "May I have this dance, lady Victoria?"

She hesitated and then nodded. Thomas took her hand and led her to the dance floor as Tristan started toward Avery. He stopped in front of her and held out his hand.

"Will you dance with me, girl?"

She smiled at him. "Aye, my lord. I will."

She took his hand and he led her to the dance floor. She rested her right hand on his shoulder as he slipped his left arm around her waist and pulled her up tight against him. He held her left hand in his right and moved her around the floor in a smooth circle.

"Thank you for the dress, my lord."

"Do you like it?" He asked a little anxiously.

"I love it. It's the nicest gift I've ever been given," she said.

"You look so pretty," he said, and then groaned at how stupid he sounded.

"You look very handsome," she whispered.

He wanted to kiss her. He wanted to lead her to his bedroom, rip off her new dress and touch and caress her naked body until she was moaning his name. He wanted to bury himself in her warm body and feel her come apart around him. He was growing hard and he could pinpoint the exact moment she felt it.

She stared up at him, her green eyes dark with need. When her mouth parted, he dipped his head to kiss her. He didn't care who was watching. She jerked against him, tripping over his foot, and they stumbled to a stop.

"Sorry," she said. She lifted up her long skirt a little to rearrange it and he couldn't help smiling at the sight of her leather work boots.

She followed his gaze and blushed, dropping her skirt to hide the boots.

"I don't have any other shoes," she said almost apologetically as he led her around the dance floor again.

"I should have asked Marshall to buy you shoes as well," he said.

She laughed. "Could you imagine, my lord? He did a wonderful job with the dress but I'm not sure I would trust him with my footwear."

He grinned at her and let go of her hand briefly to tug on one of the curls that framed her face. "I like your hair tonight."

"Thank you. Maya braided it for me."

He pulled her even closer and inhaled. It had been days since he had touched her, had smelled her own unique scent, and he squeezed her tightly as she began to tremble against him.

"It's been a wonderful party has it not?" she said. "Sophia has been having so much fun. She will remember this night her entire life."

She glanced at the couch that was pushed up against the far wall. Sophia was on the couch with her small head cushioned on a pillow and her body covered with a blanket. She had fallen asleep over an hour ago while Tristan had held her and danced her slowly around the room. Despite the noise and light, she had not stirred since.

"You're having a good time then?" he asked.

"Aye!" She gave him a dazzling smile that took his breath

away. "This is the most fun I've had since before Daddy died."

He smiled down at her. "I am pleased to hear that."

She looked up at the ceiling, staring at the small twinkling lights, and he had to smother an urge to place a soft kiss on her milky white throat.

"So many people have asked me to dance tonight." She gave him a very child-like grin of delight and he was helpless to stop his answering one. "Even at Daddy's parties, very few people would dance with me. I would dance with my father and my younger brother of course, and once, a very nice old man danced with me, but I normally just watched the other people dance."

She looked around at the people swaying on the dance floor. "Tonight, I've danced with all the Tomlin boys, Marshall, Lord Barton, Hendrick and Rory."

"Aye." He gave her a mock glare. "You danced twice with the Barton boy."

She laughed and smacked him lightly on the shoulder. "Rory is Maya's age, Tristan. Do I have to make you promise me that you will not punch him?"

"I'll try to control myself," he said with a small grin.

"Good. The Bartons seem nice. Lady Barton was very kind to me earlier."

He didn't reply and she hurried on. "Rory told me that his father was keen on taking me in to help his wife around the house. He said that his father was going to speak with you about me leaving with them tomorrow."

When Tristan remained silent, she squeezed his shoulder gently. "Did he speak with you, my lord?"

"Aye." He pulled her closer, resting the side of his head against hers.

"Will you let me go with them, Tristan?" she whispered.

She tensed against him when he shook his head. "Not tomorrow. You're still needed here. But I will take you there myself in a few weeks."

"Thank you, Tristan. I can't tell you how much I -"

"Enough," he said curtly. "I do not want to speak tonight of you leaving. Can we not just dance?"

"Aye, we can," she said.

He closed his eyes, lowering his hand until it was resting on her hip and holding her hand tightly in his other.

AVERY SMILED HAPPILY AS SHE WALKED DOWN THE DARKENED hallway. Mrs. Lanning, drunk on too much wine, had informed them that they could clean up in the morning and she was anxious to get back to her small room. She wouldn't take the dress off, not yet, but she would lie in her bed and relive the evening.

She was nearly to the kitchen when Hendrick stepped in front of her. "Good evening, Avery."

She groaned inwardly but smiled at him. "Good evening, Hendrick."

"Did you have fun this evening?"

"I did." She gave him another polite smile. "And you?"

"Very much so." He stepped closer and stroked her arm. "You are looking very lovely tonight."

"Thank you." She stepped back, frowning when he followed her.

He leaned in and kissed her cheek. "Come back to my room with me tonight, Red."

She shook her head and he scowled as he wrapped his hand around her arm. "It is not a request."

"I will not," she said. "Let me go, Hendrick."

He squeezed her arm. "You would be wise not to defy me, Red. My sister will soon be married to your master and it would be prudent of you to be friendly to me."

"Let me go," she repeated.

"And if I don't?" he sneered at her. "What will a little girl like you do if I don't?"

Avery slapped him as hard as she could across the cheek. The sound echoed through the quiet hallway and he stared at her in disbelief.

"You will pay for that, you stupid little fool," he gritted out.

He raised his hand to hit her as a hard voice spoke. "Let her go, Hendrick."

Hendrick turned to see Marshall with Maya at his side, standing behind him. "Good evening, Marshall."

"Let her go," Marshall repeated.

Hendrick dropped Avery's arm and she brushed past him and stood next to Marshall. He put his arm around her and glared at Hendrick. "Go to bed, Hendrick. You're drunk and embarrassing yourself."

Hendrick paused, gave them a sarcastic salute, and then sauntered down the hallway and into the darkness. Avery let her breath out in a trembling rush and leaned against Marshall. Maya reached across him and squeezed her arm. "Avery, are you all right?"

"Fine." She smiled shakily at her and then squeezed Marshall's waist. "Thank you."

He nodded. "I'm going to speak to Tristan about this right now."

"No, do not, Marshall. I beg you," Avery said.

He frowned. "He needs to know about this."

"No, he does not." She gave him a pleading look. "Please,

Marshall. Do not say a word to him about this. It will not end well - you know it will not."

He glanced at Maya who gave him a small nod. He grimaced. "I do not like this."

Avery squeezed his waist again. "Hendrick was drunk and being stupid. I will avoid him until he leaves Tristan's home. There is no need for Tristan to hear of this."

CHAPTER 21

Avery took the pan of dirty water out the back door of the kitchen. She carried it a few feet away from the door and threw it onto the frozen ground. She stared up at the dark sky. The stars were out, shining brightly and the nearly-full moon was large in the sky. She turned around to go back in the house and gave a soft shriek of surprise. Tristan was standing in front of her, staring silently at her.

"My lord?" She hesitated. It had been three days since the party, and she'd hardly seen him and not spoken to him at all. There was something off about him tonight. He looked bigger and stronger, his shirt sleeves were straining at his arms, and his usual dark scruff was almost a full beard.

She took a step toward him. "Tristan?"

She placed her hand on his arm and let out another soft shriek when he whirled her around and shoved her against the side of the house. He put his hands on either side of her head and leaned in until he was almost, but not quite, touching her. He dipped his head and inhaled deeply.

"I can smell how much you want me, Avery." His voice was deeper and rougher than usual, and she shivered a little.

"Tristan, what's wrong?"

"The moon will be full tomorrow," he said hoarsely.

She stared at him. The last full moon had been during his trip to his mother's. She had questioned Maya about it and Maya had shrugged. "They didn't seem much different to me, honestly. Marshall didn't touch me at all, would not even hold my hand, and both he and lord Tristan seemed more restless but that was all."

Maya had frowned, thinking back. "They kept Sophia away from me all day, I know they were working on teaching her how to control the shift, and that evening they took her and Tristan's mother and went hunting. They did not come back until the morning, and then all of them slept the entire day. Later, Marshall said that although he would never hurt me during the full moon, Lycans who lived with humans always stay away from them during the night of the full moon - just to be on the safe side."

Avery reached out and touched Tristan's shoulder timidly. "Do you – are you feeling all right?"

He grinned at her and she leaned back against the wall, a little alarmed by his grin. "I feel perfectly fine, girl."

He stretched and she heard his spine crack. "You smell so good to me, Avery."

"My lord, should you be out here with me?" She kept her voice calm.

"Probably not." He stared hungrily at her. "Especially since what I really want is to bury my cock in you."

Her stomach gave a nearly painful throb of desire and she trembled visibly. "Tristan, do not say that to me."

"What?" He dipped his head and kissed her neck. "Should I not tell you how I lay awake at night thinking about your breasts? About how perfectly they fit in my hands, and how much I enjoy sucking on your nipples?"

"Tristan," she moaned. Her hands twisted in her skirt as she fought to keep from touching him.

"Should I not tell you how I lie in my bed each night and think of reasons to have you sent to my room so that I can fuck you? How every time I close my eyes all I can see is your tight pussy sliding down my cock?"

He kissed her neck again, growling softly, and then cupped her breast in his hand. She moaned and arched her back. Her hands grabbed his arms and squeezed as he suddenly angled his mouth over hers and kissed her hard. She opened her mouth and let his tongue slide between her lips.

With a sudden groan, he pulled away from her. He stared at her as she leaned against the house, her legs shaking madly.

"I'm sorry, Avery," he rasped. "I should not have done that."

She nodded and took a few deep breaths, trying to slow her racing, thudding pulse.

"Tomorrow is the full moon. Go to your room now and do not leave it until we go hunting tomorrow night. Do you hear me, girl?"

"Mrs. Lanning will not -"

"I will speak with Mrs. Lanning. Stay in your room for the day," he said.

"Tristan, I do not understand why." She gave him a confused look. "You said before that you could control the shift, even during the full moon."

His nostrils flared and he stepped closer to her again. "That was before you denied me the pleasure of fucking you."

She swallowed hard as he gripped the back of her neck and leaned his forehead against hers. "Go to your room and stay there until we have gone hunting." He gave her a pleading look. "Promise me – please, girl."

She nodded and a look of relief crossed his face. "Thank the gods."

He hesitated and then kissed her again, his lips cold but his mouth warm as he licked at the inside of her mouth. He squeezed her breast roughly and then pushed away from her, standing with his back to her. "Go, girl. Now, before I change my mind about fucking you."

Avery turned and bolted into the house.

THE WOLVES HAD WORKED TOGETHER QUICKLY TO TAKE DOWN the frightened deer. The smallest one sniffed curiously at the dead deer as the large grey wolf grinned and panted at her. He nudged her toward the throat as the others joined her. They tore into the flesh of the deer, growling and snarling as they fed.

The wolf stepped forward to join them and then hesitated. He turned and lifted his large head to the sky, staring rapturously at the full moon as he inhaled deeply. He caught a scent in the air, one that raised his hackles and forced a low growl from his throat. He turned and slunk into the darkness of the forest, not noticing when the small, cream-coloured wolf left the deer and followed him.

"GODS BE DAMNED. I HATE THAT WOMAN. THIS IS ridiculous." Avery grumbled to herself as she picked her way carefully through the trees. Once the Lycans had left to hunt, she had left her room to help the others with dinner. Mrs.

Lanning had sent her out after dinner to pick berries. She had heard that Victoria favoured the berries, which were ready to be picked only when the weather had turned cold, and she had chosen Avery to leave the warmth of the house and search for them.

She hadn't even bothered to protest and ask to wait for the morning. Mrs. Lanning had been in a mood for days and a part of her was glad to leave the house.

The night was cold, and she could see her breath as she walked deeper into the forest that surrounded Tristan's home. The full moon was huge in the sky, so bright that even through the trees it provided enough light for her to see easily.

She glanced up at it, wondered briefly if Tristan was still hunting, and then shook her head with disgust. Of course he was still hunting. They wouldn't be back until the morning. She stumbled over a root, nearly falling flat on her face, and forced herself to pay attention to her surroundings. The sooner she could find the berries, the sooner she would be back in the warm house.

She squinted through the trees, searching for the bushes that Laura had described to her. Concentrating, she didn't notice the man until she was almost upon him.

"Good evening, child."

She looked up, stumbling back and screaming breathlessly.

He held up his hands and smiled at her. "I'm sorry. I did not mean to frighten you."

She took a deep breath, waiting for her runaway heartbeat to slow down as the man took a step towards her.

"Tell me, child. Do you live in the house that sits just on the edge of the forest?"

She took a step back, her brow furrowing. There was

something off about the man. He was dressed in a suit with his long hair braided neatly. She stared curiously at his hands. They were pale and his fingers were slender with long nails.

"Why do you ask?" She took a second step back as he moved closer.

He shrugged, smiling easily at her. "I am lost and hungry and seek shelter for the evening. Perhaps you could take me to your home and offer me solace?"

"It is not my home to offer," she said.

The hairs on the back of her neck were standing and her pulse, which had returned to a normal pace after her scare, was speeding up again sending the blood pulsing through her veins.

"That is sorry news indeed. I am very, very hungry." He suddenly grinned at her and she reeled back at the sight of his long, sharp fangs shining in the moonlight.

"Stay away from me, leech!" She cried and turned to run.

Before she had taken more than two steps, he was on her, pushing her back against a tree and pinning her there with a terrible, inhuman strength.

He sniffed her neck delicately and frowned. "I smell Lycan on you, child. It is offensive."

"Get off of me!" She pushed at his body, fear threading through her when it was like pushing against a rock.

"Of course, it is not so offensive that I won't drain you." He grinned. "I am so terribly hungry."

She opened her mouth to scream as he lowered his face to her neck, but he clapped one strong, cold hand over her mouth. She screamed against his palm as he sunk his fangs into her throat and drank. He suckled loudly at her neck as she kicked and struggled.

He released her neck with a loud pop, and she stared terrified at him as he licked her blood from his lips. "You taste delicious, my child. Perhaps it's because you're a Red?"

He leaned in but before he could latch on to her neck once more, there was a loud snarling and the vampire was torn away from her. She sunk to the ground, staring with wide eyes at the large grey wolf that was standing protectively in front of her.

The vampire climbed unsteadily to his feet and hissed at the wolf. "Lycan! Leave now and no harm will come to you."

The wolf howled loudly, and Avery clapped her hands over her ears, wincing. The vampire licked his lips, glancing quickly at Avery, before turning back to the Lycan.

"It is only one human," he said plaintively. "Give her to me and I'll feed quickly and leave your land. Do we have a deal?"

The wolf crouched low to the ground and bared its teeth in response. Avery watched in horror as Tristan launched his body at the vampire. The vampire flew across the ground and grabbed the wolf's rough pelt. He threw Tristan into a tree, and she screamed as he collapsed on the ground in front of it. The wolf howled with pain and anger and leaped to his feet.

With a loud snarl he dove on the vampire and pinned him to the ground. The vampire screeched as Tristan bit deep into its throat. With another loud snarl, he ripped the head of the vampire from its body. As the vampire's body and head burst into ash, Tristan raised his snout to the sky and howled piercingly.

Avery closed her eyes as tears slipped down her cheeks. There was a soft popping sound Tristan's warm hand cupped her face. She opened her eyes and smiled weakly at him.

"Shh, my love. You're safe now." He tugged her to her feet, and she rested against the tree, staring silently at him. He wiped the tears from her cheeks and turned her head to the right and then to the left. He frowned at the blood-ringed holes in her neck and surprised her by dipping his head and licking the blood away.

He shivered with delight at the taste of her blood before staring solemnly at her. "How do you feel?"

"All right. Are you hurt?" She tried to smile at him, but it came out more as a grimace.

He shook his head and then kissed her, softly at first, but it quickly turned into something else. She returned his kiss, wrapping her arms around him and stroking his naked back as he pressed her up against the tree.

He pulled his mouth away and checked her neck, frowning when he saw that the holes from the vampire's fangs were still there.

"You're not healing."

"I will," she murmured. Tristan was staring at her with that same hungry look from last night and despite the fear still running through her from the leech attack, she could feel the slow cycle of heat starting in her belly.

"My lord, I should not be around you right now," she whispered.

"Perhaps not," he replied.

He ran his hand down her body and grasped her dress in his hand. He pulled the edge of it up, pushing his hand underneath it and trailing his fingers along her smooth thigh. She stared wide-eyed at him as he stroked the front of her thighs.

"Open your legs," he demanded.

"Tristan, you told me to stay away from you," she said.

"Open them." He worked his fingers between her thighs and pushed. She opened her legs and moaned when he immediately rubbed her clit.

He kissed her hard on the mouth, his tongue pushing

between her lips and stroking hers while he shoved one hard thigh between hers and forced her legs open further.

"You taste so good, my love," he whispered against her mouth. "You smell good, you feel good."

He wound his fingers through her hair and yanked her head back. He kissed her throat, licking and sucking gently before he moved his hand and easily slid two fingers into her warm wetness. She cried out, her hands digging into his back, and he grinned at her.

"I love how quickly I can make you ready for my cock," he whispered as he buried his face in her throat and inhaled. He pushed her dress up around her waist, and she whimpered as the cold air washed over her naked skin. Before she could start to shiver, his body was covering hers and he was raising her thigh around his hip.

He entered her with one smooth motion, both of them groaning in unison as he filled her completely. He fucked her with long, slow movements, watching her face as she panted and moaned.

She opened her eyes, her breath catching in her throat at the fierce green light radiating from his eyes. He dipped his head and nuzzled her neck. She could feel his teeth against her throat, and she held her breath as he licked a slow path from her jaw to her collarbone.

He looked at her throat, smiling with satisfaction when there was no trace of the vampire's bite. He nuzzled her neck again.

"Are you frightened of me, girl?" He withdrew and pushed into her slowly.

"No," she moaned, thrusting her hips at him.

"If I bit you would you turn? Or would your body heal you from the Lycan virus?" he asked.

"I do not know," she whispered.

He kissed her throat again, nipping lightly without breaking the skin.

"I confess that I would very much like to find out," he growled against her throat. He was still moving within her, his hard cock rubbing against her wet walls, and she stared mesmerized at him as he looked up at her and gave her a predatory grin.

Avery's body was filled with a weird and fascinating combination of fear and pleasure. She stared into his eyes as he thrust harder within her, feeling the hard bite of the bark against her back and the cool air on her naked thighs.

She was so close to coming. Every nerve in her body was singing with pleasure as he moved within her. He inhaled sharply when she suddenly kissed him hard and then lifted her chin, tilting her head and baring her throat to him.

She realized with wonderment that she wanted him to bite her. She wanted to feel his teeth sinking into her as she came against him and as a low rumbling growl started in his chest, she whispered, "Bite me, Tristan."

He bent his head towards her neck, his teeth bared, and she dug her nails into his back and waited breathlessly for his bite.

Before he could bite her, before his cock could give her the release she was looking for, he was staggering away from her. He turned away, his hands in fists at his side and his entire body shaking violently.

She pushed her dress down and approached him, laying a hesitant hand on his back. "Tristan?"

He twitched away from her. "Do not touch me, Avery."

She recoiled, jerking her hand back as if he had burned her. "Tristan, I am sorry."

He looked back at her, his entire body was shaking and

shuddering as he started to shift. "Go back to the house – now."

She shook her head. "No, Tristan, please I -"

"For the love of the gods – go!" He suddenly roared at her and she turned and fled. Behind her, his roar became a long, torturous howl and she stumbled to a stop and turned to look. Tristan had shifted to a wolf and he was looking at her with a human-like look of misery. He barked once sharply, and she ran for the house again as he turned and disappeared into the trees.

———

VICTORIA STEPPED OUT FROM THE TREES. THE AIR WAS COLD against her naked body, but she took no notice of it. She approached the tree that Tristan had pushed Avery against, and she inhaled, her nostrils flaring with anger at the combined scent of their bodies. Her eyes narrowed as she watched Avery's retreating back before she suddenly shifted back to her wolf form and slipped silently into the woods.

CHAPTER 22

Carefully balancing the two trays, Avery stopped in front of Tristan's room. She set one of the trays on the floor in front of his door and then carried the other to Victoria's door. She knocked lightly. When there was no reply, she opened the door and stepped into the room.

It was early evening. The Lycans had returned from hunting early this morning and had immediately gone to bed. Mrs. Lanning had sent her with trays of food and drink for when they woke.

"Make sure you build their fires up." She glared at Avery. "They'll have let them burn down while they slept, and we don't want lord Tristan's houseguests uncomfortable."

She poked Avery in the back. "And if lady Victoria wakes and wants anything – a bath drawn, more food – make sure you get it for her. I don't want to hear any complaints about you."

Now, Avery set the tray down on the small table in the room and quickly built up the fire. Mrs. Lanning had been right – the fire was only a few embers. Victoria was a quiet, sleeping lump under the blankets on her bed and Avery left quickly before the woman could wake.

She entered Tristan's room without knocking. He was lying on his back in the bed, the covers around his waist despite the cold room. She smiled a little. She had lain next to him and knew how warm he was, but she built up the fire anyway, not wanting him to catch a chill.

She stared at him from across the room. He was sleeping deeply, his broad chest rising and falling in an even rhythm and she waited for a few moments, hoping he would wake. He had saved her life last night and she had not even said thank you.

When he didn't wake, she sighed and moved to the door. She reached out for the handle and stopped, staring at the door for almost a minute. With a trembling hand, she reached out and turned the lock on the door before walking toward Tristan's bed.

She would just cover him up. Pull the blankets up and make sure he didn't get cold while he slept. It was the least she could do for him. She stared down at his sleeping form. He was so beautiful, she thought wistfully.

She reached for the bedcovers but instead, found herself stroking his lean abdomen. Her thoughts turned back to the night before – to the moment he had pushed her up against the tree and entered her - and she gave a low shuddering sigh of need. She had spent most of the day in a state of arousal so deep it nearly hurt. She had tried to ignore it, tried to pretend she wasn't aching to finish what they had started in the woods, but deep down she knew that she had been waiting all day for this very moment. She took another deep breath and let her long pale fingers smooth over his chest and back down to his abdomen.

He had saved her life. She would say thank you in the

way she knew he would like best and then she would not touch him again. She was hurting no one but herself by doing this, and she decided she could live with the hurt.

Quickly, before she could change her mind, she stripped off her clothing and eased into the bed beside him. He didn't move and she slid her hand under the covers and stroked his lower abdomen. He sighed in his sleep, and she smiled and placed a soft kiss just above his navel.

She pulled the covers down to his thighs and pressed small light kisses across his abdomen and around his hips. He groaned as she took his hardening cock in her hand and stroked lightly. She watched his face as she caressed and touched him and when his eyelids started to flutter open, she bent her head and took him into her mouth. He cried out, waking fully at the feel of her warm, wet mouth and started to sit up.

"Avery?" he whispered hoarsely.

She pushed him back down on the bed and increased the rhythm of her mouth. He shuddered under her helplessly and a feeling of exhilarating power rushed through her.

"What are you doing, girl?" he half-moaned and half-sighed. She licked the head of his cock, rubbing her tongue in small circles across the top, as his hands clenched into the bed sheets and he stared down at her.

She kissed the head of his cock. "Saying thank you."

She slid her mouth down over his cock, gripping the base of him in her hand and twisting her wrist back and forth in a gentle motion as she sucked hard on the shaft.

"Oh gods, girl…please," he moaned again.

She licked his cock with warm, long strokes of her tongue as his hands threaded through her hair. He held her head and she smiled a little when he pushed gently on it, urging her to take his cock into her mouth again. She obliged willingly enough, opening her mouth wide and sliding her lips down his cock until she could feel the head of it against the back of her throat.

Tristan continued to groan as Avery licked and sucked and squeezed his rock-hard cock. His cries were growing louder and his body tensing under hers, when he suddenly sat up and grabbed her shoulders. She squeaked in surprise when he pulled her from his cock and pushed her onto her back on the bed.

"Enough, girl. I want to be in you."

He pushed her thighs open, and she hooked them around his hips as he knelt between her legs and pushed his cock into her. They both cried out, but Avery was surprised when instead of starting the quick, rough rhythm she was expecting, Tristan propped himself up on his elbows above her and laid perfectly still.

"Tristan," she sighed and wiggled her pelvis against him, but he didn't respond to her movements. He surprised her again by kissing her tenderly.

"I've missed you."

She smiled at him, blinking back the sudden tears. "I've missed you too."

"Last night…"

His eyes were troubled, and she shook her head and silenced him with a kiss.

"Make love to me, Tristan. Please." She kissed him again, probing at his lips with her tongue, and he groaned into her mouth and moved within her.

"Oh," she sighed. "Like that…it feels so good, Tristan."

"You're so warm, my love." He held her hands, linking their fingers together and staring at her as they rocked against each other in a slow, natural rhythm.

Avery could hardly breathe. The way Tristan was looking

at her, the way he was moving so gently inside of her as if she was made of some exotic glass, was making her throat ache. Tears slipped down her cheeks and he frowned and stopped.

"Am I hurting you?"

She shook her head and smiled. "No, don't stop."

He kissed her tears away, each kiss soft and tender, and she suddenly wrapped her arms around him and crushed her body against his. He buried his face in her throat, and she gasped with pleasure when he quickened his pace within her.

Little bursts of ecstasy were radiating through her pelvis and down her legs. She urged him on with small bird-like cries of need, and she squeezed him tightly with her limbs and mouthed the words 'I love you' into his neck as she climaxed.

His face still buried in the warm curve of her neck, he kissed her soft skin, his body trembling and twitching against her as warmth flooded her insides. He relaxed against her for a moment, his warm breath blowing on her throat, before he sighed and lifted himself away.

He tucked them both under the covers and lay on his back. He put his arm around her as she curled up against him, wrapping her arm around his trim waist and resting her head on his chest.

They were silent for a few moments, and then he squeezed her hip with his warm hand. "What did you mean by thank you?"

She kissed his chest. "You saved my life last night."

His hand moved to her throat, his fingers stroking her skin and feeling for any trace of the leech's bite. "Last night I," he said hesitantly, "I could have seriously hurt you, Avery."

"You didn't," she replied.

"But I could have," he said.

"But you didn't," she repeated.

"Why did you ask me to bite you?"

When she didn't reply, he tugged gently on her long hair until she looked up at him. "Why?"

She wanted to tell him the truth. She wanted to tell him that a part of her - a surprisingly large part of her - had hoped that his bite would turn her. That if she became a Lycan, perhaps she could stay with him forever.

But there was such a look of pain and misery on his face that she couldn't bring herself to say the words, and so she only shook her head and gave him a small and melancholy smile. "I do not know."

"Never ask me that again." He gripped her chin and gave her a heartbreaking look of desperation. "Promise me, Avery."

She nodded, knowing it was an easy promise to keep – she would be at the Bartons by the next full moon. "I promise, Tristan."

He searched her eyes until, satisfied with what he saw in them, he nodded and gave her a brief, hard kiss.

He relaxed against the pillow, his hand stroking her long hair, and then spoke again. "Why were you in the woods last night?"

"Mrs. Lanning had heard that Victoria was craving some berries. She sent me out to pick them for her."

He cursed loudly. "I'm dropping that crazy old bat at the outskirts."

She gave him a look of horror. "You cannot do that. She's been in your household for years."

"I don't care. She almost got you killed last night."

"Please, Tristan. I'm begging you not to send her to the outskirts."

She rubbed his chest anxiously and he shook his head.

"She's been after you since the moment she met you. I cannot let it go on any longer without some type of punishment."

"The outskirts are a death sentence," she said.

"She has been nothing but horrible to you. Why do you fight so hard for her life?"

"She cannot help who she is. Please, Tristan."

He kissed her forehead. "I will do as you ask, but she will be punished." He stared at the ceiling, his hand rubbing her arm. "I will assign Marian as the head housekeeper. Mrs. Lanning can take orders for once."

"She will not like that," she said.

He laughed and kissed her forehead again. "I do not care."

They laid in companionable silence for a while until the silence was broken by Tristan's stomach growling.

Avery sat up, the sheet falling to her waist. "You're hungry."

"Aye, I am." He grinned wickedly at her and cupped her bare breast.

She rolled her eyes and pushed his hand away. "I brought you some food." She started to climb out of the bed, and he put his hand on her wrist.

"Stay here. I'll get it."

He walked naked to where she had left the tray of food, his tanned skin glowing in the light from the fire, and brought it back to the bed. He set it down carefully and then lit the three candles clustered together on the small stand next to his bed.

She sat up, scooting back until she could lean against the headboard. Her lips twitched and she suppressed her smile when he frowned and pushed her forward so he could tuck a pillow behind her back.

"Better?"

She nodded. Aye. Thank you, Tristan."

He climbed into the bed, leaning against the headboard as well and dragged the tray towards them. He tore the bread in half and held it out to her.

She shook her head. "No. The food is for you."

"Eat," he insisted.

Sighing, she took the bread from him and nibbled on it. He grunted with satisfaction before handing her some cheese. She watched as he took a thick slice of the cold meatloaf Mrs. Lanning had placed on the tray and ate it in two large bites.

He quickly finished off most of the food on the tray and she grinned a little. "Hungry, my lord?"

"Aye. The shift burns up energy. I'm always hungry after." He set the tray on the floor beside the bed and rested his hand on her blanket-covered thigh.

"Do you not eat what you hunt?" she asked.

"Aye. But I was distracted last night and by the time I returned to the pack, they had finished the deer."

"I'm sorry."

He frowned and took her hand, stroking her wrist with his thumb. "You have nothing to be sorry about. Saving your life was more important."

He squeezed her hand and then climbed out of bed, disappearing into the bathroom. With a soft sigh, Avery began to dress. She had been in Tristan's room for nearly two hours and she was shocked that Mrs. Lanning hadn't sent someone to find her. She looked out the window. It was dark but she could see the trees at the edge of the forest swaying in the wind. It would be a cold wind and she shivered a little, knowing that as soon as she showed her face in the kitchen, Mrs. Lanning would send her outside for more wood for the cook stove.

She bent and picked up her dress from the floor before

pulling it over her head and gathering her hair into a loose bun. She would definitely be taking a warming rock to bed tonight, maybe two. Even in Tristan's room, with a fire burning in the fireplace, it was chilly. Her room would be as cold as a crypt.

She was just pulling on her boots when Tristan came out of the bathroom. He frowned. "Where are you going?"

She smiled and put her arms around his waist, squeezing affectionately. "I must go, my lord. I'm surprised Mrs. Lanning hasn't sent poor Laura to find me."

She planted a kiss on his bare chest. "Besides, I need to warm up some rocks for my bed." She winked at him, trying to make him smile, but he frowned again and put his arms around her waist.

"Stay with me tonight." He glanced out the window. "It's too cold to stay in your room."

She grinned. "That's what the rocks are for remember? To keep me warm."

"I'll keep you warm," he whispered. He pulled her up against him, dipping his head to trail a meandering path of kisses down her throat.

"My lord, I -"

He held her upper arms and shook her lightly. "Why did you come to my bed tonight, girl?"

"I told you – to say thank you for saving my life."

He was angry, she could see it in the set of his jaw and in the way he looked at her, and she pulled free of his grip. "I'm sorry, my lord. I was trying to be nice."

"Nice?" He arched his eyebrow at her. "You thought it would be nice to deny me what I want most for weeks, then out of the blue crawl into my bed, fuck me once and skip merrily back to your own bed?"

He cupped the back of her neck. "I don't like games,

girl."

"I'm not playing games," she protested. "I wanted to show my appreciation and I thought this would be what you would want. I made a mistake. I'm sorry."

He leaned his forehead against hers. "Do not be sorry. It is what I want, and I should not be taking my frustration out on you."

He kissed her on the mouth. "I wish to ask a favour of you."

"What?" she whispered.

"You will be leaving me soon. Will you spend one last night in my bed? I promise after tonight I will not touch you again."

She ignored the tingle of dismay that went through her at the thought of Tristan never touching her again and nodded. "Aye."

He grinned delightedly and suddenly picked her up, making her squeal softly in surprise, before carrying her toward the large, overstuffed chair beside the fireplace.

VICTORIA SHUT THE DOOR TO HER ROOM AND SMOOTHED down her dress. She was wearing a light blue silk dress that matched her eyes and she took a moment to adjust the neckline, ensuring that just the right amount of cleavage was showing.

She had woken nearly an hour ago and after mulling over what she had seen in the forest the night before, had decided on a plan. Tristan was infatuated with the Red - that was obvious even before last night. Although he had told her he was selling the Red to another, she had decided that it wouldn't hurt to show him exactly why and how she could please him better than the Red ever could. Once he'd had a taste of her body, he would forget the Red entirely.

She crossed the hallway and knocked lightly on Tristan's door. "Tristan, are you awake yet? May I come in?"

TRISTAN RUBBED AVERY'S LOWER BACK AS SHE STIFFED against him. She was bent over the back of the armchair, her legs spread wide and her pale, naked skin glowing in the light from the fire. He was behind her, his large body nestled between her spread legs, and he let out a soft groan of pleasure as he lifted her hips so he could slide even further into her.

"Tristan, wait," she said.

He leaned forward and cupped her breasts before kissing the back of one pale shoulder. "What's wrong?"

"Did you not hear the knock?"

Before he could shake his head, there was a second knock and Victoria's voice drifted through the door. "Tristan, may I come in?"

"Tell me you locked the door." Tristan breathed just as the doorknob turned back and forth.

Avery nodded, and he breathed a sigh of relief as she straightened. The change in position made her tighten around Tristan's cock, and a loud groan tore from his throat before he could stop it.

Tristan clamped a hand over his mouth, his dark eyes wide. Avery's body was shaking, and she covered her mouth as a spat of giggles escaped. He frowned at her and made a shushing gesture, but it just made her laugh harder.

"My lord, you are the strongest and most fearless man, I know. Yet, you hide from a woman," she whispered teasingly.

"Hush, girl," he said.

She snorted and buried her face in the crook of her arm as Tristan's hands tightened around her hips.

"Tristan? Are you sick?" Victoria rattled the doorknob and knocked again. "I know you're in there. Let me in please."

He cleared his throat. "I'm sorry, Victoria. I'm not feeling well. Could you let the others know that I will not be joining them this eve -"

He let out another loud moan as Avery, grinning wickedly at him over her shoulder, thrust her pelvis back and forth with hard, quick movements.

"Stop that!" he muttered. He pulled out of her and stepped back. She turned toward him, and he took another step back at the look on her face.

"Don't you dare, girl," he warned quietly and reached for her. She ducked and dropped to her knees, taking him into her warm mouth.

"Tristan, if you're sick and your healing powers are not helping, you need to be looked at. Let me in so I can help you." Victoria's voice was thick with frustration.

"Tristan? This is ridiculous – let me in." The door rattled in its frame when Victoria pounded on it.

Tristan stared down at Avery, watching her lips slide back and forth over his throbbing cock. He groaned and threaded his fingers through her hair. He meant to push her away but as his fingers tightened, she sucked hard and he groaned again, his hips thrusting helplessly against her mouth.

Faintly he could hear Victoria talking through the door, but he was consumed by the sight and feel of Avery's warm mouth. He watched, his groin tightening and his legs beginning to tremble as Avery sucked and licked and squeezed the base of him with her fingers.

There was a loud banging on the door and with a grunt of anger he shouted, "I am fine, Victoria. I just need to sleep. Leave me be, for the gods sake!"

"Fine, lord Tristan," Victoria snapped through the door. He could hear the loud click of her heels as she stomped down the hallway, and with a muttered curse he grabbed Avery's shoulders and pulled her to her feet.

She grinned cheekily at him. "Something wrong, my lord?"

He spun her around roughly and bent her over the back of the armchair once more. "You deserve a spanking for that, girl."

He ran his hand over her ass, smiling a little at the way she quivered beneath him. He squeezed the firm flesh and then slipped his hand between her thighs. She moaned and immediately spread her legs apart. He placed a warm kiss in the middle of her back as his fingers found her swollen clit and rubbed gently. She gasped and sighed with need, clutching the armchair as her hips moved against his fingers. When she was close to coming, he stopped.

"No, please!" she cried out and he smiled again as he pulled her up straight and pressed his cock against her soft ass. He reached around her body and cupped her breasts, kneading and rubbing the pale globes before tugging on her hard nipples.

"Tristan, please," she begged.

He turned her to face him and picked her up. She wrapped her legs around his waist, rubbing herself against his cock as he carried her to the bed. He sat down on the edge of it and as he lifted her and slid his cock deep into her warm pussy, she cried out and clutched at his shoulders. He plunged in and out of her, watching her face flush with pleasure until she suddenly stiffened and then climaxed.

The pleasure pulsating through her body pulled his own orgasm from him. As their bodies shuddered against each other, he gathered her against him, burying his face in her neck and wondering if he would be able to send her away.

"WATCH WHERE YOU'RE GOING, YOU STUPID GIRL!" VICTORIA pushed Laura away from her and then slapped her across the head. The woman gave a frightened squeak and pressed back against the wall.

Victoria scowled at her. "What are you doing slinking around the hallways?"

"Forgive me, my lady," Laura said breathlessly. "Mrs. Lanning sent me to fetch Avery. She was bringing food to you and lord Tristan and has been gone for nearly three hours now."

Victoria stared at her. "Has she now?"

"Aye. Did you not find the tray of food in your room?" Laura asked.

"Aye, it was there." Victoria looked behind her and when she turned back to Laura, the woman blanched and shrank against the wall. She knew her eyes had turned yellow, and a low growl rumbled from her chest.

She shook herself and stared down at the smaller woman. "Tell Mrs. Lanning that Tristan is not feeling well this evening. I believe Avery is," she paused, her lips curling back from her suddenly very white and very large teeth, "taking care of him. I would not expect to see either of them until the morning."

Laura nodded mutely as Victoria swept down the hallway. "And find my brother and send him to me, you stupid cow."

CHAPTER 23

A very shivered and wrapped the scarf more firmly around her throat. She crouched and tugged another potato from the hard, cold ground, tossing it into the basket at her feet before lugging the basket a few feet down the row.

Two rows down, Laura and Renee, both huddled against the cold wind, were busy digging potatoes out of the ground as well. It was the last of the potatoes and Avery was glad. Although she usually enjoyed being outdoors, the days were growing so cold that it was pure misery to be outside.

She pulled her fingerless gloves up more snugly, sighing a little at the sight of her red and chapped fingers. She used to have pretty hands – the nails perfectly manicured and the skin soft and smooth. Now, months of scrubbing and cleaning and digging in the dirt had made her hands rough and her nails broken and jagged. She smiled ruefully. There seemed to be a permanent row of dirt under her broken nails that refused to disappear no matter how hard she scrubbed her hands.

At least she was warmer than normal. Tristan had demoted Mrs. Lanning like he threatened and replaced her with Marian. In the last week Marian proved to be tough but fair. She had divided up the chores evenly amongst the slaves, and Avery bit back a smile at the memory of Mrs. Lanning scrubbing the floor in the dining area. Marian still assigned Avery to the west field to pull the remaining potatoes before the ground became too frozen, but unlike Mrs. Lanning who often sent Avery out in just a dress and thin sweater, Marian ensured that Avery was warmly dressed.

It was a shame that it had taken so long for Mrs. Lanning to lose her position as the head of the household. The last week had been almost pleasant and if it weren't for how much she missed Tristan, she might actually have considered staying. She rubbed her forehead, leaving a smear of dirt across her brow, and then angrily yanked a potato from the dirt. She'd promised herself she would not think about Tristan or how she wished he loved her. He'd kept his promise and not approached her again since the night after the full moon, and now there was a coolness emitting from him that hadn't been there before.

It was for the best. In three days, he would deliver her to the Barton's home, and she would not see him again. He'd been so sweet and gentle with her the night she had come to his room that she'd allowed herself to almost believe he cared for her the same way she cared for him.

She'd just been fooling herself, of course. The ease with which he entirely dismissed her now, proved that she was making the right choice. He'd only spoken to her once. She was in the kitchen, about to start washing the dishes when he had cleared his throat behind her. At her nervous hello, he nodded and then told her that he would be taking her to the Bartons before the week's end.

His eyes were blank of any emotion and his voice nearly serene when he told her. He hadn't waited for her reply, just turned and left the kitchen, leaving her to stare at his retreating back while hot tears pricked at her eyes.

Since then, he'd avoided her. She knew he was spending most of his free time going riding with Sophia and Victoria, and she was made herself scarce whenever they were in the house together. But two days ago, just before she retired for the night, Marian sent her to the common room to grab a forgotten sweater. Her stomach dropped and her face paled when she saw Tristan and Victoria on the couch closest to the fireplace. They were simply sitting together, his arm across the back of the couch and her body curled into his with her hand resting on his leg, but it had been enough to send a shot of pure jealousy through her.

It would have been better if she'd caught them kissing, she decided. Somehow the casual comfort they were displaying with each was worse. It was much too easy to imagine them building a life with each other, raising children and growing old together while she remained alone and pining for Tristan for the rest of her life.

She'd muttered an apology, grabbing the sweater as Victoria rubbed Tristan's leg and smiled smugly at her. Tristan had glanced her way, the look in his eyes unreadable, before staring into the fire. She'd fled the room, sick to her stomach, and practically thrown the sweater at Marian before escaping to her cold room, crawling into her bed, and crying bitterly.

She dragged her basket of potatoes toward the end of the row. Jeffrey, who was standing guard, approached her and picked it up easily.

"Thank you, Jeffrey," she said.

He nodded and she trailed after him as he carried the basket to the wagon and dumped the potatoes into the back of it. As he was handing it back to her, the sound of horse hooves could be heard in the cold, silent air and he turned and looked behind him, frowning a little.

"What's this then?" he said half to himself. Avery peered around his stocky frame to see a rider on a horse, running hard.

"I think that's Marshall, is it not?" she replied.

"Aye. He seems to be in a hurry."

They stood together and watched as Marshall grew closer. He pulled his horse to a stop beside them and as Jeffrey grabbed the horse's halter, Marshall shouted, "Avery, you need to come back with me – right now!"

"Marshall? What's wrong?" She could feel a thread of fear in her belly at the sight of his pale face and wild eyes.

"Sophia's been hurt. She was out riding with Tristan and Victoria and the horse was spooked. She fell off her horse and at first seemed fine but now she's -"

He stopped, swallowing convulsively and Avery ran to his horse. Jeffrey boosted her up and she slid onto the horse behind Marshall, wrapping her arms around his waist as he wheeled the animal around and urged the horse into a full run toward the house. Avery buried her face in his back, saying a silent prayer for the little girl.

TRISTAN PACED ACROSS THE NURSERY, STARING SILENTLY AT Sophia in her bed. She was pale and sweating, groaning softly every few minutes as her grandmother sponged her forehead with water.

He stood next to the bed and rested a shaking hand on the little girl's leg. She was so small and fragile, and he gazed helplessly at her as she opened her eyes and stared at him.

"It hurts, Papa," she whispered.

"I'm sorry, baby." He swallowed hard and rubbed her leg. "You'll feel better soon."

She closed her eyes and groaned again as he crossed the room to the window.

"Tristan, sit down." Victoria put a cool hand on his arm. "You cannot even see the west field from this side of the house."

He shook her hand off as Hendrick approached him from the other side, glancing at his sister. "Lord Tristan, I don't mean to question your judgement, but should we not be going for the doctor? I do not understand why you have sent for the Red. Sophia needs medical care, not some spell from a witch."

"Avery isn't a witch," Maya said. She was standing at the end of Sophia's bed and her face was pinched and worried looking. She boosted Nicholas up on her shoulder and patted his back as she glared at Hendrick.

Hendrick ignored her and continued to stare at Tristan. "Let me go and get the doctor."

Tristan turned abruptly and stared at him. Hendrick took a step back, holding his hands up as Tristan snarled, "The nearest doctor is in the village – a half day ride at least. Sophia will be dead before you return."

Victoria put a hand on his back. "Tristan, darling, do you think it's wise to let the Red practice her magic on your child? If she is indeed a witch like the humans believe she is, what is to stop her from -"

"She is not a witch," Tristan ground out. "She is -"

The door to the nursery flew open and Avery ran into the room, followed closely by Marshall. Her face was bright red from the cold, and she had a large smear of dirt on her forehead. She ran to the bed, tearing off her coat and gloves as she looked at Maya.

"What happened?"

"She fell off her horse and at first she seemed fine. She bruised her knee a little and she said her stomach hurt a bit, but other than that she was perfectly normal. Then an hour ago, she started complaining of a stomach ache. I was about to tuck her into bed when she just – just collapsed," Maya said. She started to cry, and Marshall put his arm around her, kissing her forehead.

Tristan took his mother's shoulders and urged her away from the bed. "Mother, let Avery look at Sophia."

Vivian allowed herself to be led away. Her face was grey, and her hands were trembling. She had seemed to age ten years.

As Tristan watched, Avery put her cold hand on Sophia's forehead. It was like touching a furnace and she kicked off her boots as Sophia opened her eyes and stared blearily at her.

"Hurts, Avery," she whimpered.

"I know it does, my love," she replied. "I'm going to make you feel better, all right?"

The little girl had already closed her eyes. Her breathing was harsh and shallow, and she had dark circles under her eyes.

Avery carefully pulled back the covers. Sophia was dressed in just her underwear and Avery sucked in her breath, a small cry escaping from her lips. Sophia's belly had swelled to twice its normal size, and bruising was blossoming like dark malignant flowers across her skin.

Tristan made a sound like a wild animal caught in a trap. Avery glanced at him and squeezed his arm for a moment before standing. Just her brief touch soothed him a little. Ignoring the others in the room, she quickly stripped out of her clothes and eased into the bed next to Sophia. She gathered the little girl into her arms so that Sophia's entire body was pressed against her. Sophia shrieked in pain as Avery moved her, and both Vivian and Maya gave their own cries of distress in response.

"I'm sorry, my love," Avery whispered into the little girl's ear. She placed her hand on Sophia's swollen belly and kissed the girl's mouth and pale face continually as Tristan crouched on the floor next to them.

He and the others watched as Avery closed her eyes and rested her forehead against the little girl's. She winced and shuddered but pressed her body even closer against Sophia.

"It will be a while," she murmured without opening her eyes.

"Can you save her?" Tristan asked hoarsely as his mother wept steadily behind him.

"I do not know," she replied.

"TRISTAN, SIT DOWN, DARLING." VICTORIA REACHED FOR HIS hand and he shook her off. He had been restlessly pacing the nursery for the last hour, staring silently at Avery and Sophia. They were a quiet, still lump under the covers. Maya had pulled the bedcovers up until just the top of Avery's head was visible and he could not see Sophia at all. Twice he had nearly approached the bed and looked under the covers, but his fear that Sophia would look exactly the same, pale and close to death, kept him away. If he could not see Sophia, he could hold on to the faith that Avery was healing her.

"This is my fault," he said as his mother crossed the room and placed a worn hand on his arm.

"It is not," she said. She glanced behind her at the bed before turning back to face her son. "Tristan, we must prepare ourselves. Sophia is gravely injured. I know you want to believe that Avery can help her in some way, but the humans' tales of the Red's being witches are only stories. We need to make arrangements -"

She stopped, her face twisting and Tristan glared at her. "She is not going to die. Avery will save her."

"Tristan, you're mad with grief," Victoria said. "It is foolish to let the Red share in your child's last moments while you watch from a distance. You and your mother should be the ones holding Sophia and soothing her right now. Would you deny your mother her last chance to be with her grandchild?"

Tristan took a deep breath as he stared at his mother. "You don't know what Avery can do. You were sick and close to death. You collapsed and fell into a deep sleep that we could not wake you from, until the next morning when you miraculously awoke feeling completely normal. That was because of Avery."

Vivian frowned at him. "Tristan, I don't know what you're talking about. Aye, I was feeling sick but my Lycan healing finally -"

He shook his head. "No, Mother, it was not your Lycan blood that helped you heal. Avery snuck into your bed the night you collapsed and held you until you healed. You owe her your life."

There was movement under the covers and coughing could be heard. Maya stood up from the rocking chair, one arm cradling Nicholas and the other held tightly by Marshall. She looked at Tristan and he nodded grimly before approaching the bed.

A combination of dread and hope filled his body as he reached out with shaking hands and tugged the covers down to Avery's shoulders. Avery, her hair very red against the extreme paleness of her skin, was lying still with her eyes closed. She didn't stir when the cold air touched her bare skin. Sophia, her eyes closed and her cheeks flushed with colour, was lying against Avery's breast.

"Sophia?" He whispered.

Her eyes popped open and she smiled at him. "Hi, Papa. I feel much better."

Tears running down his face, he pulled her from Avery's embrace. As he lifted her, he looked at her belly. It had returned to normal, the swelling completely gone, and there was no trace of the bruising seen. He hugged her against him hard until she squirmed and complained loudly. "Papa, you're squishing me. I can't breathe."

"Gods be damned." Hendrick said faintly as Vivian staggered forward and stared at Sophia.

"I – Sophia?"

"Hi, Grandmamma!" Sophia said. "My tummy doesn't hurt anymore."

"I'm glad," Vivian whispered. Her face was so pale, and she was trembling so hard that Tristan was afraid she would pass out. Still holding Sophia, he wrapped his other hand around his mother's arm.

"Take some deep breaths, Mother." He kissed Sophia's soft cheek.

"I'm hungry, Papa," Sophia said.

"Then we will get you something to eat, my love. Whatever you want." He smiled at her, knowing in this moment that he would have given her anything she asked for.

Maya was wrapping Avery in a blanket, and Marshall lifted her from Sophia's bed and carried her toward the door. As Vivian and Hendrick approached, both of them staring with wonder at Sophia, Tristan called Marshall's name.

"Is she all right?" He asked as Marshall paused in the doorway.

"I'm fine. Stay with Sophia." Avery's voice was weak but steady.

"Maya, go with your sister," Tristan said.

Maya handed Nicholas to Vivian who took him without a word. She was still staring at Sophia, her face a combination of shock and delight.

Tristan watched them leave the nursery, as Sophia ran her small hand over his long hair. "Papa, I'm hungry."

He grinned at his child. "Let's get you something to eat."

CHAPTER 24

"How do you feel?" Maya kissed Avery's forehead and rubbed her back. They were lying in the bed in Avery's room, a stack of blankets piled on them, and Avery snuggled closer to her sister.

"Better. What time is it?"

"I'm not sure. Early morning – the sun is about to rise," Maya replied. "You've been asleep for hours."

"Is Sophia all right?" Avery asked.

"She's fine. In fact, she's better than fine. Marshall stopped by last night and said she had eaten a large dinner and she was running around the living room, trying to goad Tristan into chasing her."

Avery smiled. "Good. Has – has Tristan come by?"

Maya shook her head. "No, dearest. I'm sorry."

"It's fine." Avery tried to sound cheerful. "There was no reason for him to check anyway. He knew you would take care of me."

Maya smoothed Avery's hair back from her forehead and rubbed the smear of dirt away. "Marshall told me yesterday morning that you were going to the Barton's household by the end of the week." Tears slipped down her cheeks. "Dearest, why did you not tell me?"

"I was going to tell you today, Maya. I swear," Avery replied.

"Why are you leaving?" Maya said. "Mrs. Lanning is no longer the head of the household. Marian will be good to you and treat you fairly. I know she will."

Avery sighed. "It's not about Mrs. Lanning, Maya. You know it isn't. I love him and I cannot watch him live his life with another. He has agreed to sell me to the Bartons, and I am glad. They are close enough that I will still be able to see you from time to time, and Mrs. Barton has already agreed to let me come back for your wedding."

"Marshall and I will be married in a month. Can you not ask Tristan to let you stay until then? Surely the Bartons can wait another month."

Avery shook her head. "They are expecting me in a few days. Besides, if I have to spend another moment watching Victoria and Tristan together, I will go mad."

"He doesn't love her. He loves you," Maya said.

"No, he does not." Avery smiled at her baby sister.

"He does," she insisted. "I have seen the way he looks at you. If you tell him that you love him, I know he will confess his love for you."

"He already knows," Avery said. "And it has not moved him to confess any type of feeling for me in return."

"Oh, Avery." Maya gave her a look of pity and Avery shook her head.

"It's fine, Maya. Do not look at me that way. My life since the slave house is turning out better than expected, is it not? I will be treated well at the Bartons, and I will still get to see you from time to time. That is all I need."

"Avery, that isn't enough. It hurts me to see you settling

this way. You need to fight for Tristan. I don't care what you say – he has feelings for you. If Daddy could see you now, could see you just giving up like this, he'd be so ashamed of you. He always said you were the strongest person he knew. Do you really want to -"

"Enough, Maya!" Avery ripped away from Maya's arms and sat up in the bed, resting her arms on her raised knees and staring out the window at the grey light of dawn.

"I do not wish to hear you speak on matters you know nothing about." She ignored the hurt look on Maya's face. "You are normal. You have a good man who loves you very much and would do anything for you. You will bear his children and grow old together, and I am truly happy for you. Please believe me that I am. But don't you dare tell me that I am weak or giving up when I have to live with the knowledge that I will spend the rest of my life as a slave, bound to serve another without any rights or choices. That I will live the rest of my life wanting and loving a man I will never have and knowing that he is sharing his life with another. I am choosing to find joy in your happiness, and in finding a home that will treat me well and not burn me at the stake for witchcraft. That is not weakness."

"Avery, I'm sorry I shouldn't have said you were weak," Maya said.

Avery stared moodily out the window. "I believe with all my heart that Daddy would be proud of me for making the best of this new life, and not wallowing in self-pity."

"He would, Avery. I know it. I should not have said what I did. I am just upset at the thought of you leaving. We have never been apart before."

"You will be fine." Avery allowed Maya to put her arm around her. "Besides, we will not be that far apart. You will just have to convince Marshall to bring you to visit me often. I will be lonely without you."

"I will, Avery. I promise," Maya said.

"VICTORIA, WHAT YOU'RE SUGGESTING IS MADNESS." Hendrick frowned at her.

"Is it, brother? Think about what I'm saying. The Red has some kind of healing power. Imagine if she had a child, a Lycan child, with that kind of power."

Hendrick hesitated. "Lycans have their own healing powers."

"Not like this," Victoria replied.

"So what?" Hendrick said. "She can heal but what of it? How will that benefit me?"

"Are you kidding?" Victoria said. "Imagine if she bore you a child who could heal the way she can. A Lycan who could heal with nothing more than a touch? Your child would be the most famous Lycan in the world. Think of the money you could make, of the power you would gain. Others, humans and Lycans alike, would flock to you for help in healing their loved ones. You could charge any price you wanted, and they would pay it to keep their precious ones alive."

Hendrick stared at her for a moment before his tanned face broke out into a wide grin. "Money and power have always been very appealing to me."

She grinned back at him. "You are attracted to the Red and with time and," she paused, "proper discipline, she will be more than willing to please you. She is young and could easily bear you many children. If you're lucky, more than one of them will have the same powers as their mother. And if they don't, you can always use the Red's powers to better your situation."

Hendrick stared thoughtfully out the window of his bedroom. "But she has already been sold to the Bartons. And I do not think your Tristan would give her to me anyway." He glanced at her. "He fancies the Red."

Victoria scowled. "The Bartons have not paid for her yet. And he fancies her only because she is a novelty to him. Once she is out of his sight, he will completely forget about her."

"Are you so sure about that?" Hendrick raised his eyebrow at her.

"Aye," Victoria snapped. "I will please him better than the Red ever could. I just need her away from Tristan, and both you and I know that the Bartons is not far enough. It is only a few hours ride from here, and I don't want to take any chances that Tristan will be able to see her whenever he likes. If she were to go with you, the long journey to your home will soon cool his desire for her."

"How will you convince him to sell the Red to me?" Hendrick asked. "Even you are not so naive to think that he will just hand her over."

"Dear brother," Victoria gave him an arrogant look, "it is simply a matter of telling a few lies."

Hendrick smiled a little. "Something you seem to excel at."

Victoria smoothed her dress down. "I have convinced Tristan to go riding with me alone this afternoon. While we are gone, you will tell the Red that Tristan changed his mind and agreed to sell her to you. Then you will leave with her before we return. I will tell Tristan that the Red attacked me during a fit of jealousy, and out of concern for my safety you agreed to take her to your household."

Hendrick pursed his lips. "Can you be convincing enough?"

Victoria smiled and withdrew a small, sharp dagger from the pocket of her dress. "Trust me, Hendrick. I'll be very convincing. Just make sure that you do your part and are gone with the Red before we get back."

TRISTAN STOOD AT THE WINDOW OF THE NURSERY. HE WAS holding Nicholas and he smiled a little when the boy reached up and pulled on his lip, babbling excitedly. The child was not his, but over the last few moons he had grown very fond of the baby. In time, he suspected he would feel as deeply for Nicholas as he did for Sophia.

He rested the baby against his shoulder and patted his back as he continued to stare out the window. In the yard below him, Maya and Marshall were playing some type of game with Sophia that required much shouting and running and hopping.

Sophia had woken this morning feeling as well as she had yesterday, and after much cajoling she had convinced Tristan and Maya to allow her outside to play. She was bundled up carefully against the cold and although her nose was running and her cheeks were red, she looked deliriously happy.

Faintly, he could hear her shouting commands to Marshall who knelt obligingly on the cold ground so she could climb onto his back. He ran around the yard with her riding piggy-back and her laughter drifting up through the cold glass. He could hardly believe that yesterday she had come close to dying.

His thoughts turned to Avery. She'd spent the night with Maya, and twice he nearly left the others and gone to her room to check on her. He forced himself to stay away, knowing that Maya would tell him if she wasn't healing, but he'd cornered Marshall and demanded to know how Avery was when he returned from her room.

Marshall clapped him on the back. "She's doing fine. She's still sleeping, and Maya would like to spend the night with her if she can."

"Of course." Tristan responded. "I will stay with Sophia and Nicholas tonight."

He'd spent the night in the nursery, turning down both his mother's and Victoria's offer to stay with him. He'd made a nest of blankets on the floor next to Sophia's bed and told her stories until she had fallen asleep. He laid awake for hours, listening to Sophia's soft breathing and thinking about Avery. When Nicholas woke in the night, cranky and hungry, he was thankful for the distraction. He changed the baby and then carried him to the kitchen in the dark to warm his bottle. He'd stared down the hallway of the slave's quarters and couldn't resist moving quietly to Avery's room. Jiggling Nicholas gently, he'd eased open the door of Avery's room and peered inside.

Avery and Maya were curled up together in Avery's bed under a massive stack of blankets. Maya's face was buried in Avery's back, her arms wrapped firmly around her sister, and he'd stared for a long time at Avery's sleeping face. When Nicholas began to fuss, he'd quietly closed the door and carried the baby back to the kitchen.

He'd returned to the nursery, feeding Nicholas and burping him before sitting in the rocking chair and holding the boy until he fell back asleep. Instead of placing Nicholas back in his crib, he held him until light crept across the land. He'd spent the entire night warring with himself and even now, he couldn't stop the clamoring of his brain.

He had promised Avery he would stay away from her and that he would send her to the Bartons. She had saved Nicholas' life, Marshall's life, his mother's life and now the life of his child. He owed it to her to follow through on his promise.

But the thought of taking her to the Bartons, of only seeing her occasionally and never kissing her warm mouth again, made him angry and anxious in a way he did not understand. The last week had been pure hell. He'd forced himself to stay away from her, to not give in to his urge to touch her or be with her, and thrown himself into trying to create a relationship with Victoria.

Victoria was pleasant enough and made it perfectly clear on more than one occasion that she was anxious to have him in her bed, but he felt nothing but a hollow sort of weariness when he looked at her. The thought of actually being in her bed, of touching her and having her touch him in return, filled him with revulsion.

He smelled his mother's scent as she entered the nursery. She stood next to him and kissed Nicholas' soft head. "You look tired, Tristan."

He grunted in reply and she followed his gaze out the window. A smile crossed her lips as she watched Sophia. "Have you spoken with Avery?"

"No."

"I sought her out this morning. I wanted to thank her for saving Sophia. She was in Victoria's bedroom, washing the floor and gathering the bed sheets." She shook her head. "She was just – just cleaning and scrubbing like it was a normal day. Like she hadn't performed a miracle and saved Sophia's life last night."

"It's not a miracle to her, Mother. It's just who she is. And it isn't just Sophia's life she has saved since I bought her from the slave house. Nicholas was a sickly baby. He would not have lasted another moon and only a day after I bought Avery and her sister, Avery healed him. Two days later we were attacked by faeries and Marshall was badly injured. He was stabbed multiple times by the faeries' swords and was dying. Avery saved him."

He glanced down at her. "She healed you as well. I did not ask her to – she chose to do it on her own."

Vivian nodded. "I believe you."

"She has saved the life of every member of my family, and the only thing she asked for in return was to be sent away from me. Yet for moons I could not even give her that. Instead I kept her here, letting her be abused and beaten by the head of my household, watching her scrub the floors of my home and forcing her to warm my bed."

"You did not force her to share your bed, Tristan," Vivian said. "She loves you."

"Aye, she does," Tristan said. "And I have treated her terribly."

"You have not," Vivian insisted. "You have been very kind to her."

His laugh was bitter. "Have I? She told me once that what I only wanted her as my whore, and to my shame, she was right."

Before Vivian could protest again, Tristan said, "I wanted to have it both, Mother. I wanted a Lycan mother for Sophia and I wanted Avery in my bed. I didn't care that I was hurting Avery or leading Victoria on. I've been incredibly selfish."

"Oh, Tristan." Vivian placed a hand on his arm. "I'm afraid this is partially my fault. I was so certain that Victoria would be the right person for Sophia, for *you*, that I pushed you toward her. I did not know the depth of your feelings for Avery."

He stared at her, his tanned face reddening. "What do you mean?"

"My sweet boy." She shook her head and smiled a little. "You're in love with Avery. Can you not see it?"

"Mother I…"

She smiled again and put her arm around him. They stared out the window as Nicholas babbled quietly in Tristan's arms.

CHAPTER 25

"Sophia, my love, it's time to go in for lunch." Maya shivered in the cold air as Sophia pouted at her.

"Just one more game, Maya. Please."

Marshall grinned. "What game this time, Sophia?"

"Hide and seek!" Sophia clapped her hands delightedly as Maya smiled.

"Close your eyes and count to fifty," Sophia demanded.

Marshall and Maya closed their eyes and began to count as Sophia laughed and ran off.

"HELLO, AVERY."

Avery groaned inwardly and turned to face Hendrick. She had just entered the barn and was about to start shoveling out a stall when Hendrick's voice had washed over her.

"Hello, Hendrick."

Hendrick stepped closer. "How are you today?"

"Fine."

"Not feeling sick after yesterday?"

"No," she replied.

"Good." He leaned against the wall of one of the stalls. "Tell me, Avery. Do you know – do you understand - just what a gift you have been blessed with? How valuable you are?"

Avery cupped her elbows nervously. "What is that you want, Hendrick?"

"I want you to join me in my household. I know Tristan is getting rid of you and I want to give you the chance to make a better life for yourself."

"He has already sold me to another," she replied.

He tipped his head in acknowledgement. "Aye, but in *my* home, you will not be a slave. You will be my wife. I will treat you well and you will have everything you want. Pretty dresses, slaves to attend to your every need, you will never want for anything again. I promise you that."

"That is very kind of you, Hendrick," Avery said, "but I'm afraid I will have to decline your offer."

A look of irritation flashed across his face before he smiled again. "You have no choice, Avery. I have already spoken with Tristan and he has agreed to sell you to me."

Avery stared at him in shock. "You lie."

"I do not," Hendrick said. "Your lord Tristan thought you would enjoy being my wife more than you would enjoy the life of a slave."

"No," Avery whispered. She glanced down at the floor in confusion, her stomach churning and her hands trembling. The air in the barn suddenly felt too suffocating, the previously large space too small, and she could hear her pulse thudding loudly in her ears.

"He would not do that," she said. "He knows that I want to be close to my sister. He would not sell me to you."

Hendrick sighed irritably. "I told you, girl, it's done. In

fact, my carriage is outside and waiting. We leave for my home now."

He whistled piercingly and two of his men appeared in the open doorway of the barn. Avery backed up as Hendrick walked toward her.

"I want to speak to Tristan right now," she said. "I'm not going anywhere until I hear it from him."

"Sweet girl, he has gone for a ride with my dear sister. You've seen how close they've grown over the last few weeks. Although I have no doubt that he will miss you, I imagine she is right at this very moment helping him to forget all about you."

She slapped him hard across the face and his blue eyes flashed yellow at her, a low growl starting in his throat. "You don't ever want to cross me, Avery. Do you understand?"

She tried to hit him again and his hard fist slammed into her temple. Her knees unhinged and the world turned dark.

HENDRICK CAUGHT AVERY WHEN SHE SLUMPED FORWARD. HE hoisted her over his shoulder and carried her toward the door. He paused, his head cocked to the side, before he handed Avery's prone body to one of his men.

"Put her in the carriage. I'll join you shortly."

The man nodded and he and the other left the barn. Hendrick walked slowly down the middle of the barn, inhaling deeply. He whistled softly under his breath before suddenly darting into the last empty stall.

He dragged Sophia out by her wrist and glared down at her. "What did you see, girl? Tell me now and be quick about it."

She stared at him, her lips trembling as her eyes turned a light green and glowed in the dim light.

He bent down until he was at her eye level and spoke softly. "If you tell anyone what you have seen, I will come back and kill your baby brother and your grandmother while they sleep. Do you understand me?"

She suddenly snarled and bared her teeth at him. Before he could move, she had sunk her small, needle-sharp teeth into his wrist.

He gave a short yelp of pain and shook her loose as she shifted into her wolf form. She backed up, snarling and spitting at him.

He straightened and stared down at her. "Remember what I said, girl."

He turned and left the barn.

"IT IS A BEAUTIFUL DAY, IS IT NOT?" VICTORIA SMILED UP AT Tristan. At Victoria's request, they had left their horses tied to a grove of trees and walked toward the lake that was at the edge of his property.

"Aye, it is," he replied.

Victoria squeezed his arm gently. "You've been quite and distant. Are you feeling well today, Tristan?"

"I feel fine." They stood at the edge of the lake and stared at its crystal blue waters. After a moment, he turned to her. "Victoria, I must speak with you."

She smiled up at him. "Of course, my darling."

"I'm afraid I have been dishonest with you about my feelings. I have led you to believe that I -"

She suddenly winced and placed a hand on her side. Tristan studied her. "Are you all right?"

"Aye." She gave him a small, trembling smile.

"Have you hurt yourself?"

"Not quite." She grimaced and rubbed at her side.

"Let me see."

She pulled her shirt up and he frowned at the small but deep cut he could see on her side. It was starting to heal but it still looked swollen and sore.

"What happened?"

She sighed. "It is nothing, my lord."

"Obviously it isn't nothing," he said impatiently. "Tell me."

She gave him a sorrowful look. "It was the Red, my lord."

His mouth dropped open. "What?"

She sighed again. "Earlier this morning I was chatting with her and our conversation turned to you. I mentioned how close we had grown and that I would not be surprised if you asked me to stay longer. And that your mother and I had already begun to plan our wedding."

"How did you get cut?" he asked.

"She attacked me, Tristan," Victoria said. "She drew a knife from her skirt and went after me."

"She would not do that," Tristan said.

"She did," Victoria insisted. "Hendrick was there and saw the whole thing. If it had not been for him, I don't know what would have happened."

He stared at her. "You're a Lycan, Victoria. You're saying you cannot protect yourself against a human?"

"I had no wish to hurt her, Tristan. I know how grateful you are that she saved Sophia's life."

"I will speak with her immediately."

Victoria rested her hand on his arm. "My lord, Hendrick was understandably upset and worried for my safety. He received word yesterday that he was needed at home and he decided to take the Red with him."

"He did what?" Tristan stared at her.

"You cannot blame him, my lord. She attacked me. He thought it would be best for all concerned if he took the Red with him. He left you a handsome sum of money for her."

Tristan turned and strode back towards the horses. Victoria hurried after him.

"Tristan, where are you going?"

"Back to the house. I must speak with Avery and your brother."

"It is too late, my lord. He spoke with me before we went on our ride and said that he would be leaving immediately."

"Then I will go after them."

Victoria placed her hand on his arm. "Tristan, I know you are upset but Avery agreed to go with Hendrick."

Tristan stared at her and she nodded. "Aye, it is true. I swear to you."

"I don't believe you."

"Really? She is in love with you and you made it perfectly clear that you wanted her for your bed and only your bed. When she did not agree to that, you turned cold and distant to her. Once she had calmed down, she jumped at the chance to leave with Hendrick."

"Her sister..." Tristan said. "She would not live so far from her sister."

"I don't know what to tell you. I believe your cruel treatment of her has overshadowed her desire to be close to her sister."

They had reached the horses and Tristan, his face a mask of anger and shock, silently helped her into her saddle before swinging his body onto his horse.

"My lord, I am sorry, but you know this is for the best," Victoria said as they rode back to the house.

Tristan didn't respond. His mind was whirling with the realization that Avery had left him.

"Sophia? You're worrying me, dearest." Maya sat on the edge of the little girl's bed. "Will you tell me what's bothering you?"

She frowned when the little girl huddled deeper under the covers and didn't respond.

"Sophia, do you feel sick?"

"No," the little girl said. "I am tired, and I wish to be left alone."

Maya placed her hand against the girl's forehead. It was cool to the touch and Sophia's cheeks were still flushed with colour.

"Tell me what's wrong, my love," she said.

"There's nothing wrong. I am tired," Sophia said.

"Sophia, you must tell me what's -"

The little girl suddenly sat up and growled at her, her eyes glowing with a fierce light. Maya stood and backed away, holding her hands up. "All right, dearest, everything's fine."

"Leave me alone, Maya!" Sophia shouted. "I want to rest!"

Her heart pounding, Maya left the nursery and went to the kitchen where she had left Marshall.

Maya sat down heavily in one of the kitchen chairs. She stared at Marshall as tears dripped down her cheeks.

"I'm sorry, my sweet." Marshall crouched next to her and rubbed her knee.

"She would not leave me without saying goodbye," she whispered.

"She was unhappy, Maya. She told you that herself. Perhaps she looked at the chance to leave with Hendrick as a fresh start."

"But she was going to the Bartons in a day or so. Why would she leave with Hendrick? He lives so far away," she said. "I do not believe she left with him of her own will. Will you speak to lord Tristan for me? Tell him that Avery would never leave me like that. They only left a few hours ago. We could saddle horses and catch up to them. Convince him to let me go after them so that I may speak with my sister."

Marshall nodded. "Of course, my sweet Maya."

TRISTAN SAT IN THE ARMCHAIR NEXT TO THE FIRE AND STARED blankly into the fire. He still couldn't believe that Avery had left with Hendrick. His hand tightened around the glass he was holding. Victoria had been right. He'd been cold and distant with Avery. He thought it was for the best, believed that if he closed himself off from her it would hurt less when he took her to the Bartons.

He was a fool and now he was paying the price. He would never see her again and it -

There was a knock at the door of his bedroom and Marshall stepped into the room. "Tristan, I must speak with you."

"This is not a good time, Marshall," he said.

"Maya sent me here," Marshall said. "She does not believe her sister would leave without even saying goodbye to her, and I agree. She wants to go after them. Do we have your permission to go?"

"No," Tristan said.

"Tristan – give Maya the chance to see her sister. Surely you don't believe that Avery would leave you or Maya to go with Hendrick. The night of the party, Hendrick tried to -"

"Enough!" Tristan roared at him. He stood and threw his glass into the fire. It shattered into tiny pieces, and Marshall stepped back as Tristan turned and glared at him, his eyes glowing green fire and his body swelling.

"She is gone! There is nothing we can do about it. Now leave me!"

———

A HALF-HOUR LATER, TRISTAN SIGHED IRRITABLY WHEN HE heard the door of his bedroom open. "Marshall, I told you to leave me alone."

"Papa?"

He twisted in his chair to see Sophia, looking very small and pale, standing in the doorway of his bedroom.

"Sophia, my love, come here." He held out his arms to her and she ran across the room and climbed into his lap. She snuggled into him and he buried his face in her dark hair and breathed deeply. Her entire body was trembling, and he frowned. "Sophia, what is wrong?"

She stared up at him, tears sliding down her cheeks. "I have something to tell you, Papa."

CHAPTER 26

Avery stared blankly out the window of the carriage. She'd woken only an hour after Hendrick knocked her unconscious. Her body had healed itself from the blow to her head while she slept. She pulled at the ropes that bound her wrists together before peering out the window again.

It was nearly dark, and she imagined they would be stopping to set up camp in the next little while. The air was cold and smelled of snow and she shivered against the leather seat, thankful for the warm coat she was wearing when she went to the barn.

She wondered if there would be a way to escape once they set up camp. If she could convince Hendrick that she'd changed her mind and was eager to go with him, perhaps he would let his guard down and she could slip away in the night.

The carriage creaked to a halt and she stiffened slightly when the door opened and Hendrick climbed in. He banged the ceiling of the carriage twice and whistled piercingly, and the carriage started with a jolt.

"Good evening, Red." He smiled at her and she forced herself to smile back.

"Hello, my lord."

He blinked a little, obviously surprised by her pleasant response, before moving to sit next to her. "How are you feeling?"

He examined her head as she forced herself to smile again. "Perfectly fine, lord Hendrick."

"I am glad. I didn't like being forced to hit you like that, you know."

"I do know," she said. "It was wrong of me to question you the way I did."

He stared suspiciously at her. "What's with the attitude change?"

"I realized that you were right, my lord."

He laughed. "Forgive me, but you'll understand if I don't quite believe you."

"Why would you not? I've had many hours to think about what you said. I would prefer to be your wife instead of a slave."

"And what of your beloved Tristan?"

"What of him?" She shrugged. "He has no interest in me other than using me to warm his bed. Given a choice between being his whore and your wife – I choose you."

"I'm glad to hear you say that." He grinned at her and reached to cup her cheek, wincing a little.

"Are you hurt, my lord?" she asked.

"It is nothing. Just a small bite on my wrist." He showed her the wound and she frowned.

"Why does it not heal?"

He grimaced. "It is from another Lycan. Our healing abilities serve us well but when one of our own kind bites us – it takes much longer to heal."

"Who bit you?"

"Do not ask me questions that are none of your concern." he snapped.

"Of course, my lord. Forgive me. Here, let me help you."

She covered the wound on his wrist with her bound hands for almost five minutes. She lifted her hands away to reveal smooth skin.

He stared at his wrist. "Gods be damned. That is amazing. I felt nothing more than a warm tingling."

She gave him a warm look. "I'm glad I could please you, lord Hendrick."

He stared at her, his voice lowering until it was nearly a growl. "As am I, Red."

He was reaching for her when there was a frightened scream from outside and something large and heavy landed on the roof of the carriage. The carriage creaked to a stop and the horses whinnied nervously as there was another scream that was abruptly cut off.

Avery gasped as something large and winged flew past the window of the carriage.

"Faeries," Hendrick whispered, his tanned face paling. He pulled Avery to the floor of the carriage and put his finger to his lips. "Be quiet."

Avery winced as the sound of men screaming filled the air.

My Lord, should you not help your men?" she whispered. "They are only humans – they stand no chance with the faeries."

He shook his head, his lips trembling. "Be quiet, girl."

She was filled with disgust at his cowardice. "We cannot hide in here like frightened children. They will check the carriage. They are not stupid."

He just stared at her, and she shook him impatiently.

"Untie me. We have to at least try and fight. I will not lie here and wait for death!"

"Shut up!" he snarled. "Let me think! I just need to -"

The door of the carriage was ripped open and Hendrick screamed pitifully as dirty, moss-covered hands reached in and grabbed his legs. He was yanked from the carriage and Avery, her legs trembling and adrenaline coursing through her veins, scooted out the door and pressed her body against the side of the carriage.

She moaned under her breath. All around her were faeries, swooping and gliding through the air as they dropped on Hendrick's men. Two faeries, their powerful bodies twisting and turning, lifted one of the men high into the air before dropping him. He landed in a crumpled heap, jagged shards of bone sticking out of his legs, and screamed hoarsely before one of the faeries descended on him. The faerie held his face and inhaled deeply. Immediately, grey mist rose from the man's mouth and within minutes he was slack-jawed, his eyes closed and his body limp as the faerie continued to inhale.

There was a loud howling and she glanced to her left to see that Hendrick had shifted into his wolf form. Snapping and growling he backed away from the faeries. He turned and ran for the woods but before he could make the trees, four faeries descended on him. They pinned him to the ground, hooting loudly and stabbing him with their spears.

Avery looked away as Hendrick howled with agony and more faeries crowded around him, tearing at his pelt with their strong fingers.

She slid along the carriage and around the back of it. If she could get to the trees, she could use them as coverage. She could hide herself deep in the woods and wait until dawn to try and return to Tristan's home.

She scanned the skies above her. Dark had fallen and it was nearly impossible to tell if there was anything flying in the sky above her. She took a deep breath and made a break for the trees.

She was nearly to the tree line when a faerie swooped down and knocked her to the ground. Screaming, she tried to twist away but he pinned her down as easily as a child and stared at her.

"Hello, Red!" He grinned cheerfully at her. "You're a pretty one!"

He brushed his hand across her face, and she spat at him before punching at him with her bound hands.

He laughed and hooted and then bent over her, holding her hands tightly in his own. He smiled at her and she clamped her mouth shut as he started to inhale.

She stared into his muddy brown eyes, feeling her body going limp and her mind dimming. She opened her mouth as he continued to inhale. A mist, blue instead of grey, drifted from her mouth and the faerie's eyes widened with delight and hunger.

"So tasty," it whispered to itself before it inhaled again.

Avery moaned as the world darkened around her. Tears were trickling down her cheeks and she breathed Tristan's name before falling into the darkness.

"WE'RE READY TO GO, TRISTAN," MARSHALL SAID. HE, AS well as Leo and Jeffrey, shifted to their wolf forms as Tristan bent down to Sophia.

"You did the right thing in telling me, my love. I will be back soon with Avery. I promise you. Do not be frightened while I am gone. Your grandmother will keep you safe."

She nodded solemnly and stepped back, taking Maya's hand as Vivian stepped forward. "Be careful, Tristan."

He nodded and was turning away when Victoria stepped out from the house. She glanced around the group curiously. "Tristan, my darling? Where are you going?"

Tristan stared at her. He had been so obsessed with getting Avery back that he hadn't even thought of Victoria. Now, staring at her, he could feel his anger and fear boiling up inside of him. There was no doubt in his mind that she had conspired with her brother to take Avery, and with an angry roar he stormed towards her. She backed up against the wall as he planted his hands on either side of her and stared down at her.

"My lord, what is wrong?" she whispered.

"I know that you and your brother have been plotting against me," he said in a dangerously soft voice.

She winced. "Tristan, I do not know what you mean."

"Stop lying to me!" He shouted at her, and she cringed against the wall of the house.

"You will gather your slaves and your things, and you will leave my house immediately. The gods help you if you are still here when I return."

"Tristan wait, let me explain," she begged. She stared at Vivian. "Vivian, please help him to understand that I did it for him."

"You would be wise to hold your tongue, Victoria," Vivian said.

Tristan stared at the blonde Lycan. "If your brother hurts her, if he even touches her, I will kill him where he stands. And then I will hunt you down and kill you as well. I will wipe your entire bloodline from the face of this earth. Do you understand me?"

She nodded, her eyes yellow and rolling in their sockets

with fear and her face covered in a thin sheen of sweat. He stepped back and looked at Ian. "Help her pack and leave. Watch her carefully."

Ian nodded and took Victoria's arm. When she tried to yank free, his eyes glowed a deep yellow and a snarl tore from his throat.

"All right," she whispered and allowed him to lead her into the house.

"It will be dark in a few hours, Tristan. Perhaps you should wait until morning to go after them," Vivian said.

"No. He's left with seven men and a carriage. They will be slow and if we leave now, we can catch up to them by nightfall."

He stared at Maya who had been pale and silent since she had found out Avery had been kidnapped. "I'll bring her back."

She nodded and gathered Sophia against her as Tristan shifted and he and the others disappeared into the woods.

THE WOLVES MOVED QUICKLY AND CONFIDENTLY IN THE darkness. The white wolf, his fur gleaming in the moonlight, whined quietly at the large, grey wolf beside him. The wolf barked sharply, his eyes glowing, and lengthened his stride. A man's scream, shockingly loud, pierced the night air from somewhere ahead of them. Marshall whined again, and Tristan snarled before they bounded forward.

"I WANT A TASTE! GET OUT OF THE WAY!" A FAERIE, ITS body covered in scars and strange markings, pushed at the faerie who was pinning Avery down.

The faerie held onto Avery's arms and continued to inhale. With a scream of rage, the second faerie drew his spear and stabbed the other faerie in the neck, pushing him off of Avery as black liquid and blood flowed from his neck.

With a hideous grin, he leaned over Avery and inhaled, his eyes closing in ecstasy as he tasted the blue mist rising from her mouth. He was so entranced by her taste that he took no notice of the sudden screaming of his fellow faeries. He leaned closer and took another deep breath. It wasn't until the first wave of hot breath washed over his face that he opened his eyes. Frowning he turned his head and stared into the glowing green eyes of a giant grey Lycan.

He reached for his spear, but the Lycan tore his head from his body with one swipe of his paw. The faerie's head, its mouth open in a silent scream, rolled across the ground before coming to a gentle stop against the torn and mutilated body of Hendrick.

TRISTAN SHIFTED TO HIS HUMAN FORM AS MARSHALL AND the others worked together to kill the remaining faeries. All around them were dead men and faeries but Tristan paid no attention to them. His hands shaking, he sat on the cold ground and gathered the limp body of Avery into his arms.

"My love," he whispered. "Wake up. Please, my love. Open your eyes."

She didn't respond. Her face was pale and cold, and her eyelids were tinged with purple. He held her against him, kissing her face and stroking her long red hair.

"You're all right. You're just fine," he whispered. "You can heal yourself of this. I know you can."

He continued to hold her and when she didn't wake, he shook her almost roughly. "Avery! Wake up! Do you hear me, girl? Wake up!"

She remained limp, her breathing steady and slow and her eyes closed. She was like a large doll in his arms and panic flooded through his veins.

Marshall approached and placed a hesitant hand on his back. "Tristan, brother - it is too late. The faeries have taken her essence."

Tristan howled in agony before rising to his feet. He clutched Avery against him and glared at Marshall. "It is not too late. Do you hear me? She will be fine. She will heal herself and she will wake."

Without looking at Marshall or the others he carried the limp and still body of Avery towards his horse.

CHAPTER 27

Tristan shifted Avery against him and stared at the ceiling of his bedroom. For the last three days he had laid in his bed and held Avery's naked body against his own. He had left her for only a few minutes at a time – to use the bathroom and check on Sophia - ignoring Maya's offer to lie with her sister for a longer period of time.

As the days passed and Avery did not wake, he could feel his certainty that she would heal herself fading. He ignored it grimly, clinging like a man drowning, to the idea that any moment she would wake and smile at him.

The door opened and Vivian, Maya and Marshall filed in. They stood around his bed, staring down at him, and fear trickled into his belly.

"What?" he asked. "What is it?"

His mother glanced at the others. "Tristan, my sweet boy, it has been three days. Never before has Avery taken this long to heal herself. I'm so sorry, my love, but I – *we* – believe that she is never going to wake up."

He stared mutely at her, his eyes dark with pain and

sorrow, and she rested her hand on his shoulder. "I am more sorry than I can say, Tristan, but you need to let her go now."

He glanced at Maya who was weeping silently and steadily in Marshall's arms. "Do you agree, Maya?" He asked bleakly. "Are you ready to give up on your sister?"

"My lord, never before has anyone survived and returned to normal after having their essence taken from them," she whispered.

"Avery is unique. If anyone can survive it, it will be her."

Maya swallowed thickly as the tears slid down her face. "She should have woken by now, my lord. I know that you want her to – to get better but even Avery is still only human. She is not immortal."

He took a deep breath and stared down at Avery's pale face. "She will wake. I am not giving up on her."

Vivian sighed deeply. "Tristan -"

"Get out!" He bellowed. "Get out, all of you! She will wake. I will not give up on her as easily as the three of you!"

The three of them backed away as Tristan's body grew larger and his eyes turned green.

"All right, brother," Marshall said. He led Maya and Vivian from the room as Tristan studied Avery again.

"HELLO, PAPA." SOPHIA CLIMBED INTO THE BED AND SAT cross-legged against Avery's body.

"Hello, little one," he replied dully.

It had been two hours since his conversation with the others and he'd been filled with anger and despair ever since. Even the sight of Sophia could not lift his spirits.

The little girl sat quietly for a few minutes before

speaking again. "I was in the kitchen today, playing with my dolls under the table."

"Oh?" He tried to sound interested. "Did you have fun?"

She shrugged and stroked Avery's long red hair. "It was all right." She rubbed at a dark bruise on her upper arm.

"How did you get that?" he asked.

She giggled. "I ran into the bedpost when I was playing tag with Marshall."

Her face dropped. "Maya yelled at him and then she started crying and couldn't stop. Marshall had to get Grand-mamma and then take Maya away. She came back later though and said she was sorry."

She brought her knees up and hugged them. "When I was in the kitchen, Renee and Laura came in and they did not know I was there. They started talking about you and Avery."

She grinned at him. "They said that you have gone mad. Have you, Papa? Mama had a friend who went mad. It was funny to watch him. Are you going to tear off your clothes and run around naked and screaming at people?"

Despite his worry and fear for Avery, a small smile crossed his lips at the look of pure glee on her face. "No, my love. I have not gone mad, and I will not start running around naked."

"But you scream at people," she said.

He stared at her and she shrugged again. "Everyone in the house heard you yelling at Maya and Grandmamma."

"I didn't mean to frighten you."

"You didn't. You're yelling because you miss Avery. I miss her too." She sighed and stroked Avery's cheek with her small hand.

He echoed her sigh and Sophia reached across Avery and patted his bearded face. "Don't be sad, Papa. You're right you know."

"About what?"

"That she will wake." The little girl smiled happily at him.

"Sophia, I don't know for sure that she will wake. I'm hoping and -"

"No, Papa. She *will* wake and soon."

"How do you know that?"

She gave him a strange look. "Because she told me she would. Has she not told you, Papa?"

He sat up a little, staring at Sophia. "When? When did she tell you this, Sophia?"

"When I sleep. Each night since you brought her back, she visits me in my dreams. She sits in the rocking chair in the nursery. The first night she could not speak or even move. She only smiled at me when I hugged her. The second night she still did not speak but she returned my hug when I hugged her. And last night..."

Sophia smiled happily. "She whispered in my ear."

"What did she say?" he asked.

"That she loved me, and she would see me soon." Sophia smiled radiantly at him before bending and kissing Avery's mouth. "I love you too, Avery."

She glanced at him. "Do you love her, Papa?"

"Aye, Sophia, I do."

"When she wakes, will you marry her?"

He nodded. "If she'll have me."

"She will." The little girl stroked Avery's hair again. "I'm going to call her mama. Do you think she would like that?"

He swallowed, his voice rough with unshed tears. "Aye, little one. She will like that."

"Good." Sophia kissed Avery a final time and then scrambled over her and Tristan. "I am hungry, Papa. Shall I bring you something from the kitchen? Marian is making fresh bread."

"Not right now, my love. I will eat later."

She frowned. "I will bring you bread anyway. Grand-mamma says you are not eating enough."

She slid off the bed and leaned against the side of it for a moment before kissing Tristan on the cheek and staring at Avery. "I will tell her tonight that you miss her. Perhaps she will visit you as well."

She walked toward the door. Tristan stared at her. There was something different about her, but his tired mind kept trying to grasp what it was, only to have it slip away. As she shut the door behind her, it suddenly clicked for him and he sucked in his breath. The bruise on her arm had disappeared.

VIVIAN SMILED AT TRISTAN. "IT IS GOOD TO SEE YOU eating."

He nodded and continued to eat the soup that Marian had placed in front of him.

"Is Maya with Avery?"

"Aye." He finished his soup and sat back, running his hand through his damp hair. For the first time in three days, he had allowed Maya to stay with Avery while he bathed and went to the kitchen to eat. "I'm going back to her now."

Vivian sat down beside him and put her hand on his arm. "Take a few more minutes, Tristan. Visit with Sophia for a bit."

"She was in my room earlier. We visited then." He stood, kissed his mother on the cheek and returned to his bedroom.

"How is she?" he asked Maya anxiously.

She eased her body out from under the covers. "The same, my lord."

She kissed Avery gently before leaving the room. He stripped and climbed into the bed next to her. He turned her carefully onto her side and curled up against her warm back, putting his arm around her waist and holding her firmly against his chest.

He yawned tiredly. Although he had done nothing but lie in his bed with Avery, his worry for her had kept him from sleeping. Sophia's childish belief that Avery would wake had soothed him for the first time since he had seen the faerie inhaling her essence. As the sun dipped below the horizon, he fell asleep, his face buried against her warm skin.

He woke some time later, staring into the dark and wondering what it was that had woken him. It took him a few minutes to realize that it was the absence of Avery's soft breathing and warm body. Fear engulfed his body and he sat up, the covers falling to his waist.

Avery was curled up in the armchair next to the fire. She was wearing his shirt, her hair wet and loose around her shoulders, and her skin glowing softly in the firelight. His heart stuttered to a stop before kick-starting again with a powerful thud. He slid out of the bed before reality hit him.

He was dreaming. Sophia's story about dreaming of Avery had brought on his own. He paused for a moment before walking toward her. He might be dreaming but he didn't care. He wanted to hear her voice and see her smile before he woke.

He knelt naked at her feet and stared up at her. "Hello, girl."

"Hello, my lord." She smiled her sweet smile at him.

"I've missed you so much," he whispered and laid his

head in her lap. Her skin was warm and fragrant with soap, and he closed his eyes as she ran her hands through his hair.

"I've missed you as well," she replied.

He raised his head and stared up at her. "Before I wake, I need to tell you something. Maybe Sophia is right, maybe this means that you'll come back to us, but if it doesn't, I have to tell you this now."

She frowned. "Tristan, you're not -"

"I love you, Avery. Please come back to me."

She blinked at him in surprise and then leaned forward and cupped his face in her hands, tears glinting in her eyes. "I love you too, Tristan."

She kissed him, her mouth warm against his, and he returned her kiss eagerly.

They broke apart, both of them panting a little, and he gave her a look of sorrow. "I'm so sorry, my love. I never meant for you to get hurt. If I had known what Victoria and Hendrick were capable of, I would never have allowed them in my home."

She traced his forehead with her fingers. "It does not matter now. We are together again – all is well."

She hugged him and he pushed his face into her neck, breathing deeply and wrapping his arms around her. He could feel her wet hair against his cheek and the softness of her fingertips as she stroked his naked back, and he marveled at the vividness of his dream.

"I don't want to wake up," he muttered against her throat.

She pushed him back gently and cupped his face again. "Tristan, you are not dreaming."

He stared at her uncomprehendingly and she stroked his face. "This is not a dream. I woke up over an hour ago."

She winced as his hands tightened painfully around her waist. He opened his mouth and she smiled at him encouragingly, but no sound came out. She brushed his long hair back from his face and kissed both of his cheeks and the tip of his nose. "You looked so tired and were sleeping so peacefully I did not want to wake you. I had a bath and I had just sat down here when you woke."

"Not dreaming," he whispered.

"That is right, my lord. You are awake."

He leaped to his feet and picked her up. "You're alive!"

"Tristan! Hush! It is the middle of the night. You'll wake the entire house." She shushed him frantically, and he grinned like a madman at her.

"I do not care! You're alive!" He hoisted her higher, his arms around her hips, and kissed her flat abdomen through her shirt before whirling her around.

She laughed and pushed at his shoulders. "My lord, put me down before you drop me."

He stopped and stared up at her without putting her down. She grinned down at him and smoothed his hair back once more.

"Marry me," he said.

The smile dropped from her face. "Do not tease me in such a manner, Tristan."

She wiggled in his grip and he placed her gently on the ground but kept his arms wrapped around her waist. "I am not teasing you, girl. I'm asking you to be my wife. Say yes."

"Tristan, I am not a Lycan. Your mother said

"I do not care what she says. I love you, and Sophia and Nicholas love you, that is all that matters. Besides, you won my mother over the moment you saved Sophia's life."

She stared up at him, her mouth trembling. "You would marry a Red?"

"I would marry *you*," he said. "I don't care what colour your hair is. I love you."

She continued to stare at him silently and he cleared his throat. "Well, girl? Will you marry me?"

She gave him a brilliant smile. "Aye, I will."

He grinned and hugged her against him. She tugged his head down to hers and kissed him thoroughly, sliding her tongue into his mouth and threading her fingers through his hair.

She sighed into his mouth as his hands tightened on her hips. She pressed against him eagerly and when he groaned and cupped her breast, she moaned with pleasure.

He tore his mouth from hers and rasped, "My love, we need to stop."

She frowned and trailed a path of warm, wet kisses down his throat. "I do not want to stop."

"You need rest," he gasped, as she licked from his neck to the top of his shoulder. She nipped the skin lightly with her teeth.

"I have been resting for three days," she murmured.

"No, you've been healing," he said. "You need more rest to make sure you are completely healed."

"Both you and I know exactly what will help speed up the healing." She kissed his throat again, sliding her hand down to grip him firmly.

"You said you missed me," she whispered. "Will you show me just how much, Tristan?"

He picked her up and carried her to the bed. "I will do whatever you ask of me, my love."

EPILOGUE

Tristan paced in the hallway. Sophia, her face grave, paced next to him and Nicholas toddled a few feet behind them.

"I want to go in and see her, Papa," she fretted.

"Soon, my love," he soothed.

He turned and cursed under his breath when he ran straight into Nicholas. The little boy fell onto his bottom with a soft thud and started to cry.

"Papa! You hurt him!" Sophia reached for Nicholas, but Tristan was already bending down. He picked up the sturdy little boy and kissed his cheek.

"You're all right, little one." He wiped away the tears from his chubby cheeks and Nicholas grinned at him.

"I want Mama."

"You have to wait, Nicholas." Sophia scowled at him. "She's having -"

She stopped and looked behind her as the door to the bedroom opened. Maya, her belly swollen with child, stepped into the hallway.

"She's asking for you, Tristan." She rubbed her neck

wearily and smiled at Sophia who leaned forward and placed a gentle kiss on her large belly.

"I want to go too," the little girl said.

"She's asking for all of you, dearest." Maya pushed the door open wide and started down the hallway. "Tell her I will return in a while. I want to see Marshall for a bit."

Tristan nodded and, still holding Nicholas in his arms, followed Sophia into the room. The three of them approached the bed and Nicholas squealed with delight when he saw Avery.

"Mama!" He reached for her and Sophia shook her head.

"No, Nicky. She can't hold you right now."

"Of course, I can." Avery, her voice laced with weariness, smiled at the little girl. "Come, Sophia. Sit beside me so you can see him."

Sophia climbed onto the bed as Tristan gently dropped Nicholas on the bed next to Avery. She put her arm around him, and he cuddled into her. "Hello, my sweet baby Nicky."

"Hello, Mama." He stuck his thumb into his mouth and leaned against her contently.

Tristan sat down on the bed beside her hip and rested a warm hand on her leg. "How do you feel, my love?"

She smiled at him. "Tired, but happy."

There was a short cry from the pile of blankets on her right side and Tristan's breath caught in his throat.

"Would you like to meet your son, my lord?"

"Aye," he whispered, "I would."

He leaned over her and with shaking hands, lifted the tiny, warm baby from the nest of blankets. His heart was thudding heavily in his chest and a wave of love so large it was nearly painful, washed over him. Sophia leaned against him, staring at the baby.

"He has your eyes, Papa," she whispered.

"Aye - and his nose and his chin." Avery kissed the top of Nicholas' head.

"And your hair." Tristan ran his hand over the baby's bright red hair before grinning at Avery.

She reached for his hand, squeezing it gently as Sophia leaned over and brushed her lips across the baby's soft head.

"What's his name, Mama?" she asked.

Avery smiled at Tristan, who smiled back before leaning over and kissing his son's smooth forehead. He looked down at Sophia. "His name is James."

He glanced at Avery. Her eyes were wet with tears and she leaned forward and kissed him warmly on the mouth.

"I love you, girl," he whispered.

"I love you too, my lord."

RED MOON RISING EXCERPT

(BOOK TWO, RED MOON SERIES)

"Red Moon Rising" takes place twenty-two years after Red Moon and focuses on Tristan and Avery's son James.

She stumbled through the forest, her body trembling violently, and her vision blurred. The sun was setting, and she could see her breath in the cold air. She had used her shirt as a bandage but the blood from the wounds on her side had already soaked through it and dark rivers of blood were streaming down her leg.

She was dying. She'd managed to kill one of the beasts, more from luck than any kind of skill, but not before it had wounded her mortally. She staggered on anyway. The other two would soon discover their dead brother and it would not take them long to find her. They would smell her blood and track her down. If the gods were merciful, she would already be dead before they found her and ripped her body to pieces.

She stopped and leaned against one of the thick trees, the bark scraping against her bare back as she took shallow, gasping breaths. The small dog at her feet whined nervously and pawed at her leg.

"Tia." Her voice was thick, and she coughed weakly, moaning when it made her sides burn. Blood coated her lips and slipped down her chin. Her ribs were broken, she was sure of it. She had both heard and felt the crack when the beast threw her against the tree.

She raised her hand and touched her face gingerly. Her battle with the beast had left her face battered and bruised. One eye was swollen shut completely and her lips were bruised and swollen from having her mouth punched. She touched her front teeth experimentally with her tongue, wincing when they wiggled loosely in their sockets. She was surprised they hadn't been knocked out completely.

"Tia." She tried again. "When I die, you have to leave me."

The dog stood and rested its small paws on her shin. It whined again and she tried to smile at the dog. "Don't stick around. They'll kill you if they see you. You have to -"

She coughed again, moaning and crying out with the pain as fresh blood poured from the wounds on her side.

"You have to run away. Find a new family, all right?" she whispered.

The dog barked once, shrilly, and she winced. "Hush, Tia."

She made herself push away from the tree. Oddly enough the pain was a little better. It had been replaced by a curious feeling of numbness. She pulled the sodden material of her shirt away from her wound and stared at the blood spurting from the four deep slashes.

"That can't be good," she whispered and then laughed weakly. She replaced the drenched material against the wounds, why she bothered she didn't know, and stared down at the dog.

"Do you hear me, Tia? Find a new family. Don't stay with me." She stared into Tia's soft brown eyes. The dog cocked its head, stared into the trees, and bolted away.

"I'm not dead yet, damn you," she muttered.

Her heart squeezed painfully. The little dog's abandonment hurt more than her broken body did, but it was for the better. She swiped a shaking hand across her mouth, stared dully at the blood on her fingers, and lurched on.

They would bring her head back and stick it on a pole beside the others. She cringed at the thought that her brother would see it. He'd screamed and raged and begged the beasts to allow him to take her place in the hunt. They laughed and sneered at him. He was too valuable to be used in hunting.

They'd stopped laughing when he attacked and killed one of them with his bare hands. Valuable or not, they would have torn him apart if she had not gotten on her knees and begged Draken to spare his life.

They hadn't let her say goodbye to him, hadn't let her hug him and tell him she loved him. The last time she had seen him he was pinned to the ground, his face red and his muscles straining against his captors as he fought to get to her.

She swallowed, tasting the metallic tang of blood as tears slipped down her cheeks. She was suddenly so weary she couldn't take another single step. She collapsed to the ground, her breath wheezing in and out as her lungs laboured to draw air into them.

She was cold and exhausted. Her eyes slipped shut and she pictured her brother's face - his strong jaw and clear blue eyes. His eyes had once danced with laughter, but it had been many months since there was anything but anger and sorrow in them.

There was snuffling beside her and a warm, wet tongue licked her forehead. She forced her one good eye open and stared at the small dog.

"Tia," she whispered.

Tia whined and looked behind her. The dying woman followed the dog's gaze, squinting at the two figures behind the dog. Dread filled her body. They had found her.

One of them crouched beside her and she realized with a faint thread of relief that it was not one of the beasts. The man was as big as her brother, his shoulders broad and heavily muscled. His eyes were a dark brown and his hair was a rich, dark red.

The second figure knelt beside him. He was blond and blue eyed and almost as big as the redhead. Even with only one eye working properly, she could see the horror and disgust on his face.

"Gods be damned, James. What happened to her?"

The redhead grunted. "I don't know, Nicky." He leaned over her. "What is your name, girl?"

She ignored his question and with the last of her strength reached up and brushed his face with her bloody fingers. "Tia. Please help her -"

A sudden, stabbing pain shot through her chest and she screamed hoarsely. Darkness crept across her vision and the last thing she saw before it overtook her, was the redhead reaching for her.

The thumping in her head was loud and irritating. With her eyes closed, she reached up and massaged at her temple. It didn't help. The thumping continued - a solid constant beat that demanded her attention.

She wanted to ignore it. Her side and head ached, and she was exhausted. She wanted to drift back into sleep, but the thumping wouldn't allow it. She frowned. Her bed was moving. Only a little, but it was definitely moving.

She forced her eyelids up and her mouth dropped open with surprise. Her bed wasn't a bed at all but a human being. She was sprawled across the body of a man twice her size. Moving carefully, she lifted her head from his chest. The thumping stopped, and she realized that it was the solid beat of his heart she had been hearing.

Not daring to move anything but her head, she looked around. She was in a tent. Cold sunlight was filtering through its walls and although she could see her breath, she wasn't the least bit chilled. The man beneath her radiated heat. It surrounded her entire body and –

She realized with sudden horror that she was completely naked, and the gods help her, so was the man underneath her. She froze, her pulse thudding and her eyes widening, as she stared at the man's broad chest. It was covered in a layer of reddish-brown hair and despite the cold weather, he was deeply tanned. His chest was rising and falling evenly, and she risked a glance at his face. He was sleeping soundly, and she studied his face. He had a broad nose and wide cheek-bones, and freckles covered his tanned cheeks.

He looked to be around her age, and he was a handsome man, she decided. He was also huge. Her small frame fit neatly on top of him with room to spare. He would be at least a foot and a half taller than her, her feet barely reached his knees. If she –

For the gods sake – what are you doing? In case you've forgotten, the man is very naked and very much a stranger. Get your naked self off of him and get out of his tent before he wakes.

Excellent advice. Moving slowly, she slithered off his body onto the blanket beside him. He snorted, his hands twitching by his sides, but didn't wake. She almost screamed out loud when a cold nose poked into her back. She twisted her head, flinching at the pain in her face, and stared into the face of the small dog.

"Tia," she breathed. The dog licked her face, her entire body wiggling.

"Hush, Tia," she said before turning back to the man beside her. She started to slide out from under the blankets that covered them and then paused, reaching for the edge of it.

What are you doing? Have you gone mad? What do you think he'll do if he catches you staring at his naked body?

She ignored the voice and lifted the blanket a little. In all of her nineteen years she had never once seen what was between a man's legs, and curiosity was winning out over her fear. She lifted the blanket higher, squinting to see in the dim light below it. Before she could fully see what was between his legs, he muttered in his sleep and turned away from her.

She stared at his naked back and ass for a moment before gingerly scooting out from under the blankets. Away from the heat of his body, she started to shiver as the cool air brought goose bumps to her skin. Her clothes were nowhere to be seen, but his were piled neatly on the ground and she picked out his shirt and slipped into it. The material was cold but soft, and it fell past her knees. Tia scratched at her legs and she reached down and petted the small dog, wincing at the pain in her side.

Lying in the Red's bed she had felt tired but there was only a dull ache in her side and her face. Now, sharp pain was radiating from her side into her back and her face was throbbing dully. She touched her face gingerly, realizing for the first time that she could see out of both eyes. The one that had been puffed shut was tender and sore, but not swollen the way it was before. She pressed her tongue against her front teeth. They didn't move and she frowned a little. They were loose last night. She was sure of it.

The evening came flooding back to her. Her fight with the beast, the agonizing pain in her side and back when he had thrown her against the tree. She paled and reached for the hem of the shirt, lifting it up and studying her side carefully.

It was swollen and bruised, and she could see four barely-scabbed over gashes where the beast had swiped her with his long claws. She blinked in astonishment. Last night they were wide, gaping slashes with blood pouring from them.

"What's happening to me, Tia?" she whispered fearfully as she dropped the shirt.

She decided that for the moment she didn't care. What mattered was getting out of here before he woke up. Her side was burning and throbbing, but she would have to move quickly. She needed to put as much space between her and the stranger as possible.

"Come, Tia," she whispered. Her eye fell on the sword lying next to his pants. She hesitated and then picked it up. It was heavy and it hurt her side to hold it, but she would take it anyway.

"Good morning."

She screamed and whirled around. The cuts on her side split open and fresh blood dripped down her side as she lifted the man's sword and held it in front of her.

The Red was sitting up in his nest of blankets. He yawned and stood, and her eyes dropped automatically. She flushed scarlet at the sight of his penis. It was partially erect and as big as the rest of him.

He walked toward her, and she stumbled back, holding

the handle of the sword tightly in her hand and giving him a warning look. He ignored it and reached for his pants, slipping into them and smiling a little at the redness of her cheeks.

"Do you know how to use that?" He pointed to the sword in her hand.

"Aye," she lied.

He reached out with terrifying quickness and knocked the sword from her hand. It clattered to the ground, barely missing her bare toes, and he scooped it up. He held it out to her, handle-first and grinned at her. "Try again."

She glared at him and snatched it from him. Her sudden movement ripped open the barely-healed cuts on her side even more, and she fought back the wave of nausea that went through her as blood soaked into his shirt. She swayed a little and he frowned.

"You're not fully healed yet." He held out his hand. "Come to me."

She backed away toward the opening of the tent.

"Do not be frightened of me, little one. I only wish to help you."

"Stay away from me," she said.

"Tia - that is your name is it not?"

She frowned in confusion at him as the dog at her feet perked its ears up and then ran to the man. Her tail wagged happily, and she rolled onto her back when the man reached down. He rubbed the dog's belly. She whistled softly and the dog, after licking the Red's hand, bounced to her feet and ran back to her.

"We're leaving. If you try and stop me, I'll kill you," she whispered.

She backed out of the tent. The man made no attempt to follow her as she stepped into the cold morning air. She trembled violently and pressed her hand against her side. It was getting hard to breathe again, and she felt weak and faint. She took a deep breath and turned to flee into the forest. The blond man, an amused expression on his face, was standing behind her.

"Good morning." He stared at the sword in her hand. "Are you planning on hunting for our breakfast?"

She lunged forward, lifting the sword and jabbing it at him weakly. He sidestepped her easily and she tumbled to the ground, crying out at the bolt of pain that went through her side. Dimly she could hear Tia barking and the blond man cursing, and then the Red's face was above hers and he was staring at her gravely.

"Stay away from me," she whispered as he plucked the sword from her limp hand.

"We won't harm you, little one," the man said.

Black edged her vision and then swallowed her whole.

ABOUT THE AUTHOR

Elizabeth Kelly was born and raised in Ontario, Canada. She moved west as a teenager and now lives in Alberta with her husband and a menagerie of pets. She firmly believes that a person can survive solely on sushi and coffee, and only her husband's mad cooking skills prevents her from proving that theory.

For more information about Elizabeth, check out her website at

www.elizabethkelly.ca

facebook.com/EKellyBooks
twitter.com/ElizabethKBooks
instagram.com/elizabethkelly_author
amazon.com/Elizabeth-Kelly/e/B00EOHZ0MS
bookbub.com/authors/elizabeth-kelly

Saving Charlotte

Shameless

The Fairy Tales Collection

Broken

An Unlikely Seduction

Holiday Romance

The Christmas Wife

The Christmas Rescue

The Christmas Nanny

Sordid Games